# Seer Society
## Book One: Clarity

Jenna Kay Pridgen

First Edition 2014

The characters, events, and locales portrayed in this book are fictitious. Any similarity to real persons, living or dead, is coincidental and not intended by the author.

ISBN: 0988298236
ISBN-13: 978-0-9882-9823-1

Edited By: Heidi Pittman

LIFELINE Press
Gainesville, Georgia
Printed in the United States of America

For we are not fighting against flesh-and-blood enemies, but against evil rulers and authorities of the unseen world, against mighty powers in this dark world, and against evil spirits in the heavenly places.

Ephesians 6:12

This book is dedicated to my daddy.

I love you.

I miss you.

I will see you again.

# Prologue

# Lukus

The bowels of Hell are drenched with cries of anguish and despair. Scorched flesh permeates the air as I walk through the dark rocky tunnels of this underground pit. Torches line the walls, lighting my path. My feet crunch atop a mixture of bones and rocks, the sound a sinister song to my ears. I exit the tunnel. A large cavern greets me. Lava pours from crevices situated in the blackened rock, cascading into a river of death. A bridge is up ahead, the only obstacle between my master and I. Flames lick at my bare feet as I make my way across, but they do not pain me.

Destination: Satan's office.

A call had come from Satan's upper room just minutes before, an order stating that my presence was requested. Immediately I'd handed over my assignment to a low-ranking demon. I felt confident that the underling could dish out the proper amount of punishment upon the cursed human soul.

Usually I had many souls to inflict pain and torment on, but today my workload had been extremely light. *Unusually* light.

Among the ranks in Hell I'm not what you consider a high ranker, but I'm also not low on Hell's totem pole. A little above the middle is where I stand. Never have I been a bottom feeder.

As I make my way to Satan's private quarters, I can't help but wonder why he's calling for me. He's never called me before, especially to his personal space. He doesn't like to be bothered by any of his bound servants. Only the elite are allowed to congregate around him.

An intense wave of terror courses through my being as I stare at the large wooden door before me. Sure, I've been called here – that's why I made the journey across Hell's fiery terrain. But what reason could there possibly be for me to see Satan?

**"Stop stalling, Lukus,"** Satan says inside my head. **"You know I don't like to be kept waiting."**

Gulping down a knot of dread, I push the door open. The loud creak sounds like metal grating against metal. I take a few steps inside the large, cavernous office as the door slams behind me.

The room is empty; Satan is nowhere in sight. For a moment I soak in the grandest room in Hell. The walls are made of sharp rock, with black torment oozing down the stony surfaces. Wails of pain flow down along the vile walls, a never-ending chorus of agony that Satan is able to drink in every second of the day. His very own personal soundtrack. His daily sustenance that feeds him nonstop.

Many steps lead up to a throne made of bones, skulls, and reptilian-shaped scepters, all twisted and wound together in a poisonous design. A vicious yet glorious throne room for the lord of iniquity.

A red-orange light bathes the room, casting shadows that seem to gyrate and move around the dark edifice. Peering up toward the ceiling, I search for the source of light, but I'm unable to find it.

**"Lukus. Kneel before your master and close your eyes."**

At once I drop to my knees, placing my forehead on the ground and shutting my eyes. "Master, I – "

**"SILENCE!"** His deep, rumbling voice instantly cuts me off, the sound slicing like a sword into my skin.

A chilly breeze frosts the air. Footsteps sound, circling around my trembling body. I'm scared, I'm frightened. For the first time in all my existence, I'm terrified.

"**You don't know what terror truly is, Lukus,**" Satan tells me, reading my mind. He makes a *tsk tsk* noise. "**I've heard good things from your superiors, but you're making me rethink my opinion of you.** "

"Master," I start with a shaky voice, "you are all powerful, much more than I will ever be. Being in your presence is simply overwhelming. I-I can't..." I'm completely tongue-tied, finding it hard to speak. A chuckle thunders around the room, assaulting my body with tremors.

"**Lukus, I know you are wondering why I have called you here, so I'm going to cut to the chase.**" When he speaks next I feel the air from his breath on top of my bald head. "**I have chosen you for a specific mission on earth.**"

"Earth?" I almost stand to my feet, but quickly remember my place.

"**Yes, earth.**"

"What is waiting for me there?"

A pause, then he replies, "**A Seer.**"

If I possessed a heart it would have come to a halting

stop. "A S-Seer?"

"**Yes**," he replies, sounding amused. "**You are afraid. Why is that?**"

With my face still plastered to the ground I admit, "I've heard about them, the *Ra'ahs*, about how they can send demons back to Hell with just one touch. I've heard the pain is … excruciating. Is that true?"

"**Yes, that is true, but your assignment will be an easy one, and you won't be alone. You will have two trained soldiers going with you.**"

"How will it be easy?" I question timidly. How can he say this mission will be an easy one? "Seers are The Almighty's human foot soldiers, and they always have one of The Guard by their sides. Even if there is a group of us, how will we be able to defeat The Light?"

Satan sighs a long, drawn-out suspiration. "**It will be an easy mission because this *Ra'ah* has no idea what resides within her. She is clueless to the unseen world and that a Guard stands with her. And she has not yet been marked.**"

"Really?" A heavy burden lifts off me, and I smile with relief.

"**Lukus,**" he begins firmly, "**do you feel capable**

**enough to get this job done?"**

Slowly, I stand to my feet and peer into the eyes of Satan, lord of darkness.

"Yes,      master.      When      do      we      leave?"

# Chapter One

# Clarity

The early morning sun sets my bedroom ablaze with life, pouring through curtained windows and instantly stinging my sleep-filled eyes. The horrible buzz of an alarm clock sounds in my ears. Slinging an arm across my body, I slap at the pesky clock, knocking it to the floor, silencing it. Today is Saturday, and unfortunately a job of cashiering awaits me.

In my opinion, the absolute worse sound you can hear on a lovely Saturday morning is an alarm clock. It's a reminder (in my case) that I will be imprisoned at Baker's Supermarket all day long. On a Saturday. Bleh, and *Bleh*.

Maybe if I got paid more than minimum wage I'd be happier about going to work. Or maybe if I'd slept longer than two hours I'd feel up to working. Though working after only a couple hours of sleep is possible. Aunt Caroline does it all the time.

A.C. (my pet name for her) works third shift as a registered nurse at Garlandton Medical Center and makes a pretty decent living. Me, on the other hand, would have to work three times as much to make what she brings home.

Why had I agreed to work a double shift? Temporary insanity, I guess. As if working Friday nights wasn't enough. Though if I didn't have a job, sucky as it may be, I might be stuck in this hick town forever. I may be depressed about working on Fridays and Saturdays, but thinking about staying in this town forever … that would be pure hell.

Plus, adding salt to my gloomy wound, this particular Saturday marks the last one of the summer. All the kids in Garlandton will soon be forced to hit the books, along with the humdrum routine of teachers, tests, and lousy cafeteria food.

Honestly, I don't mind the teachers or the work. Academics have never been a thorn in my side. Most of my headaches revolve around snotty teenage girls that think they're better than … well, *everyone*. Of course I know I'm not the only one who has to deal with that junk. Snot-nosed bullies are in every school around the world.

Not looking forward to that. Not. At. All.

Beams of yellow and orange continue to flood through

my windows, the rising sun causing my eyes to flinch. I should be jumping out of bed and getting ready for my workday. Instead, I decide to take it slow for a moment and bask in the renewed light. I listen as birds belt out their early morning melodies, a perfect soundtrack in honor of a new day. A rooster crows in the distance, surely rousing its owners from their beds.

Even with this beautiful morning, I can't help but feel weighed down with sadness. With my favorite season drawing to a close, my thought train starts chugging through all the lasting memories I'd made the last three months.

Many nights had been spent hanging out with my friends and partying up a storm. During the day we would take dips in the cool, refreshing waters of the swimming hole, then walk in the endless fields of sunflowers. At night we'd venture to Granny Mae's Ice Cream Parlor located on the town square, then head to whatever party was taking place, where a beer bottle would become permanently glued to the palm of my hand. All the fun would be worth it, even when the imminent hangover attacked the next day.

I'd miss the earthy aroma of freshly cut grass in the mornings, and the stray showers that cool off the sticky hot afternoons; I'd miss picking honeysuckle and tasting its sweet, summery flavor.

Yes, all these things I'll miss once summer flees town, allowing school to enter the picture. But there's one thing I'll especially miss, and that one thing is staying out all night with Brenton Sparks.

As an image of Brenton's handsome face, light brown hair and bright smile skirts across my vision, my heart begins its usual barrage of flip-flops in my chest. Those chocolate brown eyes of his always sends excitable shivers up and down my spine.

Brenton and I have been best friends since our diaper days. We've known each other our whole lives. And since the beginning of summer, we've been a couple.

It makes sense, us being together. Our parents had always been close friends, every weekend enjoying cookouts, and every summer taking vacations. Though vacations and cookouts don't take place anymore. Not since Mom and Dad died...

Immediately I slam the brakes on my *woe-is-me* thoughts. I have no time to take a drive down Deplorable Lane. After all, when my shift ends at eight tonight, I'll be jumping in my car and racing to a teen-infested bonfire. All of my friends will be there, along with the rest of Garlandton's teenagers, to celebrate the last throw-down of the summer. Thinking about my dead parents is not on the schedule.

Sighing, I order my tired bones out of bed, their cracking and popping singing off my bedroom walls. I step over a mound of dirty clothes. A curse slips off my tongue as my big toe connects with the dresser.

Finally, after trekking through my untidy room (I'm a bit of a slob), I make it to the cluttered bathroom. I stare at the reflection in the mirror, attempting to put my game face on. A tortuous day of dealing with this town's country bumpkins was about to start, and boy, am I beyond excited ... *not*.

Yep, here I come. A mind-numbed zombie behind a register.

\*\*\*

Baker's Supermarket is located right before entering the town square. The brick building is ancient, housing three checkout lanes. The parking lot is small with only a handful of spaces. Inside the ceiling is low with big square tiles, which need replacing. Every single square has yellowed with age, mostly from the leaky roof, which also needs fixing. Stanley Baker, the owner, is my boss, and he's the best boss ever. He reminds me of good 'ol Saint Nick, with his white beard, chubby stature, and rosy red cheeks.

Oh, and he's single. He shares a one bedroom apartment with his cats, Salt and Pepper. He's gone on dates, but those are rare. Most women in Garlandton are either married, widowed, or not interested in a chubby supermarket owner. Kind of sad, really, though he never shows he's missing a female companion. After all, he's got Salt and Pepper – who else does he need?

The day started off well, though late afternoon births annoyance.

"Your total is $49.95," I inform a customer.

The customer, an old lady sporting a bright yellow housecoat with brush rollers in her gray hair, replies in a sing-song voice, "Wait a minute! I've got *coupons*!"

With that said, she dumps out a handful of crumpled coupons. I sigh as I go through them.

"That's wonderful," I say, forcing a smile. Sneaking a peek at the long line of impatient customers, I sigh again. "Just wonderful."

The old lady laughs, and I hold back a horrified gasp as I take in her wide, toothless grin.

The day drags on, and before I know it the clock reads 8 PM. I'm beyond excited! It's closing time, and as soon as I finish my cleaning duties, the party is on!

While I'm counting down my drawer, my best friend Kora Dodd strolls in. Appearing sleek as usual, with a black tank top, skinny jeans, combat boots and spiky black hair, I gift her with a nod of approval. She's the only person I know who can pull off that style.

Hyper as always, she bounces up to the counter, battering me with her bright green eyes and her contagious smile.

"Hi ya, Clare!" She leans her elbows on the counter. "How's your day been?"

I moan. "Horrible, crazy, sticky, *insane*! And you know what the best part of all was? Janey and Casey called in sick. I've been alone all day, except for all the dingbat customers."

Kora nods. "Uh-huh, uh-huh ... wanna tell me more about it?"

"Absolutely not," I smirk.

"We all have bad days," she begins. Scooting up and

sitting on the conveyor belt she recounts, "Why, just last night I had the enjoyment of cleaning up a mountain of soggy popcorn off the theater's floor. Come to find out these imbeciles were attempting to make a volcano using cola and popcorn. People can be such morons!"

"Wow, that *is* bad – and dumb!" I laugh, realizing that my job isn't so bad after all.

Kora works at the Garlandton Movie Theater, and when I say works, I mean she busts her butt almost every night. She kind of has to, so she can keep a roof over her and her mother's heads. With an alcoholic parent who can't hold down a job, she has no choice but to bust her hump.

"So, are you ready for the party?" There's an energized lilt evident in her voice – Typical, *ready-for-a-good-time* Kora.

"You know it!" I respond, giving her a high-five. "But I gotta sweep the floor – want to grab a broom so we can get out of here?" I wink, hoping she takes the hint.

She shakes her head. "No … but I will anyway."

# Sam

Perched on the rooftop of Baker's, I keep a close eye on

my Charge, Clarity Miller. She's changed out of her yellow work smock and into less modest attire. I don't understand why teenage girls feel the need to show off their flesh. They don't recognize that their actions will lead to dire circumstances with men.

Lustful pleasures are a big hit in this fallen world. Humans allow their sinful natures to take root, causing them to believe that having multiple sex partners is okay. Sadly, that path leads to destruction and death. So few know the truth. Most choose not to hear it. And that's exactly how Satan wants to keep it.

The roar of Clarity's engine hits the air, along with booming racket blaring from the vehicle's speakers. The noise hurts my celestial ears.

I've been Clarity's Guardian her entire life. Growing up she'd been such a cheerful delight. A happy child, one who loved God, her family and friends. However, that all changed the night her parents died in the car crash. That same night was the night she turned away from God. Her heart became frozen and hard, and she kept a constant guard up. To this very day she doesn't speak to the Father.

Soon all that will change.

Spreading my wings, I prepare to follow Clarity and her friend to a bonfire. Alcohol and drugs will be in attendance there, along with jealous and lustful spirits. I'm unable to do much in the terrestrial field, but I can do plenty in the spiritual realm.

After all, I am her Guardian. That's my job – to keep a watchful eye on her and make sure she doesn't cause herself and others any harm. She's the reason of my existence. Soon she'll know me, but now isn't the time. She wouldn't understand. Not yet.

Sniffing the air, I know the enemy is close. *Too* close.

In the distance lightning flashes across the darkened sky, following up with a rumble of profound thunder. This isn't a natural storm, though. This one contains an otherworldly presence, and it's heading right toward the little town of Garlandton.

Change is coming to Clarity, something so prominent and complicated that she'll have no other choice but to trust again. She'll have to learn to trust me.

More importantly, to trust God.

# Chapter Two

# Lukus

The sign reads *Welcome to Garlandton, A Friendly Place To Live!*.

I snarl, shaking my head in disgust.

"There is no place on earth that is *friendly*," I spit out. "Foolish, deceived mortals."

"These human skins are itchy!" complains Markus, my Hellhound companion.

His brother, Stone, agrees in his deep, unearthly voice, "Yeah! My fur keeps knotting up!"

Turning around, I cackle at the sight of them. Before we made our journey from Hell to earth we had to pick out human disguises, so as to blend in amongst the mortals. However, Markus had chosen a look that causes him to stick out like a sore thumb.

Markus wears a male Caucasian skin, one that's well over six feet tall and extremely wiry. His attire consists of tight-fitting leather pants, a leather vest, and black boots.

Tattoos of serpents twist and wind around his skinny arms. A tall platinum mohawk sits on his head, and with it he appears to be even taller.

Stone chose a dark-skinned disguise. He stands almost six feet tall, wearing all black, though instead of hair he's chosen to go bald. He'll blend in the best, thanks to his conservative style.

As for myself, I'm a six foot three white male with longish black hair and hard, toned muscles. I can understand the Hellhound's discomfort, because these bodies are way smaller than our natural ones. Lucky for me I don't have the thick fur tangling under my skins.

"Quit your complaining," I snap at the underlings, keeping my focus straight ahead. "It's only for a brief time."

Stone walks up beside me, his hands scratching awkwardly at his human disguise. "When, Lukus? When can we bring down the *Ra'ah*?"

"Yes, when?" Markus adds, standing on the other side of me. "This itching is excruciating!"

Glancing to Stone, then Markus, and lastly toward the town of Garlandton, I reply, "Soon, my brothers. Soon."

# Clarity

Arriving at the party, pulling my late model Honda into the massive hayfield, a surge of hot adrenaline electrifies my veins. Cars and trucks of every make and model fill up the space in front of the big red barn, which has been decorated with Christmas lights and streamers. Music screams from inside the structure, the bass vibrating the ground we tread on. Smoke from the bonfire lingers in the air. I take a big whiff, loving the scent of burning wood.

Ahh, the three S's – sights, smells, and sounds of a summer in the south. Time to drink, dance, and be merry! More importantly, to escape the reality of a seriously drab life – that's what every teen in town yearns to do. Elude the sense of realism.

"This is going to be great!" I exclaim cheerfully, my eyes darting back and forth. I'm searching for one person and one person only – Brenton.

Kora wholeheartedly agrees. "Yes, it is … though I won't be drinking."

"What?!" I grab her arm and halt our steps, her *way out there* revelation leaving me completely stunned. Then I

13

consider her words, perceiving that she's most likely joking. "You're pulling my leg, right?"

"No, not at all."

Viewing her solid expression, digesting her forthright words, I at once know she's telling the truth. The only question tossing over and over in my head is ... why?

As if reading the question drafted all over my face, she begins explaining, "Kevin doesn't like drinking. Says it makes people act stupid. And since I've been going to church with him I've decided to give up alcohol."

Again, I'm baffled. How could I have missed something like this? She's my freaking best friend!

Considering what she just admitted I pry, "Wait, what are you talking about? You've actually been going to church, like, God and all that stuff?"

"I'm giving it a shot," she points out, shrugging her small shoulders. "Besides, Kevin is into it, and since we're together now, it just feels, I don't know ... like the right thing to do."

I continue to ogle my best friend with unrelenting perplexity. Church. *Really*? Party girl Kora Dodd has given up drinking to sit in a church pew? My simple brain is having a difficult time downloading all this inconceivable info.

When Kora started dating Kevin Davis, the football team's corner back, four months back, everyone – myself included – had been collectively shocked. Don't get me wrong. If they're happy with each other, then good for them. It's just, well ... they're so very different, like comparing apples to oranges.

Kevin is a straight-laced, straight-A student, a Christian guy who works his tail off on his family's farm, while Kora is your typical C student who cares none about her future. She could care less about getting into a good college, and care more about hooking up with some random guy.

That is, she *used* to be that way. Her relationship with Kevin has changed her for the better, blossoming her into a happier, more confident girl. Way better than her last boyfriend, who turned out to be a total whack job.

I should be happy for her, and really, I am. A little.

In a weird sort of way, with her changing her ideals on life, I feel like I'm losing my best friend. Reality, though, shows that I'm not losing her. It's just a life adjustment, and I have to support her no matter what. Like everything in life, I will learn to deal with it.

If Kevin makes her happy, then I'll be happy. Even if I don't agree with the whole religious aspect.

"Hey!" Kora cries out, jolting me from my contentious thoughts. "There's Kevin!"

I sigh, feeling a little deflated. "Go ahead. Run off with church boy."

"Meet up later?" she wonders, waiting expectantly.

I nod. "Yeah, I'll be the drunk girl in the corner." I begin walking away from the barn.

"Hey, where ya going?" Kora calls out. "The party's this way."

Without a glance back I loudly reply, "That's the last place Brenton will be."

Brenton and I have a lot in common. Really, we do. We both love watching cheesy black and white movies, sitting on my roof at night, gazing up at the stars and talking about the future, and Sponge Bob – don't laugh, adults love him, too.

The ultimate one thing that Brenton and I constantly disagree on is this – Brenton and his dislike for parties. In my opinion his only flaw.

Forging my way behind the barn, the thick brush that makes up the field pulling at my feet, I spot a lone figure sitting on top a large bale of hay. I know straight away that it's Brenton.

The glow of the moon hovers directly above him, spotlighting his entire form. His head tilts back as he takes a drink from an amber bottle, most likely cheap beer.

Lightning in the distance strikes, along with a faraway rumble of thunder. Guess a storm is headed this way, which is very common for this time of year.

Sneaking up behind him I shout, "Boo!"

"What the...?!" he exclaims, and I laugh as he almost tumbles off the hay. When he finds out it's me, he jumps off the bale, his facial exhibits severe.

"Did I scare you?" I query, gazing up at him as I innocently twirl a strand of my long brown hair.

"What do you think you're doing, huh?" He pelts me with a maddening glare.

Crossing my arms at my chest and raising an eyebrow, I pragmatically tell him, "You are not really mad at me."

He sneers, his dark eyes fixated on mine, and for a brief moment I'm nervous that he's really peeved with me. I relax when he breaks out into a wide grin, his dimples appearing on his tanned face.

"You're right," he admits, slowly stepping towards me. "I can never stay mad at you. You look beautiful, by the way."

Brenton is wearing his usual gear – blue jeans, flip-flops, and a tight-fitted t-shirt that shows off his muscular arms. His brown hair, which has lightened a little over the summer, is wavy and unkempt. Just the way I like it.

I soak in his appearance and nod an approval. "And you are as handsome as ever."

Getting nose-to-nose with me he whispers, "What took you so long?"

"Work, people, junk," I nonchalantly reply. Pretending to almost kiss him, I snatch his beer instead. It's half full, so I knock it back in three gulps.

He frowns. "*Man*, that was my last one!"

"So." I shrug, dropping the bottle to the ground. "Let's go inside and get more."

He shakes his head. "No way. I'd rather stay out here and do this."

Raking a hand through my hair, he pulls me closer and kisses me. I kiss him back, passionately, wanting him as close to me as possible. I place my hand on his face, feeling the coarse stubble on his skin. The cologne he's wearing is tantalizing, causing me to melt even more into him.

A few moments pass by before we slowly break apart, keeping our foreheads touching. I feel total peace, but then he goes and takes it away with the words he speaks.

"You know what Monday is, right?"

"First day of school," I answer, but I know that's not what he's bringing up.

"Come on, Clare. You've got to face it."

His statement sends an electric shock through me, then an overwhelming amount of anger forces my hands to push him away. He stumbles back, his face harboring a confused look. I openly gape at him, furious that he's ruined our special moment.

"Why are you bringing them up?" My teeth are clenched so tightly my jaw starts to hurt.

"Because you need to face it," he says again, his eyes regarding me with caution.

Outraged, I continue to stare at him, unwilling to admit that what he's saying is true. Yes, I do need to face what Monday represents. But the truth is, I don't want to. With each year that passes, this day is one I wish I could skip.

The day Mom and Dad were killed in the car crash.

"Five years," I say softly. I order myself to feel no emotion. "They've been dead for five years."

Brenton nods. "Five years, and you're still angry – "

"I am not angry!" I scream, my emotions beginning to get the best of me.

"Clarity..." He reaches for me, but I back away, shaking my head. He releases a sigh. "You've got to let this go."

"I *have* let it go," I spit back. "I've come a long way since then. I've dealt with it the best way I know how, by – "

"Partying and drinking," he reveals, finishing my sentence.

A silent moment passes. "You know me well."

"Clarity." He walks up and wraps his arms around my waist, pulling me to his chest; I, in turn, let him.

"Clarity," he repeats, breathing into my hair, "you say you're over it, but you're really not. You haven't grieved them. That very night I watched you shut down. You became hard as stone." Leaning back so as to peer into my eyes he adds, "I love you and I want you to be at peace. The thing is, you can't find that peace in a bottle."

I study him curiously, then whisper, "Depends on the bottle."

Before he can offer a response, a loud crash sounds from within the barn. The music shuts off almost immediately. The only noise coming from the barn are screams of terror.

Something has just gone terribly wrong.

# Chapter Three

# Clarity

"What was that?" I glance toward the barn, then back to Brenton. The consternation painting his face informs me that he's as concerned as I am.

"I don't know," he responds, then grabs my hand. "Let's go check it out. It sounds like someone is hurt, and in a bad way."

Hand-in-hand we race to the barn, entering from the back. Gasps of shock and dismay travel around the room, but one voice peals above all others.

"Arrrrg! Get it out! Get it *out!*"

A circle has assembled around a fallen teenager. Brenton pushes through the crowd, which lands us right in front of the dire situation. My hand flies to my mouth as I force down a building shriek.

Don Freeman, a burly football player with a mop of curly red hair, is sprawled out on the dirt floor. The disco ball that was strung up on the ceiling has broken free, shattered

23

into thousands of pieces. A few wooden beams have fallen, some splitting into sharp, smaller pieces and resting on the ground. Except one didn't make it with the rest. Rather it had become embedded in the palm of Don's hand. The worst part? It appears that the stake-like piece of wood in his hand has him pinned to the ground!

We watch as Cole Parks, Garlandton's star quarterback, falls to his knees next to his fallen friend.

"Don, dude," sputters Cole, "your hand! It's... "

"Shut-up and pull it out!" Don yells, his chubby face burning crimson. Beads of sweat cascade down his face, while a multitude of veins pop out of his neck.

"Okay, okay," repeats Cole. Wrapping shaky hands around the base of the wood, he gazes down at Don, his face showing fear. "I'm gonna count to thr – "

"JUST PULL IT OUT!" screams Don, the harrowing pain fueling his temper.

Upon Don's outburst, Cole quickly yanks it out of his hand. Don yelps, then his eyes roll back inside his head. The extracting of the splintered wood renders him unconscious.

An uneasy silence ticks by, all eyes focused on the out-cold Don. We're all a little shocked – in complete disbelief, actually. Especially Cole, who has turned pale as a ghost. A cold, eerie feeling wraps around me, causing a shiver to rack my body. Brenton, noticing my sudden movement, places his arm around my shoulders and draws me nearer to him.

"Shouldn't he be on his way to the emergency room?" Mary-Ann Greenway, a cheerleader, squeaks out in a small, timid voice. Her words shake us out of our dazed reveries.

"She's right!" exclaims Cole. Gesturing to a couple of guys nearest him he orders, "You two – help me get him up and into my truck."

The crowd parts, allowing room for the boys to exit. Cole and his two helpers carry the comatose Don out of the barn. A restless quiet fills the atmosphere, the mood of the party turning cold and dreary. Then the DJ proclaims, "Party time!"

Suddenly the music turns back on, and everyone quickly forgets about Don, including myself. Dancing and drinking commences, along with couples making out in the shadows. I bend over a cooler and withdraw two bottles of beer.

Brenton's dumbfounded expression leads me to ask, "What's wrong?"

"Don just had a brush with death," he promptly responds, shaking his head, "and now everybody is acting as if it didn't happen. It's kind of disturbing, don't ya think?"

"Brenton." I lock my arms around his waist, still holding the bottles of beer. "He's fine. It was only a piece of wood stuck in his hand – "

"That had him pinned to the ground, Clare!" he strongly interjects, his tone swamped with frustration. "It stabbed through his hand – what if it had stabbed him in his heart or neck? What if one of the heavy beams holding this place up had crushed and killed him and the people closest to him?"

Sighing, I stand on my tiptoes so I'm eye-to-eye with him. "But nothing like that happened. He's alive, not dead." Brenton attempts a rebuttal but I hurriedly continue on. "He's fine, Brenton! Plus, this party is the last throw-down of the summer! We can't let one unfortunate incident halt our fun."

"But – "

I shush him, placing a finger on his lips. "It's over. Now let's have some fun!"

Before he can do or say anything, I kiss him hard on the lips. When we break apart, I gaze up at him adoringly. Finally he smiles and takes one of the beers. Grabbing his arm, I drag him into the mosh pit of slam dancing kids. After a few minutes we find ourselves lost in a whole new world...

**Two hours later...**

"Where ... am ... I?"

My feet stumble over the dense field. I hear music, but the sound is far, far away. The moon is gone, leaving the sky dark and cloudy. I scream when a lightning bolt flashes before me, the rumbling thunder hitting almost instantly. I try to take a sip of beer, but the bottle is empty.

"Ahh man," I mutter, throwing it to the ground. At that same moment a tangled bushel of weeds catch my feet, sending me face first to the earth.

Rolling onto my back, I begin roaring with laughter, not knowing what's funny. Just laughing.

The wind starts howling, causing shivers to roll up and down my body. A storm is fast approaching, but I'm not afraid. I'm too drunk to be scared.

Really, I should be getting up, sprinting to the safety of the barn. I should be finding Brenton so I can cuddle in his warm arms. But then I realize something...

Right now, I don't care about ... *anything*.

Closing my eyes, I settle into the softness of the uncut field. With the wind swishing the hay back and forth, I'm surprised to feel a comfort and peace wrap around me. Even with the upcoming storm, the calm I feel has me unafraid, bold...

Fearless.

A scent I've inhaled my entire life smothers the air – lavender.

This smell has always been able to find me in certain times of my life, though I've never seen it growing anywhere in town. Never thought about it, really. Never cared.

"Why do you do this to yourself, Clarity?"

My eyes fly open, and my heart beats wildly as fear begins to engulf my body. When I peer up into the face of a young man, the panicked jitters recede, giving way to ease. I sniff the air, the lavender scent that hangs in the air calming my anxious nerves. Another strike of lightning hits the sky, the thunder shaking the ground. A gust of wind hits my face. Instantly I recognize where the calming scent of lavender is coming from.

"You smell like lavender," I whisper, then laugh. "Craziness. Pure craziness."

"Why do you do this to yourself?" the mysterious boy inquires once again, gazing down at me, his expression that of sorrow.

Confusion lurches across my wayward mind. "Do what?"

He leans down, giving me a good look of his face. It's a bit fuzzy because of all the beer I'd downed, but somehow I can make out every detail of his face. Extremely pale, strong cheekbones, rosy full lips, black hair, and glowing blue eyes – wait, glowing? How can that be?

"Your eyes, they're … they … "

"You were bought for a price," he gently continues, his lavender-induced breath caressing my face. "Your body is a temple created by God. He's not happy with how you're treating it."

My face contorts into disgust as I snarl, "God? Oh *please*, spare me the sermon. And besides..." I roll over, showing him my back. "I'm only having some fun. Please – leave me alone."

A couple of ticking seconds pass before I hear him

reply, "Very well."

A warm, bright light forms around me. Even with my back to him, the light burns my corneas. Quickly I flip back over, only to see that the young man and the light are gone.

"What the...?" Where is he? It's almost like he disappeared. And what about the light? Where had that come from? Another question: Did I just have my first alcohol-forced hallucination?

Yeah, that's probably it.

"Clarity!"

That voice, it … sounds familiar.

"Brenton, is that you?" I call out, eventually figuring out whose voice it is.

"Where are ya, Clare-Baby?" There's a hint of worry evident in his tone. I find it sweet and enduring.

"Over here!"

Trying to stand, I quickly see that my legs are way too wobbly to work, which causes me to fall back on my bottom. Goofy laughter bubbles up and out of me as I stare up at the dark sky. Amazed, I observe the many jagged streaks of lightning painting the darkness. However, this time there's no thunder to accompany it – only more flashes of bright bolts.

Finally, Brenton's face pops into my peripheral vision. I smile widely up at him.

"Brenton!" I excitedly express. "Where ya been?"

He lets down a hand. I grab it as he replies, "I've been looking for you, that's where I've been. What are you doing out here?"

"I needed ... I needed some air – Whoa!" With my equilibrium being way off, I start to lose my footing. Luckily Brenton's right there to catch me. "Yikes! Everything is spinnin'..."

"Yep, I think it's time to get you home." In one swift move, he picks me up and cradles me close to his chest, then adds an extremely pointed, *"Now."*

"No!" I protest, my head shaking from side-to-side. "We can't just *leave*! This is ... this night is the last ... last ... " I pause with frustration, then inquire, "What am I trying to say?"

"No clue, Clare-Baby," mutters Brenton. He then adds, "I hate parties."

I want to argue, to fight back, but I'm already to that point of utter fatigue; complete listlessness. Brenton carries me across the field, past the noisy barn, the whole while with me snuggled to his chest. And I'm loving it.

A moment passes, then Brenton halts his steps and says, "That's weird."

"What?" I grumble, keeping my face buried in his shirt.

"The storm," he responds, his voice filled with awe, "it's gone. The stars are out, and so is the moon."

With my curiosity peaked, I lean my head back and gaze upward. Brenton's right – the storm is gone, and the sky is clear. The moon appears bigger and brighter than before, and the wind has died down.

Brenton continues, still in wonderment because of the changed weather. "We were about to get pummeled with rain and who knows what. And in the blink of an eye it dissipates. That's just freaky."

"Yeah, it's really interesting," I boringly remark. Cupping his cheek in my hand, using a seductive tone, I ask, "You wanna make-out or what?"

This gets his attention. He stares at me, searching my face, then laughs. "No, dear, I don't think so. You skipped the 'make-out' stage of the party when you decided to drink all the way to the 'plastered' stage." He starts walking again, straight toward his truck.

I frown at him, batting my eyelashes ... at least I think I'm batting them. Could have dirt in my eyes. "But I'm not plastered."

"You're right," he agrees, then adds, "You're not plastered. You're completely bombed."

I giggle. "Okay, maybe a little." Observing his handsome face I whisper, "You're my hero, Brenton."

He laughs, showing off his dimples. "I'm no hero – I'm just a glutton for punishment."

"Huh?" I ask with raised eyebrows.

"It means I love you." He gives me a wink.

"Love you..."

I stop right there. Can't talk anymore. The liquor I'd downed is finally taking its course. My world turns fuzzy and I close my eyes, feeling safe and secure in Brenton's arms.

# Sam

Viewing from the barn's roof, I watch as Brenton pulls out of the field with my Charge, Clarity. He will get her home safely, I'm sure of it. He's a good guy, though he's lost, just like Clarity.

Brenton had been right about the storm. The way it started up then quickly diminished had been a little unusual. He can't conceive that the storm had been part of the enemy's plot to get Clarity. They'd almost had her, too, until I'd shown up. When they got a touch of God's light, they'd split, which I'm glad they did. Smart move on their part. But now I'd have to be on guard. They know who Clarity is – they also know how close she is to being marked.

Puffing out my chest, I allow my wings to emerge from my back. It feels good to liberate them, to set them free. It feels … exceptional.

Crouching down, I spring into the air, straight toward the moon. I've been Clarity's Guardian all of her life. With the enemy so close, my job was about to get interesting.

# Chapter Four

# Clarity

*I'm thirteen, sitting on the couch next to my best friend, Brenton. An old black and white monster movie is playing on the screen, one of our favorites. The lights are turned off, which allows us to see the storm brewing outside. The lightning envelops the room. The thunder shakes the house. A perfect night for some old horror flicks.*

*A.C. is in the kitchen popping some popcorn, her long brown ponytail swishing back and forth as she moves. She's babysitting us while Mom and Dad are out to dinner, spending what they call "quality time" together. I try not to think about them alone, hugging, kissing and holding hands. They're parents – they shouldn't be doing that. Totally gross.*

*The doorbell suddenly rings. I jump up to answer the door, assuming Mom and Dad are home. On regarding the flashing police lights outside the window I realize it's not them. As I open the door, two policemen are standing there, both wearing grave expressions on their faces.*

"C-Can I help you?" I ask timidly, not knowing what to expect.

"Are you Clarity Miller?" one of them inquires.

Unease starts streaming through my veins as I retort, "Yes, I am." Brenton and A.C. slowly walk up behind me.

"We have ... some bad news." The officer removes his cap and rubs a hand over his bald head. His eyes lower to the ground, like he's having a tough time looking at me.

"What?" I press, becoming frustrated.

"Your parents," he says. I jump when he starts to laugh. The other officer joins in, both of the men laughing so hard they're bent over.

Anger begins rising inside me. "What?! What about my parents?"

The officer lifts his gaze, shooting a look of malice right in my face, all the while keeping his cackling strong and unwavering.

"They're DEAD!" he shouts.

"No!" I shout back, not wanting to believe.

Laughing sounds behind me. I turn around and I'm shocked to see that A.C. and Brenton have fallen in with the laughter.

Confusion and fury mix together as I prepare to attack with severe words, but I'm stopped when a flash of lightning gives me a *glance of their faces. They are no longer A.C. and Brenton – they are no longer human! Horns protrude from their foreheads and their eyes … their eyes are as black as the night sky.*

*As they continue their laughter, I back away from them. The fear is overpowering, trapping me in its indestructible grasp. I bump into something … something solid and enormous. Slowly, I turn and find myself trapped by a horned, red-skinned monster with blood-red eyes. A scream of terror rips from my mouth...*

I wake screaming, jumping off the bed and falling to the floor. I scoot across the floor until my back hits the wall, shaking all the pictures that hang on it. My heartbeat is out of control, pulsating in my throat, making it hard to breathe. I feel like I'm dying.

With my eyes darting back and forth, I absorb my surroundings. Harsh yellow walls, dark hardwood floors, wooden dresser, nightstand, closet door with clothes spilling out – yes, this is my room. It had only been a dream, one that has left me soaked to the bone with sweat.

I'm not at all surprised that I'd dreamed of my parents. After all, the anniversary of their death was just a day away. Five years, and I'm still having nightmares of that night. Though this nightmare had been way different than the ones in the past. This was a first with monsters in it – or maybe they had been demons, which is totally preposterous.

Demons aren't real.

Standing up and crossing my room to the window, I stare at the rising sun. Orange and red hues of light warm my body, the sun casting its radiance around my bedroom.

My parents used to tell me that a sunrise is just one of the many ways God shows His love for His children. The beauty of a brand new day is found in a sunrise. A colorful visual of a renewed day.

Too bad I don't believe in renewability.

Too bad I don't believe in God.

***

Monday morning has arrived, bringing an end to summer and marking the first day of school. Our freedom licenses were in the process of being revoked, landing us in school limbo for the next nine months.

The morning is sunny and cloudless, a beautiful first day of school. But for the students at Garlandton High, no amount of sunshine could sweep over the dark clouds of depression looming over the school. From my vantage point in my rust-bucket car I can tell that even the teachers appear crestfallen. They, like us students, are wishing for more recuperation time between school and summer. Three months is not near enough time to relax and unwind.

At least for a few of us this is our last year. Knowing that certain detail helps ease the pain ... a little. That one detail helps, especially in my case, to suck it up and get it over with. Graduation day will come and I, like lightning, will bolt to the county line and keep going, never looking back.

I find a parking spot next to the fence, not far from the school building. As soon as I open the door I hear my name being called.

"Clarity!"

Kora runs up wearing a broad smile on her face. I'm about to respond when my eyes spot the change on top of her head. Her hair color is different, changed from black to bright red.

"Wow," I express, a little taken back by her appearance. "You ... you dyed your hair red."

"*Raspberry Blush* to be precise." She strikes a pose, her green eyes sparkling. "What do ya think?"

"Um..." I strive to think of something nice to say, but

instead I go with, "Truthfully, the color reminds me of a shiny baboon's – "

Kora clamps a hand over my mouth, ceasing my degrading thought. Besides, she knew where I was going with that sentence.

"On second thought, I don't care what you think." She's grinning, with her hand still on my mouth. I shock her by licking it.

"Gross!" she cries out, yanking her hand away and wiping it on her skinny jeans. "You're so sick!"

I smirk with raised eyebrows. "Teach you to try and shut me up again."

"Yeah, like that could ever happen," she mutters, rolling her eyes.

We start walking through the parking lot, making small talk. I update her on how wild everything got after Don Freeman's accident and about how I didn't remember getting home that night. Kora listens quietly, her expression unreadable. Usually after raging parties like that we have plenty to talk and gossip about. Now, since Kora's dating Kevin and attending church, she's not as jovial about drinking and parties. Kind of sad, really. Kora has always been the party girl. Lately she's been a downer.

As we reach the steps leading up to school, we stop walking and stare. The two-story, seventy-five year old building looks like a prison without bars. And we're about to start our sentence.

"I can't believe summer is over," Kora remarks, breaking the silence.

"At least it's our last year," I point out, attempting to lighten the mood.

Kora sighs and says, "True dat, Clare."

We link arms and hike up the concrete steps, heading directly to our impending doom. Once through the doors, the school smells punch me right in the face. You know, that mixture of disinfectant, sweat, feet, and an unidentified musty odor that takes over every school in the world. Yeah, *that* stench.

"Man, absolutely nothing has changed."

Kora snorts. "I don't think anything has changed here since the sixties."

The school's interior is painted an off-white color, which is chipped here and there. The green and white checkered industrial tiles still hold scuff marks from last

school year. Dust about two inches thick coat the lockers –
apparently they haven't been touched for the last three
months.

Yep, this is our school. Home of the Bovines.

Seriously. We're the Garlandton Bovines. Our home
away from home.

Home sweet *whatever.*

Pulling out our schedules, we both groan in unison.

"Really? Our first class is World History?" My
expression sours. "This is gonna suck."

"In total agreement with that statement." Kora nods,
adding, "Come on, let's go." We start off to class as fast as a
herd of snails.

A mass of childish excitement jams the hallways. Kids
who haven't seen each other the last three months find it easy
to sink back into their little cliques. On one side of the hall
cheerleaders are gossiping about anything and everything,
while on the other side a jock is beating the crap out of an
underclassman. A group huddles at the end of the hall next to
the exit doors sharing a cigarette, while one guy keeps a watch
out for any teachers passing by.

Like every school on earth, you have your different

types of cliques. At Garlandton the list goes as such: Jocks, Cheerleaders, Goths, Emos, Geeks, Hippies, Rednecks, Introverts, and Butt Kissers. I've always found it bizarre that there's such diversity under one roof. All together, trapped in one great big fish bowl of imperfection. In my opinion, an extremely dangerous combination.

Arriving at the classroom, Kora leans in and whispers, "I really hope Nick isn't in any of my classes."

"If he is, I'll protect you," I offer with a wink, which makes her laugh.

Nick Reece is one of the richest boys at school. He is also Kora's ex-boyfriend. Not only that, but he's a deranged psychopath.

Kora had dated Nick for a few months. Everything had been going great, until he became abusive to her, mentally and physically. The last time he pushed her around, he'd given her a black eye. After that he tried showering her with gifts in hopes of earning her forgiveness. His ploys didn't work. She dumped him, and since then moved on.

Seven months have passed since she broke up with him, but he still calls her everyday, trying to win her back. Total stalker, if you ask me, but Kora's not at all worried. After all, she's got Kevin Davis, the ultimate strongbox. He'll protect her from the insanity that is Nick.

Taking seats in the back, we fling our backpacks on our desktops and sit. I place my history book on the desk when Kora makes a horrible moaning sound.

"What's your problem?" I inquire, feeling concern for my friend.

Lifting her chin she replies, "That's my problem." Following her gaze, I quickly realize what the problem is, or rather *who* it is.

Strolling in is Daria Phipps, captain of the cheer squad, Homecoming snob, and queen over all mean girls of the world. With her perky chest, blonde hair, and perfect teeth, she's every boy's dream, and every girl's nightmare. Her skin is the perfect shade of a Caribbean vacation all year round, her blue eyes the color of the deep sea.

Daria has it all – beauty, popularity, money – and she knows it. If there was a picture next to the word "snob" in the dictionary, her perfect smiling face would be there, along with the words "tramp" and "slut".

Alongside Daria is Gerran Greene and Melinda White, fellow pep squad snobs. Gerran is tall and skinny, with short, curly red hair that bounces up and down when she walks. Melinda has dark skin and long, shiny black hair.

Gerran and Melinda mimic everything Daria says and does. They act like puppets, with Daria their puppet master, engineering every move they create.

From day one, Kora and Daria had despised each other, and no one knows the reason why. It's as if they had been born mortal enemies.

Daria and her friends pick seats in the front of the class. For a moment I'm relieved, thinking that Daria doesn't see Kora in the back. In that certain moment I think that maybe she has grown up over the summer and is done bullying Kora. That thought quickly dies when she shifts her gaze to the back, her eyes directed on my best friend.

"Why, Kora," Daria calls from the front, her lips curling upward, "love your new hairstyle. Every hooker in town will be following your lead!" She throws her head back and guffaws, her cheerleader minions following suit.

Leaning toward Kora I say, "Ignore them, Kora – they're so not worth it."

Right after those words exit my mouth, Daria adds, "How many boys will become men this year, Kora?"

Kora, with a matter-of-fact expression, says, "How can I ignore them when they don't ignore me?" Before I can respond Kora calls out, "Look everybody! Satan has World History, too!"

Snickers formulate all across the room. Daria sneers, her face turning tomato red.

"*Whatever*," Daria snarls, then her and her friends take their seats, whispering amongst themselves.

Fixing my gaze on Kora, I grin and say, "Wow, that's the best comeback I've heard in a long while. You're getting better, babe."

A pleased look crosses her face as she responds, "And just think – I've got all year to come up with even better ones. All year long." Reclining back in her desk, she fixes her hands behind her head.

Shaking my head, I think to myself that this is going to be the longest year of my life.

# Sam

Clarity has handled this day pretty well, way better than most. She's gone through all the motions of a teenage girl in high school – girlfriend, friend, student – without anyone knowing of the turmoil boiling underneath her skin.

I've stayed by Clarity's side all day. When she'd dug in her locker and cursed because she couldn't find what she was looking for, I was there. At lunch with her friends, I'd watched and listened to all the nonsensical words they all spoke, the whole time sitting next to my Charge. When she and Brenton concealed a kiss between classes, I'd been there. And now, at this very moment, placing flowers on her mother and father's graves, I am by her side.

Her features show no emotion, her eyes empty of tears. The wind blows her long brown hair in her face, but she's not fazed. Unmoving, she's kneeling in front of their graves, peering at the gravestones. No thoughts pass by in her mind – she's completely impassive.

Five years has passed, and Clarity still has not found the peace she needs to move forward. The only time she cried over their deaths was the night the car wreck occurred. After that, walls were built up inside of Clarity, thick with anger, hurt and resentment.

That night she became a hollow shell with a frozen heart. Not letting anyone in, especially God. She has all of her friends fooled, even Brenton, though I do believe her love for him is genuine. Her problem is she doesn't know how to trust. She's too afraid of being hurt again.

Only I know of her destructive thoughts, and the pain she's buried deep within her heart. She doesn't sense that I'm here by her side, an unseen force that comforts her when hostility begins to rise to the surface, threatening to take control of her life.

Clarity doesn't know me, not yet.

But she will.

Soon.

# Chapter Five

# Clarity

"Where have you been?" inquires Janey Thomas, my friend and fellow cashier at Baker's Supermarket.

"None of your business, Miss Nosey," I snidely answer as I tie my yellow smock around my waist. "Besides, I'm never late. That's Casey's job."

Janey looks thoughtful a moment, then giggles, flipping her strawberry blonde hair off her shoulders. With a twinkle in her hazel eyes she states, "Yep, that's my Casey."

"I'm here!"

We turn to find Casey swinging the doors open, hitting the tiny bell that dangles from the ceiling. His usual spiky blonde hair appears matted down with sweat, like he'd ran the whole way to work. Strolling toward us, he puts on a goofy grin.

"Speak of the devil," I mutter under my breath while pulling my hair into a ponytail.

"Who's a devil?" Casey wonders, glancing from me to

49

Janey.

"You are!" exclaims Janey. She wraps her arms around his waist and they kiss.

Rolling my eyes I jib, "Yuck, gag me!" I stick my finger in my mouth, making a sick noise in my throat.

When they break apart, Casey says, "You're just jealous because *Sparky-Warky* doesn't work here."

"Mr. Baker doesn't pay us to make-out in the stockroom," I crudely point out.

"Speaking of making-out," Casey begins, knotting his yellow smock behind his back, "have y'all heard the latest on Don's hand?"

Janey and I glance at each other, then let out a collective "*Eww, gross!*"

"Casey, come on!" Janey says, shuddering. "That is so wrong."

"What did I say?" questions Casey with raised eyebrows.

"Don and making-out does not need to be in the same sentence," I stormily point out. "And honestly I'd rather eat dog vomit than ... uh, never mind." I blanch, my stomach rolling.

"As I was saying," Casey continues, his tone wet with irritation, "his accident will keep him from playing his last year of football."

"Wow, that's gotta suck!" proclaims Janey, her eyes wide with disbelief.

"It does," Casey nods. "This will hurt his chances for a football scholarship."

"If you ask me, he's getting what he deserves," I declare nonchalantly.

"Clarity!" Janey's mouth drops open with shock. "How can you say that? You can't mean it."

Flinging my gaze her way I respond with, "Well, Janey, if what I heard is true, that being Don getting on top of the disco ball and riding on it like a horsey, then my opinion is this: He deserves the *Moron of the Year* award."

Casey lets loose a low whistle. "That's cold, Clare. Ice cold."

"Yeah, totally cold," echoes Janey, with her head shaking back and forth.

"Okay, is it true?" I twine my arms together.

"Is what true?" Casey inquires.

I clarify with, "Is it true that Don was swinging on the

disco ball yelling 'Yee-Haw'?"

"Um..." Janey peeks at Casey, her teeth combing over her bottom lip.

A brief pause ensues before Casey finally admits, "Yes, it's true. We were there."

Plastering a pleased know-it-all grin on my face I say, "So I'm right. Moron with a capitol *Idiot*."

I'm not a heartless or detached person, but what Don did is his fault and his fault alone. Anyone with half a brain can see that. Obviously the common sense gene isn't a predominate trait in his family tree.

Before the two of them can offer a rebuttal, Mr. Baker waddles out of his office, whistling as he walks. The three of us glance at each other and stifle laughs. I know we're all thinking the same thing. It's his pants – and how they're pulled up to his armpits.

"Good afternoon, Mr. Baker!" Casey calls out, his voice quivering with amusement. "Beautiful day, isn't it?"

Inwardly I groan, feeling a tinge of annoyance. I've known Casey for a long time. I know when he's being real and being phony. Right now he's being immeasurably fake, but Mr. Baker doesn't see that in Casey. He eats the pleasantness right up, clearly believing that Casey Anderson is an outstanding young man.

Boy, is he duped!

"Yes, Mr. Anderson, it sure is," replies Mr. Baker with a smile on his face. Beads of sweat congregate on his shiny red forehead. He presses forward with, "I have a job to ask of you and Miss Thomas."

"Anything for you, Mr. Baker," Casey says, continuing to brown nose the boss.

"What needs to be done?" pipes in Janey.

"The stockroom is in complete disarray," answers Mr. Baker, his head shaking back and forth. "Too much work for one person alone. And since customers are few and far between, I thought the two of you could work together and – "

"Don't say another word!" Casey tells Mr. Baker, lightly slapping him on the back. "Janey and I got this."

Janey grins, nodding her head. "Absolutely. Consider it done."

Hurriedly, the couple sprints to the stockroom, appearing enthusiastic to start their workload. In reality their speedy getaway is just a ploy to not give Mr. Baker any second thoughts on the two of them working in the stockroom. Alone. *Together.*

But I know better.

Sometimes I wonder if the old man is clueless, or just plain senile. He knows they're dating – he's caught them kissing before. I mean, why else would he put the two of them alone in a stockroom, especially if he wants work to actually happen?

No work would be done back there today. Unless you count tongue wrestling as work.

Gross with a huge *Nasty.*

"Miss Miller, I've got a job for you as well."

Breaking my focus off the gruesome twosome, I turn to Mr. Baker and say, "Alright." My nose isn't as brown as Casey's.

He smiles, not noticing my bored attitude. "I want you, when you're not attending to customers, to clean the store from top to bottom. Floors, windows, shelves, bathrooms – everything. Can I count on you to make the store sparkle, Miss Miller?"

Do I really have a say so? Nope, sure don't.

"Yes sir, you can," I reply with a smile, swallowing

down a snarky comment.

He smiles and pulls his pants up higher, which I thought impossible – what is he trying to do, pull them over his shoulders? Geez, that would be one massive wedgie!

"Alright, then," he says. "I'll be in my office if you need me."

"Cool," is all I say back.

Mr. Baker totters back to his office, closing the door. Right after that he starts up some music over the speakers, which continuously plays the oldies. The station did seem like the right kind of noise to play, since the store decor was still stuck in the fifties.

With my orders bestowed upon me, I begin busying myself with making the store, ahem … *sparkle*. Dusting and arranging shelves, washing windows, scrubbing toilets, disinfecting counters – anything to keep me far away from Casey and Janey in the dreaded stockroom. I'd most likely be scarred for life if I walked into something disgusting there.

Two hours go by without a single customer. Fine by me. I've gotten everything done, besides the floors. First sweep, then mop – easy as pie. Grabbing the broom, I start sweeping, humming along to an oldies tune. Maybe I can leave work earlier than expected. I'm worn out!

That one thought is crushed when the bell above the doors ring, signaling in a customer. After two hours of no customers, one decides to show up, ruining my chances of going home early.

Sighing, I dredge up a fake smile, though I don't have much energy left to make my face work. Spinning around, I prepare to greet the customer who's going to make me work even harder. My smile dissolves into a frown when I find the person is Nick Reece, Kora's ex-boyfriend.

Nick tromps up to me like he owns the place, his smile so arrogant I want to punch it off his face. He's wearing dark jeans and a red, untucked silk shirt, probably designer labels. Wisps of dark blonde hair fall over his intense green eyes, his bright white teeth blinding under the fluorescent lights.

I hate to say it, but Nick is a good-looking guy. No doubt about that. His attitude, however, smells worse than dog farts.

"Hello, princess," he smirks. "Doing a little sweeping, I see."

"Hello, *Nicky*," I snootily retort. "Doing nothing but taking up space, I see. Business as usual, huh?"

The grin on his face fades. He glowers, his eyes as cold as a winter's day. "Funny as always, Clarity. Funny as always."

Rolling my eyes, I turn away from him, placing my concentration on cleaning the floor. "What do you want, Nick? I'm a little busy here."

"I think you know why I'm here," he answers, his tone darkening. He moves closer, so close I feel his breath against my cheek. It reeks of alcohol.

Flashing him a sideways glance I sarcastically remark, "Oh, looking for the tampon aisle, are you?" A cackle sounds from my mouth, and I mentally congratulate myself for my witty satire.

All of a sudden he grabs my arm and jerks me around so as to face him. I drop the broom in the process, the *clank* of the wood echoing throughout the store.

"Don't get smart with me, Miller," he grinds out angrily, his features twisting into undeniable rage.

"Or what? You gonna tell your daddy on me?" I yank my arm out of his grasp, rubbing at the soreness. I'd definitely have a bruise there tomorrow.

As if realizing what he'd done, he takes a step back and

rakes a hand through his disheveled hair. A blank look appears in his eyes.

"S-Sorry, Clarity, I … I'm …"

"Drunk?" The word expels before I can stop it. I glare at him and say, "Nick, I've got a mega-amount of junk to do before I can go home, so – "

He instantly cuts me off. "Why did you make Kora break up with me?"

His crazy proclamation bowls right over me. *"Excuse me?"*

"Kora broke up with me," he persists bitterly, "and immediately started dating that Davis guy – and *you* are to blame."

I stare at him in utter amazement. Is he for real? Or just insane?

"Are you serious right now?" I bark out a laugh, my head unable to perceive his distorted thinking.

"I'm always serious," he reacts, his expression stone cold.

This guy has lost his marbles!

"I didn't make Kora break up with you. I don't have that kind of power over her. But I can tell you that she broke up with you because you're an egotistical spoiled little rich kid who thinks he can control people with loads of cash. Plus, *Nicky*, she got tired of all the verbal and physical abuse you constantly caused her." Feeling brave and indestructible, I get nose-to-nose with him. "She figured out she deserved better than a snot-nosed brat that's never worked a day in his life. Kevin, on the other hand, knows about hard work, and he genuinely cares for Kora."

"No he don't," he states gruffly. "He's after one thing, just like every guy alive."

Idiot. What a freaking idiot.

"Whatever," I mutter. "Get out of my way and out of my life."

I make a move to pass by him, when he grabs my shoulders and throws me up against the wall, knocking the breath from my lungs. Clamping his hands tightly on the sides of my arms, he has me trapped between him and the wall. His lips are curled into a sneer, his bloodshot eyes turning dark and wild. My stomach lurches when his rank liquor breath drifts up my nostrils.

I've always thought of him as a joke, but with his hands squeezing my arms so firmly, fear begins to snake through my limbs, weaving in and out of my ribs. An ice cold blanket starts to cover my skin, from my head down to my toes.

"Listen here, girlie," he speaks hoarsely, his face just an inch from mine. "You can say whatever you wanna say, but the truth is this: You bad-mouthed me to Kora and set her up with your boyfriend's best friend. You whispered lies, you conned her into dumping me, which leaves only one conclusion – *You* are the problem."

A lump of terror has become wedged in my throat, but I force it down. I'm stronger than he thinks. I'm not weak. And I will not show fear.

"I didn't con her into doing anything," I tell him with an unwavering voice. "She's not a puppet. She's smarter than that."

"Smart?" He abrasively laughs, and I wince at the sound. "She's dumber than a box of nails. And you ..." His drunk eyes roam over my face, landing right on my lips. He adds in a whisper, "You're even dumber than her."

Nick leans in, attempting to kiss me, but that's not happening. Not in this lifetime, or ever! I squirm and kick, but I can't get him to release me. He's too strong. I push back against the wall and shake my head side-to-side, but he won't let up.

Why is he doing this? What is he capable of?

This can't be happening! This can't —

"Let her go."

# Chapter Six

# Clarity

Nick releases his hold on me, his menacing eyes glaring at the newcomer. I flex my head ... and my heart stutters in my chest.

Standing by the magazine rack, holding a biker magazine in his hands, is the most gorgeous guy I've ever seen. He stands around six feet tall, with a lot of muscle definition. His skin is pale, his black hair falls right above his eyebrows, and if I had to guess I'd say he's around my age, maybe a little older. He stares at Nick with unnatural blue eyes, his expression firm and unyielding.

A rock has formed uncomfortably in my throat, pulsating along with my heart. I can't shake the feeling that I've seen this boy before, but deep down I know I have not. He has a face that no one could forget. Still, there's a familiarity about him...

The mysterious boy's focus leaves Nick, then finds me. When our gazes meet, a sense of calmness roves through my veins, making the altercation with Nick seem miles away. Lavender permeates the air, overtaking the lemony disinfectant I'd used to clean the store.

Lavender. The scent that's been around for as long as I can remember. And this guy smells like he's rolled in it.

Weird. Extremely, undeniably weird. And yet, somehow, extremely *normal*.

When the young man smiles, I automatically smile back. My feet, which had felt cemented to the floor a second before, starts moving, pulling me forward. Relief and peace is all I feel.

Of course that's when Nick wrenches my arm, dragging me back to him. My blissful trance is broken, bringing me back to the unsightly present.

"Come back here, princess," growls Nick. "We're not done talking."

"Yes, you are," the boy tells Nick, his jaw set in a serious lock. He places the magazine down, then walks over. Squaring his shoulders with Nick he says, "And if I were you, I'd take my hand off her. *Now*."

Surprisingly, Nick drops my arm, then clenches his fists at his sides. He's boiling mad, his face as red as a cooked lobster. I shudder, hating what's about to happen. Nick loves a challenge, anything to physically wound a person. And he never backs down.

"Hey," I say to the boy, my voice tired and weak, "you don't have to do this." He only smiles.

"I'm not worried, Clarity." His voice is soft and velvety – and he knows my name. How does he know my name?

Nick snarls. "Yeah, you might wanna listen to her. She's seen me in action before and – "

The boy sharply cuts his eyes to Nick and declares, "That's enough. Now go home and rest your polluted mind. Tomorrow you will be able to think clearer."

An uneasy, squeamish few seconds skate by in silence. My eyes flick back and forth between Nick and the boy. I try closing my eyes so I'm unable to watch the inevitable beat down that's coming, but my lids won't shut. And just when I think Nick's about to wail on him, the biggest shock of the night takes place.

Nick slowly turns around and strolls out of the store, his face blank and expressionless. Never in my life did I think I'd see Nick back down from a fight.

Finding my will to speak I inquire, "How did you do

that?" My heart skips a beat as his blue eyes caress my face. A wave of lavender flows through the air, which is driving me crazy. Where is it coming from?

"Do what?" he softly inquires.

Dubiously, I gape at him, my jaw dropping. "Keep Nick from grinding you into pieces! He could have beaten you to a bloody hump, but he listened to you when you told him to leave!"

A grin colors his face, and I'm nearly knocked off my feet at its beauty.

"Looks can be deceiving," he says mysteriously, winking.

Studying him a moment, I wonder if he's playing me or being serious. There's a sincere quality to his being, but trusting people has always been my downfall, especially strangers. Double especially when it comes to *handsome* strangers.

"Who *are* you?" I marvel, crossing my arms at my chest.

"Sam," he promptly responds.

"How do you know my name?"

Sam doesn't answer. Instead he states, "You need to

keep your distance from that young man. He's got demons all over him."

Demons? What is he talking about? Is he insane? Probably so. All the beautiful guys are stinking crazy.

Laughing undulates off the walls of the store. Janey and Casey are exiting the stockroom, sounding happier and more in love than ever. Sickening, really.

Shifting my gaze toward their voices I say, "That's Janey and Casey. I'll introduce you to them. I know they'd love to meet the guy that Nick backed down from."

I smile, looking back to Sam. The smile drops from my lips as a gasp escapes my mouth.

Sam is gone.

# Sam

"Where'd he go?"

Clarity's brown eyes are wide with concern, and she's feeling a large case of bafflement. She doesn't realize that I'm right next to her, quietly observing as she searches every aisle. Hoping she finds me because she has lots of questions, and expects lots of answers, which I cannot disclose at this time.

Not yet, that is.

When the two other humans showed up, I had no other choice but to disappear, to become invisible. Unseen. Yes, no other choice.

"Clarity, you did an immaculate job!" the human named Janey cries out. I watch as she stops in front of a mirror, playing with her long, frazzled hair. She's too busy primping herself to notice Clarity and her frantic behavior.

The other human, Casey, takes notice right away. "Hey, Clarity ... what ya doing?"

Clarity stiffens, turning her attention to Casey. Janey has walked up next to him, and the both of them are wearing curious expressions. Thoughts are running rampant in Clarity's mind:

*Should I tell them about Nick and how he'd put his hands on me? Should I tell them about the mysterious boy named Sam who showed and made Nick leave, just by telling him to? How can I explain how Sam was there one second, and then gone the next, vanished into thin air?*

Yes, a battle of thoughts wage in her mind. I can hear every single one. In the end she decides to keep it to herself, which is a smart move on her part.

"Just making sure things are … in order." She smiles at her friends, hoping they believe her story.

"They look in order to me!" Janey investigates the floors. "Except for sweeping – here, I'll sweep for you while you get the mop ready." She picks the broom up and starts brushing it across the floor.

Clarity smiles, relieved. "Sounds good to me." Turning to Casey she inquires, "How's the stockroom? In shipshape?"

But Casey doesn't hear her. His hands are touching the glass and he appears fascinated by something outside. All Clarity sees is his hands dirtying up the windows she'd wiped down.

"Casey!" she squeals, running up and punching his arm. "I've already cleaned that – "

"Shh." He gestures with one of his hands. "Check out the sky."

Clarity groans, taking a look out the window. Her eyes grow wide.

"Wow, that's so *weird*."

"What's so weird?" inquires Janey. She bounces up next to Clarity and gasps. "Is that lightning?"

"Yeah," murmurs Casey, still in complete awe.

Clarity shakes her head. "It's jagged and sideways. I've never seen the sky like this, with nonstop lightning."

"And no thunder," adds Casey. The three teens share a look, then continue to watch the lightning.

Little do they know that this lightning is of the supernatural kind. The bad kind.

Closing my eyes, I reopen them when I'm outside, standing in the parking lot of Baker's Supermarket. My wings open wide and I leap into the night sky, directly into the storm. Though this isn't a storm made by mother nature. This is a storm made up of demons – three demons to be more precise.

I know what they're doing. They're preparing for battle, and their prime target is Clarity. I can read it in their minds. Time is of the essence, and I'm running out of it.

Tonight has to be the night.

The night Clarity becomes marked.

# Chapter Seven

# Clarity

*The small room is congested with teens dancing to loud techno music. They have their arms above their heads, swaying them back and forth. An assortment of colored lights flash, pulsating off their faces. With eyes closed, they concentrate on the psychedelic beat, their expressions bare of any emotions. They move the same way, the same rhythm, in unison with one another.*

*All of them but me.*

*Feeling like a lost sheep, I stand motionless in the heart of the crowd. I'm alone, stranded in a mist of deep abandonment. My heart pounds, seeking to escape my chest. My nerves are frazzled and frayed.*

*A door to my left hooks my eye. It's off to the side of the cramped room, far away from the dancing teenagers. A white light seeps through the cracks of the door, shining in my eyes and instantly grabbing my attention.*

*I start weaving in and out of the thick of people, the light beyond flickering like a lit candle, beckoning me to come closer.*

*"Clarity ..."*

*A voice sounds behind the door, calling out for me. On trembling feet, I walk over until I'm standing right in front of it. Examining the door, I don't see anything spectacular about it. It's just a door, a wooden door with a few cracks and a brass knob.*

*Warmth races up my arm, spreading like a wildfire through my body, as I take hold of the knob. I twist it slowly, opening it slightly. The white light is so brilliant I have to shield my eyes using my free hand. A sense of uncertainty pounds away at my conscious. I'm unsure if I want to open the door further. What if there's something calamitous awaiting me on the other side? What if there's something I've buried deep down in my heart long ago that I don't want to face?*

*With all these thoughts traversing around in my head, the voice speaks again.*

*"Do not be afraid, Clarity. Open the door. Come in."*

*Taking in a shaky breath, I do as the voice commands. I swing the door wide, and a gasp crawls out of my mouth. My eyes are forced shut, the blinding light swallowing me whole, overtaking the darkness and the dancing teens. The music ceases and silence greets me. All is calm. All is still.*

*The scent of lavender wraps around me like a soft blanket,* and a sense of peace follows. I open my eyes to find Sam standing in front of me. His face shouts relief. His blue eyes glow steadily. He smiles, his teeth almost as white as the light around us.

"You did it, Clarity." His voice is soft and pure, devoid of any negativity. His statement, though, has me confused.

"What did I do?" I inquire. My voice sounds distant, like an echo.

His smile continues to shine. "You walked through the door, taking your first steps toward your destiny."

Sam reaches out and places a hand on my shoulder. Instantly I'm subdued with calm and serenity. Tranquility seems to emanate from him, along with the sweetness of lavender.

Dropping his hand from my shoulder, he reaches out with both hands and says, "Give me your hands."

"Okay." I comply with his order, though I'm hesitant. He catches on to my discomfort.

"It's okay, Clarity," he reassures, giving both my hands a squeeze. "You've got to trust me."

"I'll … try, I guess." Trust? I don't know him at all! But what choice do I have? I have no idea where I am or what's going on. I have to trust him, whether I like it or not.

A rumble sounds, rocking the room. Low, steady vibrations

*can be felt under our feet. Gazing up at him, I see that urgency is illustrated all over his pale face.*

*"We don't have much time." His voice has become deep, almost angry, though his smile stays put. "They're trying to interfere by using a storm."*

*"Who are you talking about?"*

*He ignores my question and says, "When I tell you to take a breath, do it. Understand?"*

*"Oh — okay." I'm still confused, but since his touch on my skin, I've landed in some sort of dreamy, comforting state. I stare into his eyes, mesmerized by their color. They hold me in their grasp, not letting me go.*

*"On three," whispers Sam. "One..."*

*Suddenly my palms start burning, my comfort zone tainted. "Um ... Sam?"*

*"Two..."*

*The heat intensifies. "Sam, wait..."*

*"Three!"*

*Quickly, I take a breath and then I...*

Wake up screaming.

"OWW!"

My hands feel like they've had lava spilled over them.

Outside a storm is brewing, the lightning illuminating the room. House-shaking thunder follows soon after, causing the window sill to rattle. But I have no time to fret over a little thunderstorm. The hotness of my hands are all I'm able to concentrate on.

Jumping out of bed, kicking my sweat-soaked sheets to the floor, I race to the sink in my bathroom and flip the light on. I turn the cold water on to full blast. Holding my still scorching hands under the flow of freezing bliss, I release a long, alleviated sigh. The water cools my hands right away, releasing them from their fiery prisons.

What the heck just happened? I've never had a dream as crazy as that one, and I've experience some real *out there* junk. And what's going on with the burn in my hands?

Switching the water off, I nervously gaze down at my hands. Horror and fascination slap me across the face, leaving me in unrestrained wonderment. Right smack dab in the middle of my palms are etchings ... better yet, tattoos of some sort.

On each hand appears a cross, with white wings folded around them. The tops of the crosses carry golden crowns. The outside of each tattoo is defined in gold.

No, this isn't real. I'm still asleep. Yeah, that's it!

Pinching my arm, I wait to wake up, but nothing changes. I'm still standing in front of my mirror, looking like I've been beat with an ugly stick. My hands ... still showcase the strange tattoos.

My heart thuds in my ears, its racing a distinct warning that a panic attack is well underway.

Lying down in the bathtub, I turn on the shower and enjoy the comforting heat that streams from the shower head. Closing my eyes, I concentrate on my breathing, seeking to chill out my speedy heartbeat.

Tattoos have appeared on my hands.

Tattoos. Have appeared. On my *hands*.

I figure if I repeat this in my mind over and over again, this whole baffling situation will make sense. However, repeating the obvious will not make the foreign tattoos go away. I know this because I just took a peek ... and they're still there. Crosses. Crowns. Wings. Right in the middle of my hands.

The dream. It had been real. Some of it, at least. The part where Sam had taken my hands and –

Wait. Sam. The stranger. The stranger who knows my

name and reeks of lavender, which I've smelled all my life. Are they connected somehow?

Jumbled thoughts wrench into illogical chatter inside the walls of my brain. I try sorting them into their correct places, but the feat seems futile. I focus on the reality of what's happened.

Maybe reality is trying to betray me. Maybe insanity is weaving its wicked threads inside my damaged soul. If I'm not going crazy, then how can these tattoos be comprehended?

Hugging myself under the hot water, I free my emotions and cry. I mean, what else can I do? Move forward and ignore the fact that I've just woken up with burning palms and tattooed hands?

"I'm not crazy, I'm not crazy, I'm not crazy," I repeat many times over, wanting to believe the phrase swimming laps in my mind.

Still, the proof is in the palms of my hands, pun *intended*.

I raise them to my face, studying them under the cascading water. Yep. Still there. Crosses, wings, crowns, all trimmed in gold.

Who knew that when I went to bed a few hours ago I'd wake up to this junk.

"I'm not crazy," I whisper. "I'm *not.*"

# Lukus

"NO!"

The windows of the abandoned warehouse explode, causing shards of glass to rain down on my vile companions and I. Rage fuels my temper, which had already been close to stewing over the top. To say I'm blistering angry is a huge understatement.

Wind and rain pour through the destroyed windows, my fury still churning in the heart of the storm. The hot madness continues to race through my veins. I pick up a nearby table and throw it against the concrete wall. An explosion of wood and metal follows, the sound almost deafening. Breathing hard, I look to Stone and Markus.

"He marked her," I grind out, my teeth grating together. "The angel sent the Heavenly Light into her, and now she's marked as a Seer!"

Markus and Stone remain silent, observing me with

their blackened orbs. Stupid, worthless underlings. Why had Satan sent these two peons to help me? I know Hellhounds aren't the brightest of demons, but could they have not used their extra-sensitive snouts to sniff out the angelic Guardian?

Silence gathers in the warehouse, and I'm finally able to calm myself. The storm subsides, all rain, wind, and thunder has ceased. With my nerves settling, I start up another plan of action, another line of attack on the newly marked Seer. Just when I'm ready to press forward, Markus opens his mouth.

"That night in the field – that's when we should have got her."

Violence inflames my blood as lightning once again flashes in the outside world. Slowly, I shift my eyes to the underling. The skittish expression he wears on his face excites me.

"What did you say?" I growl with narrowed eyes.

Markus, in a quivering voice, replies, "I-I said the night the *Ra'ah* was inebriated we should have – "

With a primal roar, I charge at Markus, my sharp black nails growing a few inches. As I reach the Hellhound, my nails swipe across his face, slashing through the tender human skin.

Markus, in obvious shock, flies back and connects with

79

a concrete wall, bouncing off of it as if he was made of rubber. He lands on his knees, his breath coming out in hefty pants.

I watch as he steadily gets to his feet, remaining in a low crouch. The skin on one side of his face is shredded, dangling in loose strips. Black hair peeks out from the pale peels of flesh, his black eyes beginning to glow red with frenzied choler. He snarls and bares his teeth, his fingers outstretched, his black claws lengthening.

Directly behind me, a sonorous growl starts to motor. I turn and glare at Stone, seeing that his black eyes are red with vile hatred. He doesn't like that I harmed his fellow brother. After all, hounds are notorious for staying united in times of trouble. When one becomes injured, the other retaliates.

I, for one, am not worried, even in the middle of two agitated hounds. I have to stand my ground and remind them of who's in charge.

"Don't try intimidating me. It will not work." I move to the side, so as to look at the both of them. I lift my chin. "I am your superior. Your jobs are to follow my orders, no matter the cost. If you two cannot handle this mission, tell me now, and I'll send you back to the fiery pit. Though Satan will regard you as failures. I don't have to tell you what he does to demons who are weak – you've seen it with your own eyes."

The two underlings do not speak. Their growls subside and they stand up straight. I watch as their claws shrink to normal. An arrogant smirk touches my lips. I know I've got them where I want them. They know this, as well.

"I need to ponder on a new course of action. You two will stay in here. I need some alone time." Walking toward the exit door, I brush shoulders with Markus and sneer, "Fix your face. We'll be walking amongst the humans soon."

Trudging out the doors, I can feel the hound's eyes burning holes in my back. That's fine. Nobody likes someone to rule over them. But they know they must obey me like the pathetic dogs they are, or suffer Satan's damaging consequences.

They know their place.

Next in line is to put the Seer in her place.

# Chapter Eight

# Clarity

School starts out like the day before, all sunny, clear, and bright. After last night's events, though, I feel like I'm in an endless fog of mystery and doubt. Catching my reflection in the locker's magnetic mirror, a wave of hapless sympathy crashes right over me, threatening to capsize and muddle my entire life.

"Should have put some make-up on," I mumble, embarrassed by my appearance. I'm severely pale, with dark circles resting underneath my eyes. A loose ponytail was the best I could do this morning. I'd struggled brushing the tangles out of my thick hair.

I feel exactly how I look – washed out and dog-tired.

Since I had awakened at four-thirty AM, sleep didn't come back to visit again. Maybe because I'd been too restless to sleep. Or maybe because my freshly tattooed hands held me so completely fixated I couldn't close my eyes to get a couple more hours sleep.

83

Luck had been on my side through it all. A.C. had been at work when my screaming fit occurred, and she'd already gone to bed by the time I was ready for school.

Closing my locker, I take a gander at my gloved hands. This morning as I'd gotten ready for school, a rampage ensued inside my closet. Clothes, blankets, and other nameless junk got caught in the line of fire, until I'd found what I was looking for.

Gloves. Black winter gloves that I'm wearing right this moment.

The only thought running wild in my overwrought brain is that I must hide these tattoos from everyone, even if they think I'm a total geek. Although, the gloves may be a brilliantly lit attraction, sort of a "Hey, look at my hands" kind of situation.

"Clarity, why are you wearing gloves?"

Swinging around, nearly hurdling out of my skin, I come face-to-face with Kora. Smiling, her hair still the color of a firetruck, she opens her locker next to mine and begins poking around, searching for the right textbook.

"Morning, Kora," I softly respond. I don't think I have enough energy to speak.

Still ransacking her locker, she persists with, "You didn't answer my question, Clare. Why are you wearing gloves when it's nearly ninety degrees outside?"

"You wouldn't believe it if I told you," I mutter. I study her, contemplating whether or not I should tell her everything. About Sam, the dream. My hands.

"What happened?" She slams her locker shut, views my dull face, and gasps. "Whoa, did you have a rough night or something? You look like crap, dude."

"Gee, thanks," I sarcastically remark. Kora has never been the type to hold back feelings and thoughts. I'm not at all surprised by her excessive bluntness.

Still, her words sting.

She eyes my gloves. "So about the gloves – new fad you're trying out? Because let me tell you, that won't catch around here."

"My hands are cold." I tell her a complete lie, my gaze dropping to the floor.

Placing a skinny finger under my chin, she lifts it up, forcing me to look in her eyes. She shakes her head, clucks her tongue, and remarks, "Bull *crap*."

Observing her point-blank expression, I have no other

choice but to let her in on my secret. She knows me all too well, especially when I harbor lying lips.

Releasing a fatigued sigh, I motion for her to follow me. "I'll tell you in the girls room."

"Okay, but we only have a couple of minutes before the bell rings." She checks her watch and bites her bottom lip, seeming distressed.

As we traipse over to the bathroom, I ask, "Since when do you care if you're late for class?"

"Oh, I don't care!" she promptly exclaims. "I'm just, you know, trying to start off this year on a good note, is all."

"Religion is really changing you," I mutter, tugging the door to the girls room open. She ignores my remark.

As I bend over and check the stalls to make sure we're alone, she pesters, "So what are we doing here exactly? Why did you drag me to the bathroom just to explain the gloves – which are totally atrocious, by the way."

Sucking in a breath, I respire it slow and easy. Am I really going to show her my hands? Analyzing her prying eyes and speculative gape, my question is readily answered.

"Alright, without freaking out or assuming I got plowed last night..." I pause, removing my gloves. "Take a gander at *these*."

Showcasing my hands, palms up, I flinch at the abnormal sight. Kora, in turn, takes hold of them. A funny look appears on her face as she studies them. What is she thinking? What will she say?

"*Riiight,*" she says after a few lengthy seconds. Her gaze lifts to mine as she admits, "I give up. What am I supposed to see?"

Floored by her admission, I stutter out, "W-What do you mean?"

Her eyebrows raise to double arches. "I've seen hands before, you know. Got a pair myself."

Hazy confusion consumes reality, leaving me in a heavy discombobulated state. "Wait, you mean you don't see what's on them? I-In the middle of m-my hands?"

My heart is banging uncomfortably in my throat, while my stomach begins twisting itself into a tight knot. How can Kora not see them? There's tattoos on my hands! Plain as freaking day!

Emitting a short breath, she flips my hands over, then back again. "Clare, doll, I don't see anything out of the norm. They're just your hands."

The pace of my heart slows to almost nothing. A discouraging trash bag of sheer grief weighs me down. Slowly I withdraw my hands from hers, gazing at them, seeing what Kora does not. Growing more tired than ever, I lean against a nearby sink, the situation a burden that's sapping me of all energy.

Kora reaches out, lightly squeezing my arm. "What's wrong? You know you can tell me anything."

An involuntary tension grabs hold of every muscle in my body. "I'm not sure I can. It will sound insane to you."

"Oh *please!*" she scoffs, shrugging her dainty shoulders. "I'm the Queen of insane. Well, I used to be, anyway."

Giving in, I begin telling her the story. "It started last night when Nick came into the store, yelling that I'd broken the two of you up. He grabbed my arm , then threw me up against the wall – "

That's as far as I got with the story.

"What?!" Kora squeals suddenly.

"Kora, calm down – "

"Don't tell me to calm down!" Kora's voice resounds off the tiled walls of the bathroom. "Nick physically put his hands on you and you didn't call the police? Clarity, where'd he hurt you?" She picks up my hands, then drops them. "Not your hands, there's nothing to see there."

Not that she can see … apparently.

"Kora..."

"Show me your arms."

"But – "

"Show me your arms!" Her face has turned an angry shade of red.

Grudgingly, I push my sleeves all the way up. Glancing at the mirror, I can see the bruised hand prints Nick left on my upper arms. Unfortunately, Kora's able to see those, which doesn't help contain the caustic hostility from cultivating like wild vines within her nerves.

"I'll kill him," she grates out, her eyes scrunched into tiny slivers.

Shrugging my sleeves down, I attempt to soothe her. "It's okay, Kora, really. I'm fine, and Nick was drunk last night. He probably doesn't remember coming to the store."

She releases an irritated snort. "Don't make excuses for the little pissant. Just because he was drunk doesn't give him the right to lay hands on you, or anyone for that matter."

The warning bell sounds, alerting students they have

one minute to get to class. Kora slings her book bag over her shoulder and slams the bathroom door open, banging it against the wall. She stalks down the hall, with me trailing behind.

Before going into class, I gently snatch her book bag strap. "Kora, wait." She groans, but turns around, her face still flushed. "I'm sorry. I should have told you. But luckily someone stopped him from seriously hurting me."

"Someone stopped him, huh?" A harsh laugh scarpers from her thin lips. "They should've beat the crap out of him, taught him some sort of lesson."

The final bell rings. Class is ready to start.

"Kora – "

"Let it go for now, Clarity. I'm fine, and thankfully so are you."

As we pass Daria and her crew of snobby cheer sluts on the way to our seats, Daria starts to say, "Well, looky who decided to –"

"Shut-up!" Kora and I both snap. Immediately Daria clams up, a shocked expression wiping over her perfectly made-up face.

Kora plops down in her seat, staring straight ahead.

She doesn't speak to Kevin, who sits directly behind her. A concerned look crosses his face, but he remains impassive.

Before I take my seat, Brenton, who sits behind me, graces me with one of his signature dimpled grins. I smile back, though it's forced. I peek at my hands, the tattoos peeking back, taunting me. I'm so messed up right now. A straightjacket is waiting for me at the insane asylum, with my name stitched across the front.

All through class my mind wanders. I think about Nick slinging me against the wall. Then Sam's face travels across my vision. How had he gotten away with telling Nick to leave? And just how did he leave the store so fast? It's like he'd disappeared into thin air...

Why can't I shake the mentation that I've known him my entire existence? And why do I feel that I can trust him with my life?

So many whys, no probable explanations.

Eventually I get tired of my chin slipping off my hand, so I settle for tuning out the teacher's droning voice. Instead of learning about the Aztecs, my swollen, sleepy eyes flicker over to the window.

That's when I realize Sam is in the room, his back

leaned against the window, his arms crossed at his chest. I stare at him a moment, with him staring right back at me with unreal blue eyes. He appears so normal inclined against the window. His attire consists of a black t-shirt and dark jeans, very casual. The sun shines down on him, giving his hair a smooth, silky effect.

I open my mouth to speak, but he beats me to the punch.

"No one can see me, so don't talk." Seriousness has edged its way inside his voice. "Speak to me through your thoughts. I can hear them."

My thoughts? Did he just say he can read my thoughts? No. Impossible.

"Oh, it's possible." He grins when my jaw becomes slack with astoundment.

I fidget in my seat and skim over the room, making sure no one is watching this peculiar debacle. Some seem engrossed in the teacher's lecture, while most appear uninterested.

Focusing on Sam, I prepare to have my first conversation using only my thoughts instead of my tongue. Still don't understand what's happening and why. I figure the best thing I can do is roll with it. Go with the flow.

*What are you? How can you hear my thoughts? Why am I the only one who can see you?*

To my utmost amazement, he laughs out loud. Instinctively, my eyes drift across the room, again ascertaining that no one has heard his outburst. Hoping he'd been heard, so I wouldn't be feeling like I'm going crazy.

"No, Clarity, they don't hear. And trust me, you don't *want* them to – they wouldn't understand me."

Lavender blows my way, with comfort and peace dancing along my skin, causing goosebumps to skitter up and down my body. Again, that smell. Is it coming from him?

"Yes," he replies, his smile still beaming.

*Are you going to answer my original questions or not?* I gift him an extremely pointed look, along with hitched-up eyebrows.

"Of course." His arms drop to his sides and he stands up straight, pacing back and forth in front of the window, his eyes on me the whole while. "The answer to your first question, I'm afraid, can't be fully answered just yet, but I can say that I've been by your side since the day you were born. Question two, I can hear your thoughts because we have a supernatural link that God the Father placed between us." He stops pacing, clasping his hands together. "As for the last question … again, I can't tell you the reason of why only you can see me. Not yet."

Frustration starts weaving an angry web inside my mind. I'm not pleased with his responses. At all.

Flipping my palms upward, laying them on my desk, I gesture at them with my eyes. *Are you the reason for these hideous things?*

Sam's smile fades. In the time it takes to blink, he's kneeling on the ground beside my desk. I clamp down the shock that wants to display on my face after his little disappearing/reappearing act. It takes all the strength I have left to not bound from my seat and foot it right out the door. When he reaches over and covers his hand over both of mine, I'm forced to swallow down a boggled cry.

What calms me down instantaneously is the warmth that travels up my arms and to the rest of my body, just by his touch on my flesh. Once more, lavender loops around me like a protective band of pure serenity.

"They are not hideous," he says softly, his blue eyes drilling all the way through to my heart. "God doesn't make such things. He creates all things beautiful and perfect. Mankind is the reason beautiful creations become tarnished."

Narrowing my eyes, attempting to ignore the peaceful tone of his voice, I tell him, *I don't believe in God.*

He tilts his head and says with certainty, "You will." And with that, he vanishes into thin air, exactly like he did the night before at Baker's.

Before I can stop it, I gasp, and that sparks the interest of everyone in the room. All eyes are on me. Heat flushes my face when Mrs. Taylor, the droning teacher, inquires, "Clarity, are you okay?"

Snickers and whispers sweep across the room, me being the primary target.

Mortified to the ultimate limit, I reply, "Y-Yes, Mrs. Taylor. I'm fine."

Satisfied with my answer, Mrs. Taylor returns to the chalkboard and continues with her lecture. A hand gently squeezes my shoulder. I jump, then quickly realize it's Brenton.

"You really okay?" he whispers in my ear.

Turning my head slightly, I nod and whisper, "Yeah."

But I'm not. I'm not okay. I just had a conversation with

someone who can read my thoughts and disappear in a flash. Someone who can calm me with one touch of his hand. Someone who reeks of lavender. The thing about it is, I'm not sure he's real or a figment of my imagination.

What had he said about the tattoos? That they were beautifully made by God or something along those lines.

I'm going insane, pure and simple.

There's no explanation. Not a one.

***

"These are for you."

Closing my locker, I find Brenton and his dimpled grin shining on me. He's brought me a bundle of sunflowers, which he has clasped in both hands.

Grinning, I reach out and take them. "My favorite, but what are they for?"

"Well," he says nervously, raking a hand through his sandy brown hair, "I meant to give them to you yesterday, you know, to cheer you up..."

"Oh, I get it." Yesterday, the anniversary of the car crash. "Thank you."

"Are you okay?"

No, I'm not. You have no idea how *not* okay I am.

"Yeah," I lie, not meeting his eyes. He palms my cheek.

"No, you're not." He kisses my forehead. "I love you."

I lift my gaze to his brown eyes and whisper, " I lo – "

My words are brought to a screeching halt. Down the hall, close to the exit of the school, a girl is screaming. I quickly realize that it's Kora's voice, and she's directing her yells at Nick Reece.

"Why can't you just get it through your thick skull!" she fumes, pushing him in the chest. "Leave me and my friends alone!"

Nick counters with, "But Kora – I love you."

Disgust is evident on her face, her head shaking back and forth. I cry out when her hand rears back and slaps Nick hard across the face, the *smack* resounding off the lockers. Students stop what they're doing to concentrate on the new attraction down the hall.

Nick is fuming, both fists clenched at his sides. Kora, who must have thrown her book bag to the floor, picks it up and storms out the doors, leaving a steaming Nick in her wake. The students, seeing that the fight is over, resume what they were doing before the interruption. Nick, Kora, and the fight flush quickly from their minds. But Nick is still there, staring at the place Kora had just stood, his face contorted with rage.

"Wow, Kora sure can pack a smack, huh?" Brenton blows a low whistle, then says, "Well, I'm off to work. Call me later?" When I don't respond, he waves a hand in front of my face. "Clarity?"

Wringing my gaze from Nick, I answer, "Yeah, I'll call ya after work."

"Sure you're okay? You're acting distant."

I peer into his eyes, wishing I could let him in. About Sam, about the tattoos, but I can't. Not until I can understand it fully.

"I'm sure," I tell him, sounding more like myself. I give him a long kiss, showing him that I'm fine; I'm such a good actress.

When the kiss is finished, he backs away with a goofy grin on his face, then turns and walks down the hall. I watch him go, feeling a little guilty about lying to him. I hate lying to the person who's been through it all with me. But what choice do I have?

Placing my book bag on my shoulder, I shoot one more

glance toward Nick. He's still standing there, but he's not alone. There's three guys huddled around him, keeping him in a tight conversation. I can't tell much about them, except that I've never seen them around school before. One of them wears a tall platinum mohawk on his head.

Yep. Definitely not from around here.

Abruptly the three new guys lift their heads and glance my direction. An instant chill wraps around me like a wet towel, and I shiver. They quickly turn their attentions to Nick, the one with long black hair placing an arm around his shoulder. As a unit, they steer Nick out the doors of the school. The one with long black hair hangs back, his head turning my direction. Though I'm way down the hall, I can see the grin on his face, but it's not a friendly grin.

It's a grin of intense malice, and it's directed straight at me.

# Chapter Nine

# Clarity

A shift in the weather brings a change to Garlandton. The leaves on the trees are mixtures of yellows, reds, oranges and browns. Wind tosses the loose leaves through the air, some capering just above the ground. Sunflowers are in full bloom, making the normally drab town a bit brighter.

Churches hold their annual bake sales and fundraisers, while the town council prepares for festivals and concerts on the square. Their hope is to have city people visit for all the fall festivities. Taking their money is also an avenue they have talked about.

Fall is one of my favorite seasons, but this year is different. I've got too many convoluted thoughts running different directions inside my skull. My brain is simply a wrecked mess.

Six weeks have passed, and it's now the middle of October.

Six weeks, and the tattoos are still there.

Six weeks, and not a sign or word from Sam.

Where was he? The last time I'd seen him was the day in class, when he'd spoke to me and heard my thoughts. After that, everything seemed to go back to normal … well, as normal as normal could be, at least. The exception is my tattooed hands, the ones that no one else can see. And they're still as bright as they'd been the day of their appearance.

Nightmares of monsters and storms plague me when my head hits the pillow at night. In every dream I'm running through woods filled with lightning and thunder. I'm running because I'm being chased by shadows – three of them, to be exact. Before they can catch me, I come alive from sleep, with the palms of my hands burning excessively.

Every waking moment I search for Sam, waiting – hoping – for him to show up. I've even called out to him in my mind, believing that since he can read my thoughts then surely he can hear my pleas for him to appear. I desperately need him to help me make sense of my life, because it had crumbled into disarray the night he crashed my world.

To my discouragement, Sam never materializes. My patience is being stripped away bit by bit, wearing down to a thin line. The weight of a ton of bricks is balanced on my back.

Inch by inch I'm drooping lower to the ground. My fear is that once I hit the ground, there will be no way for me to get back up. That I'll forever be buried underneath the complications of an upside down, implausible life.

Like an aggressive cancer, that fear continues to grow.

Day after day.

After day.

***

A knock sounds on my bedroom door, and I yell, "Come in!"

A.C. pops her head in. "You busy?"

"Nope," I reply, laying my flat iron on the desk. "Just finished doing my hair."

"Cool." She staggers in and flops onto my bed, headfirst into my bright yellow comforter. She's wearing Halloween-themed hospital scrubs, with white ghosts and orange jack-o-lanterns floating on the fabric.

Sitting down next to her, leaning my back on the headboard, I say, "I see you're wore out as usual."

"You have no idea," she snips, her voice muffled from talking into my comforter. Rolling over onto her back, she stares up at the ceiling. "I worked a double shift last night and was planning on getting a full night's sleep, but the hospital called a few minutes ago. Suzie's out sick and I'm the only one available to take her shift."

A.C. is eleven years older than me, but with dark bags under her eyes and mousy brown hair that's always styled in a loose bun, she looks way older than her twenty-eight years. She works nonstop, always third shift, and always doubles. I tell her every day that she needs to cut back on her hours, because these late hours will one day catch up to her. Then she'll be the one laid up in a hospital bed.

"Why don't you call them back and tell them you can't work after all?"

"Not possible. I'm nothing if not dependable." Her tired hazel eyes peer up at me. They quickly grow wide. "Why are you so made-up? Big date tonight?"

"Nah, just going bowling with Brenton, Kora, and Kevin."

"Ooooh, a double date!" She breathes out a sigh, once again staring up at the ceiling. "Must be nice."

I study my aunt, wishing she would get on with her life. A.C.'s been my legal guardian for the last five years, giving up her hopes and dreams. She'd been engaged once, but that dude split the day she signed the papers stating that she'd take care of me.

Sure, she's been on dates since then, but all of them turn out to be frogs instead of princes. When they find out that I'm in the picture, they quickly run the other way. And it's all my fault.

"I'm sorry life hasn't turned out like you thought it would." A sliver of guilt stabs my heart. "In a few months I'll hopefully be in New York, and you can get on with your life."

"Clarity, shut-*up*." She scoots her back up the headboard, then wraps me in a hug. "My life is perfect just the way it is. I love you. And besides, life is what we make it – whoa, you've got an amazing rack!"

A.C.'s sudden change of topic has me gushing with laughter. However, her expression remains equable.

"Seriously, when did you grow those?"

I gawk at her. "Omigosh, now it's my time to say shut-up!"

She laughs, then gasps when her eyes latch on to the clock on my nightstand.

"No, actually it's time for me to hit the road." Jumping

up in one solid movement, she's almost out of the room, when she stops and leans back in. "Be careful tonight and no drinking."

My jaw drops and I make an offended noise in the back of my throat. "A.C., I never – "

"Clarity," she swiftly interjects, raising a hand up. "Don't. I'm smarter than that. I trust you can make the right decisions." And with her lecture out, she turns around, tromping down the stairs. When I hear the door slam, I know she's gone.

I blow out a relieved sigh and say aloud, "Boy, that was a close one." I didn't need a lecture about alcohol and not drinking it.

Standing to my feet, I walk over to my vanity to primp a bit more. Taking in my appearance, I can't help but suffer a vain moment. The smoky eye shadow and black mascara I'd chosen makes my brown eyes seem even darker. My red v-neck shirt and jeans fit me to a superb tee, hugging tightly to all the right places. A pleased smile caresses my shiny-glossed lips. Brenton's going to have one hot date tonight!

Finding a wisp of hair out of place, I lift my hand to put it behind my ear. The mirror reflects my tattooed hand, and that's when reality brings me off my conceited high. A frown overtakes my smile. I still have no idea what they mean or why they have appeared, but I'm not allowing them to steal all my teenage fun. No matter what, tonight is about bowling, drinking, and maybe a few kisses goodnight.

I think about A.C. bringing up the whole drinking subject. She's not stupid. She knows exactly what teens do for fun in this town. When Don injured his hand, she'd been working in the emergency room that night. Also, she knows what goes on at the bowling alley on the weekends and –

I shriek as a cold hand grips the back of my neck. Swinging around, I become annoyed when Brenton starts laughing hysterically. He's wearing dark jeans, with a blue and white striped shirt. His chin has a little stubble on it, and his dimpled grin causes my stomach to give a flutter. He is just so cute, but at the same time so nerve-racking.

"Brenton!" I cry, delivering a punch to his arm. "How did you get in without me knowing?"

"A.C. let me in as she was leaving." He rubs his arm. "Uh, and by the way – Ow!"

"You about gave me a heart attack, you jerk!" I frown up at him, my hands landing on my hips.

He raises his hands. "Hey, don't freak! I was only trying to get a rise out of you. Did it work?"

"What do you think?" I spring on him a steely-eyed glare.

"Well..." His chocolate brown eyes roam down my body, then back up. "I do believe an apology is in order, and I know the perfect way to show you how sorry I am." He motions with his head towards my bed, hitching his eyebrows up and down. "What do ya say?"

I fight not to roll my eyes, but the gesture happens anyway. Brenton and I haven't gone "all the way" yet, but the thought is always in the back of our minds – mostly on his, though. Lately he's been dropping hints, hints that I'm not buying into. He's ready, but I'm not. Not at this particular moment, anyhow.

"I think," I begin, standing on my tiptoes, my lips hovering just an inch away from his, "we need to get on with our date ... at the bowling alley."

He studies me a moment, his grin fading. After a few seconds, he sighs and says, "Alright, have it your way, but remember that the offer is on the table."

I laugh, stealing a kiss. "Yeah, I know."

# Sam

From the roof of Clarity's house, I watch as she hops into Brenton's truck. When they speed down her long driveway, my wings break free from my back and I take off after them. They're going to the bowling alley, a place chock-full of demons out to steal, kill, and destroy. Especially the young people in the small town of Garlandton.

The sun is beginning to set, casting orange and red hues over the earth. Humans take something as simple as the sun setting for granted, not understanding that God is showing His love and grace within the warm rays. However, most humans have turned their backs on the Father, though He hasn't given up on them.

Lightning flashes in the distance, close to the bowling alley. It's already starting. Those flashes are just warnings of what is coming. The enemy knows what Clarity is, about the divine power she holds within her. They also know she has no idea what she carries or what she's capable of.

Clarity thinks I've abandoned her, when in actuality I'm right by her side, guarding her from iniquity. They've been stalking her, trying to break through the heavenly band God personally wound around her. Their attempts have failed miserably, except for the dreams. That's the only way they've been able to touch her. But Clarity's freewill will soon come into play, and that will dictate the path in which she'll walk. It will depend on future decisions whether or not they will be allowed to torment her.

Clarity will get a taste of what she's in for soon. I can tell by the dark rumbling cloud that hovers over the town. The evil ones are already riled by her getting marked.

Tonight they will be out for blood. I'll be there fighting the good fight.

Always.

# Clarity

Entering Garlandton Lanes is like taking a step back in time. Aromas such as dust and mildew float up your nostrils with every breath you take in. The bright orange color of the walls hit your eyes like massive blasts of sunlight. Big round light fixtures hang excessively throughout the building, reminiscent of the sixties.

The bowling alley is a popular place for teens to congregate, especially on the weekends. The owners always take off Fridays and Saturdays, leaving the alley in the capable hands of their teen employees. Little did they know that alcohol, cigarettes, and pot was brought in on the weekends.

Though the place is outdated and stinks with cigarette and pot smoke, it's a pretty cool place to chill. Well, as cool as it gets in this backwards town of ours.

"Do you see Kora and Kevin?" I ask Brenton, yelling over the loud music and rowdy teens. The crowd is thick and reminds me of a concert mosh pit.

Brenton does a quick scan over the alley, then hollers back, "Over by the lockers!"

Like tumultuous waves in the ocean, we pass and swim through people in various stages of merriment. Some are goofing off and laughing, talking and drinking, while others are openly locking lips with each other. Next to the exit door in the back, close to the bright blue lockers, the stoners have grouped together, and by their vacant stares it doesn't take a genius to figure out that they are so high they have left the planet.

Finally we make it over to our friends, who appear to

be in deep conversation.

"Hey guys!" I greet, showing them a charming smile.

"Clarity!" Kora launches from the bench she's sitting on, then adds, "I've got to talk to you."

"Okay." What could she possibly want to talk about?

Kora hauls me to the girls bathroom. We slip by a group of girls who are primping and reapplying lip gloss. Filing into the last stall, she closes the door, locks it, then eyes me with saturated graveness.

"What's wrong?" I inquire right away. Immediately I'm concerned for my friend.

"Nick is here, and you won't believe who he's with."

"Who?"

She leans closer, her green eyes blaring, and nastily replies, "*Daria.*"

My mouth falls open. "No way!"

"*Yes* way!" Her head shakes laboriously from side-to-side. "Out of all the girls in town, he chooses my number one enemy."

"What a scuz!" I remark with astonishment. Then a thought pops up in my brain. "Wait – why do you even care? You've got Kevin. You've moved on."

"Oh, I know, and I'm not upset about Nick moving on, it's just..." She blows out a sigh. "In Daria's mind, she probably thinks she's beaten me, you know? Like she's won something by gaining Nick. Does that make any sense?"

"No." I can't stop the chafed look that falls across my features. "Nick treated you like dump, and you broke up with him. You're now with a guy who treats you like a princess. Why do you care if Nick and Daria go out?"

Kora opens her mouth, then shuts it. I can tell she's pondering my question, digging deep into her mind full of fuddled thoughts.

"Huh," she reflects after a fast moment. "You're right. I've got Kevin, and he's awesome. No one has ever treated me with the respect he gives. Why should I care about Daria and Nick?"

"Exactly," I agree. "Plus, think about – Nick's arrogance and Daria's beastliness – they totally deserve each other!"

We share a laugh, then exit the bathroom stall. Brenton and Kevin are waiting for us outside the girls room.

"Can we bowl now?" Kevin wonders. He wraps his arm around Kora's shoulders, and she snuggles close to him.

I study them, observing their love and devotion to one

another. Sure, Kevin's six foot three and outweighs her by a hundred and fifty pounds, but witnessing the adoring look in his blue eyes I realize how perfect they are together, and how much he cares for her. With his strong cheekbones, short dark hair, and tanned skin –

Nope, going to stop right there. Yes, Kevin is cute, but I have a good-looking guy standing right next to me.

"Aww, ain't they sweet!" Brenton comments, mocking sweetness.

"They sure are." I peer up at him. "I know how much you stink at bowling, so are you ready to get your butt handed to ya?"

# Chapter Ten

# Lukus

I sniff the air, experiencing a mixture of fervor and satisfaction. Gazing across the hydrosphere of human bodies, a sense of authority overwhelms my demon self. Devils of all shapes and sizes are in attendance, whispering in mortal ears an array of lies and deceit. They're busy at work planting slimy circumstances and viscous situations in their young minds, stirring a pot full of fleshly evils and desires.

Heavy metal music pours out of large speakers, which delights my infernal ears. I suck in a breath, tasting all the immorality infusing the air. I get lost in the weighty bouquet of pure obscurity. All this debauchery and potent evil under one roof is great sustenance for us demons, keeping us strong and unbreakable. And the best part is no angels are allowed in – they remain uninvited by almost every human in this diabolical place.

Gazing to my left, then to my right, I find that my Hellhound comrades are flanking me. After the confrontation where I'd put them in their places, they'd become extremely compliant, obedient and eager to please. Just the way they were created to be.

"Your orders, sir?" Markus's query rips me from my trance. By my bidding, Markus has trimmed his tall mohawk down, so as not to draw too much attention from the humans. Stone stays completely stoic, his black orbs trained on the unruly crowd.

"There's only one thing to do." I lift my hands high above my hand and clamor, "Unleash some Hell!"

# Clarity

"What the – you gotta be kidding me!" Brenton stares at me with wide eyes, wonderment sketching into his features. "Another strike?"

I crack an uppity grin. "Told you I'd kick your butt."

"You're beating all of us," Kevin points out, his blue eyes grazing the scoreboard that hovers above us. Standing to his feet, he runs a hand over his hair, then picks up his ball.

"What can I say? I'm sizzlin' tonight!" I drop into the seat next to Brenton.

Brenton smirks. "No, you're like a super bowler, or whatever they're called."

Noticing his glazed eyes, I inquire, "A little drunk, are you?"

"Just a little," he admits, lifting his hand and gesturing with his thumb and pointer finger. His action causes a giggle to elude my mouth.

"Get a strike this time, baby!" Kora calls out. She's seated on one of the tall seats, swinging her short legs back and forth. She seems to have forgotten that Nick is here with Daria.

Good.

Kevin gives her a wink and says, "This one's for you."

Kora grimaces when Kevin only knocks three pins down. In a satirical tone she jabs, "Gee, *thanks*."

Kevin shrugs his shoulders, broadcasting a goofy look for all to see. Kora smiles, running up and rewarding him with a hug.

Before I realize it, Brenton pulls me onto his lap and kisses my neck. He peers up at me, his expression soft and tender. In return, without breaking eye contact, I take a long draw from my bottle of beer – my *third* bottle of beer.

When the bottle leaves my lips, Brenton quickly plants his on top of them. Catcalls and whistles interrupt us.

"Woo-hoo! Go get'em, Sparks!"

"Yeah, get a room already!"

Embarrassment floods the both of us, our faces burning crimson. The guys barging in on our private moment are football jocks from school, one of them being Don Freeman. I shoot them all a dirty look.

Don Freeman opens his fat mouth and shouts, "Yo, Clarity, why don't you drop Sparks and get with a *real* man?" He starts dancing around in a circle, shaking his butt back and forth. His pants slide down, revealing his unsightly butt crack.

"Yo Don!" I shout back, forcing myself not to laugh. "Got crack?"

Don stops dancing when he realizes his cheeky butt is showing. His face turns beet red as his jock friends and everyone nearby points and laughs at his bare rear end. Hurriedly he tries pulling them up, but it's a hard feat to accomplish with one hand. After all, his other hand is wrapped up and damaged, still healing from surgery.

"Ha-ha, good one, Clare!" Kora flings a thumbs-up my way.

Before I can fling one back, a loud *boom* sounds from outside, shaking the entire building. Startled screams ring throughout the alley as the lights cut off, the music silenced. We are left in quiet, stark darkness. I cling to Brenton, digging my face into his chest. His arms wind tightly around my waist, keeping me close and secure.

Suddenly, the lights flicker back to life, along with the loud tunes. Hoots of laughter and relief are heard all over the alley. I look up at Brenton and smile, then turn my gaze toward Kevin and Kora. They're okay, laughing and play fighting with each other. I glance across the room and...

Turn ice cold.

The world around me fades away. My body is assaulted with shivers. Icy fingertips dance over every square inch of my flesh. However, the palms of my hands are blistering hot, on fire ... and glowing bright red!

Though my glowing and burning palms terrify me to no end, it doesn't top the atrocious spectacle set before my eyes right at this second. My heart lobs itself viciously against my chest, trying to escape its tight confinements. Puzzlement and awe has taken over all of my senses as I attempt to digest the unimaginable sight.

Creatures, of different shapes and sizes, have materialized all over the room. Some are only a few inches tall with red bodies, horns on their heads, and black wings on their backs. They fly and swarm around certain individuals, some sitting and whispering in people's ears.

Others are over seven-feet tall, with long black fur covering their thick, muscular bodies. They remind me of the drawings I'd seen of the fabled Sasquatch. These bigger creatures cling close to certain people, like Don Freeman, which has one of the hairy dudes standing right behind him, watching his every move. Don has no idea, though. He is oblivious to the hairy giant behind him, and so is everybody else. They don't see these hideous ... *things*.

With my heart continuing its strident thump in my chest, I realize there's a multitude of creatures walking around. One has a human body with a boar's head, and another has a dog body with a human head. A loud, noisy hum drifts across the building, along with deviant cackles. They talk with each other, walking amongst the crowd of partying teens, and I'm appalled that no one seems to see them.

No one but me.

Deep down, I know that I'm the only one able to see these repulsive beasts, and Brenton proves that to be true.

"Hey, alright, it's my turn!" Brenton exclaims. He pushes me into the next seat, not noticing my fractured expression. I watch as he picks up his ball and strolls over to our lane. I'm hit by a wave of fuddled dismay as I watch him walk straight through one of the tall hairy beasts. Right through it! He doesn't see it...

How come he doesn't see it? How come everyone is unaware of these morbid anomalies?

Why are my tattooed hands glowing red and as hot as magma?

A smell so horrible hits, a decaying, roadkill smell – the worst stench I've ever had envelop me whole. Nausea does somersaults in my stomach, and any minute I know chunks will be flying.

Leaping from the seat, I rush as fast as humanly possible to the restroom. Along the way, I hear the little creatures whispering wretched, disgusting words. Evil chatter and laughter enter my eardrums, a sound so abrasive and unnatural I start seeing stars.

I make it to the bathroom just in time. Running to the

last stall, I empty my stomach of all its contents. The whole time I can still hear the chitter-chatter of the little monsters.

Flushing the toilet, I stand to my feet and stare at the yellow-tiled floor. Goosebumps line my arms and entire body. I'm freezing, like I've been buried under five feet of snow, except for my hands. Thoughts blow around like tumbleweeds in my head.

I don't know. I don't know what's happening or why. I don't know why I'm seeing these things and smelling death all around me. I don't know why I'm the only one seeing, hearing, and smelling things no one else can.

They're oblivious – Brenton, Kora, Kevin, and every teen in the building – they don't see what I see, or smell what I smell, and...

Why are my hands still burning and glowing red?!

I'm losing it. I've finally gone over the deep end, and I don't ... know ... why!

Splashing water on my face, I gaze at my bewildered expression. Wide, frightened eyes and a pale face reflect back at me. Lifting my hands up, discouragement pummels into me. The tattoos are *still* glowing red, *still* burning, and *still* very much *there*.

I've got to get out of here.

With nerves doubly electrified, I slowly shuffle out of the bathroom in a complete daze. Music is still blasting from the speakers at ear-splitting levels, throbbing like drums in my skull. I bump into someone, and that person suddenly pushes me against the wall. The air is knocked from my lungs. I'm stunned, but I snap out of it quickly when a face wearing an ugly expression pops into view.

"Watch it, skank!" insults Daria. Her blonde hair is bushy and tangled, her mascara runs down her face. Alcohol leaks from her breath.

"I...I'm..." Words are having a tough time forming on my tongue, most likely because I discover that Daria has one of those little red things lounging on her shoulder. It whispers in her ear – her lips part in a cynical grin.

"Idiot," she breathes out, spinning around. As she stumbles to the bar, the little imp-looking thing glances back at me and snickers.

What the heck is going on here?

A voice catches my attention, causing my blood to run cold.

"There she is, Nick. There's the one who's caused you

pain. Are you going to let her get away with it?"

Directing my concentration toward the eerie voice, Nick comes into view. He's glaring at me with eyes brimming over with hate and madness – and he's not alone.

Three other guys stand around him, two white and one black. The memory of the day Kora fussed out Nick and slapped him in front of the entire hallway crosses my mind. Those guys had been there, waiting for him after Kora ripped his pride to shreds.

Nick's unblinking eyes have me pinned in placed, my feet super-glued to the floor. The tall, muscular guy with black, shoulder-length hair is talking to him. The other two guys I can't tell much about. It's as if a dark fog has them cloaked, keeping them from being seen. I can't hear what's being said, but I'm sure it's something bad. I'm also sure it pertains to me.

Abruptly, the one talking to Nick ricks his neck, gazing directly in my eyes. An icicle of terror stabs straight into my heart, making it skip a beat, as my tattooed hands heat up another few degrees. The pale guy grins at me with eyes that are pitch black ... black!

When he starts making a move toward me, I holler at

my feet to move, but they aren't listening. A scream begins building in my lungs, but before it's released, something amazing happens.

A bright white light flashes, bathing the whole bowling alley with warmness. The smell of lavender overtakes the dying smell, and a peace wells up from my soul. Shrieks and moans of tortured pain resound through the air, piercing my eardrums. I cover my ears while fighting to keep my eyes open. I want to see what's happening; I want to understand why it's happening.

In deep enthrallment I see the monsters, big and small, explode into a grayish dust, as if the light is too much for them to endure. For some reason, my eyes switch to Nick and his new friends. A dark, rumbling cloud of smoke enshrouds him and the other three guys. They're completely covered, out of sight, and I cry out as an invisible wind blows and scatters the cloud. Where Nick and his friends once stood is now empty. They're gone, vanished right before my eyes.

Daria falters by carrying two bottles of beer. She heads over to the corner Nick had just been seconds before. Halting her steps, she looks to her left, then to her right. A perplexed expression pencils in her face as she calls, "Nick! Nick, where are you?"

"Clarity."

I hear my voice being called. Forcing myself to look directly into the source of light, I find that it is slowly dimming. A figure appears from the light. Astonishment rages in my blood when the figure comes into sight.

There, kneeling on the ground, searching me out, is Sam. But he doesn't look like Sam. Well, he does, but he has a little something extra going on.

White fluffy wings protrude from his back, extremely large in size. His eyes are glowing an incandescent blue. The scent of lavender is consuming all reality, and I feel the pull of warmth and peace pouring out from his presence. When he stands, my feet finally listen to my mind and start moving.

The word *angel* reverberates in my mind. Can it be true? Is Sam an angel?

Running to find Brenton, pushing through the flock of teens, my emotions get the best of me. Tears of frustration cascade like raindrops down my face.

While running I notice that everyone is covered with gray dust, from head to toe. What the heck?

Reaching Brenton, I demand, "Take me home." Brenton

is also covered in gray dust.

He turns around, and his outgoing smile fades. "Clare-Baby, what's wrong – "

"NOW!" I scream at the top of my lungs.

The crowd stops what they're doing and aims all their attention on Brenton and me. I hadn't meant to be so loud, but my emotions had boiled over the top. I'd had enough.

Concern flits across Brenton's face, and he begins to say something, but I don't give him a chance. Spinning on one foot, I once again push through the crowd and hightail it out the door, leaving footprints on the dusty floor.

# Chapter Eleven

## Sam

Falling from the sky, I land on the pathway leading up to Clarity's house just as she runs up the steps to her front door. Brenton is trailing behind her, with worry coursing through his system. For good reason, too. She'd been through something that most mortals wouldn't believe, and if she tells him the truth, he will think she's lost it. Listening to Clarity's thoughts, I'm relieved to hear that she's not going to try and explain her outrageous, unbelievable dilemma.

Closing my eyes, then opening them, I now stand on the porch beside Clarity, watching their interaction with curiosity. How will she handle this?

"Clare, wait," Brenton says, his breath coming out in sonorous pants. He'd had to sprint to catch up with her.

She swings around. "Brenton, it's like I said. I got sick, and right now I need to go to bed!" Her outburst causes Brenton to flinch back, then frown.

"Is there anything I can do?" he pleads, palming her

129

flushed cheek.

She closes her eyes, lifts her hand, and closes it around his. "No, Brenton. There's nothing you can do."

"I feel like you're leaving something out. Whatever it is you can tell me." He waits for her response on bated breath. He's genuinely concerned for her, and I know his love for her is real.

Clarity keeps her eyes closed, rubbing his hand with hers. Thoughts circle around in her mind.

*Should I tell him? If I do, what will he say? Will he believe me? Or think me nuts? Because if he did, I'd have to agree with him.*

Opening her eyes, she forces a smile. "There's nothing else going on. I think I may have drank too much." Her heart skips once the lie is off her tongue. She hates lying to Brenton.

"Your girl's in a bit of a mess, huh, Sam?"

I focus on who the voice belongs to, then break out into a wide grin. Another angel has shown – Brenton's Guardian, and she's standing by his side.

"Sarah," I say, nodding my head. "You know as well as I that this day would find her."

"True," she admits. Her long brown hair sweeps across her back. The white sundress she wears dances around her feet. Just like me, her eyes glow a soft blue, though I see vexation living in hers.

"What is wrong, Sarah?"

"This." She gestures toward Clarity and Brenton. When my eyebrows lift, she clarifies, "She's marked as a Seer, a foot soldier for The Light. But Brenton ... he's a normal, not one called by our Father to harbor the power."

"Sarah, you know that things can change in a matter of seconds." I switch my gaze to the couple. "They love each other, you know. And it's real. There has been many marked who is linked to unmarked humans."

"Yes, yes, I know that. It's just..." She pauses, looking to her Charge. "He has a long road ahead of him, and I do not know if he'll be strong enough."

I place a hand on her shoulder. "God's will, no matter what, will be done in their lives."

"You are right," she agrees, staring up at me. "And whatever comes, I hope the both of them are ready."

The sound of the door closing catches our attention, and I release my hand from her shoulder. Brenton holds a hand to the door, wanting so badly to help Clarity, but then drops it. Letting out a sigh, he shifts his feet and jogs down the porch steps. Sarah's wings sprout from her back, and she's about to ascend when I say, "Walk in faith, Sarah."

Glancing back, her wings softly fluttering, she responds, "Always." With that said she takes to the skies, following her Charge home to safety. I look toward the house, praying to God for direction.

# Clarity

Shutting the door, I recline back against it, trying to steady my wobbly legs. Brenton will wonder what's really going on – he knows when I'm feeding him lies. But how can I allow him in if I don't understand what's happening?

If I'd been real and honest with him, he for sure would believe me insane. I, for one, don't want to wind up a comatose zombie sitting in a mental hospital ingesting pills that's handed out in little floral cups.

Alcohol. Yeah, that's it. That's what I need. A quick fix, something to numb my bleeding mind.

Rapidly I head to the kitchen, going straight to A.C.'s hiding place, which is under the sink. She hid all her liquor behind bottles of cleaning supplies, figuring that would be the best place to conceal her drinking habits.

But I'd found it – three years ago. And to this day she has no clue I dip into her mind-altering stash.

Digging under the sink, I retrieve a bottle of tequila. Unscrewing the lid, I tip the bottle back, ready and willing to escape the rest of this night. Before a single drop can land on my tongue, a voice inquires, "What are you doing?"

Startled, I cry out, the bottle slipping from my grasp. It explodes, sending glass and liquid all over the floor. I fall back, running into the counter next to the sink. Pain shoots up and down my spine. A great astonishment forces its way throughout my brain.

Sam has manifested inside my house, and he's fast approaching, his feet moving soundlessly against the floor. A concerned expression mantles his pale face, his blue eyes clear and aglow. He's wearing a white tee and jeans. The wings he'd worn at Garlandton Lanes are gone, giving him the appearance of a normal teenager. Though he is far from normal.

Again, for the second time that night, it becomes clear that my feet don't want to listen to my mind's excessive orders to move, so I stay put. Lavender coils around me, but it's not a comfort this time.

Gently grabbing my shoulders, he gets face-to-face with me and demands, "Don't drink that poison. After all, your body is a temple in which the Spirit of God resides. The Word says, *Wine is a mocker, strong drink a brawler, and whoever is led astray by it is not wise.* Be wise, Clarity. Don't destroy your temple."

His words come out soft and sincere, though I'm struggling with a mountain of trepidation. I'd just seen monsters at the bowling alley, and wings protruding from his back. I'd watched said monsters explode into dust, and Nick disappear in a cloud of smoke with three guys, and one of those guys had black eyes. And now I'm being preached at, which makes my predicament worse.

This is too much. Too much.

With my body shaking like a leaf on steroids, I do the first thing that comes to mind.

I scream.

Somehow, I yank out of his firm yet tender grasp and sprint to the stairs. Taking steps two at a time, I make it to my room and slam the door, locking it. Going a step further, I push my dresser over until it's flush with the door. Out of breath, I lean on the wall, only to catch sight of my tattooed hands.

Rather than glowing red, they're glowing green! Oh, why is this happening?

"Because he chose you."

At the sound of Sam's voice inside my room, I make a move toward my closet, tripping along the way. Crawling on hands and knees, I reach in and seize my aluminum baseball bat. A bullet of sheer panic lodges in my heart, piercing deep in my tortured soul.

With the bat posed and ready to swing, I threaten, "I-I'm warning y-you. Stay back or I'll – "

"I'm not your enemy."

A soft, fluttery wind blows, and suddenly he's standing in front of me. Apprehension has me immobilized, my body quivering with dread.

"I'm not your enemy," he insists again. He takes hold of the bat. I release my grip. The reverberating sound of the bat hitting the hardwood floor makes me realize that this could be it. This may be the night I die.

"You're not going to die, Clarity," he assures, listening to my thoughts. He then adds in a quiet tone, "And I will never hurt you."

*Why?* I inquire of him, using my thoughts.

He replies, "Because you are precious to the Father, therefore you are precious to me."

Tears build, and the dam bursts. "I'm going crazy."

A sympathetic smile invades his pinkish lips. "You may be feeling unsure of yourself. You may be feeling a little discomfort." His eyes travel down to my hands. Taking them in his, I'm stupefied when the touch of his bare skin relinquishes the biting sting in my palms. His gaze rises back to mine, and still clasping my hands he affirms, "You may be thinking many sporadic thoughts, and feeling many foreign pains, but believe me when I say that you're not crazy."

After the last sentence is spoken, my knees buckle and I fall into Sam's arms. In one quick step, he picks me up, then places me lightly on my unmade bed. I suspiciously study him as he sits on the end of the mattress. We don't break eye contact. Silence bounces off the walls, but not an uncomfortable one – a peaceful one.

"What *are* you?" I ask after a full minute passes, not hiding the wonderment in my voice.

"What does your heart tell you?" His voice is soft and

even as he speaks.

Another round of tears fall down my face. I swiftly wipe them away, then admit, "It's not saying anything."

"Yes it is." The smile on his face fades, his tone drenched in relevance.

My head rocks back against the pillow. "I-I don't know! Tonight at the bowling alley, seeing those hideous *things*..." I pause, squelching down a huge sob that's begging to be released. Sucking in a breath, I softly say, "And seeing you with wings, and that bright, luminous light you stepped out of, I think ... I think you're an angel."

There, I said it. But do I believe it?

"Believe it," Sam tells me.

After a brief pause I marvel, "You're an angel – a good guy – and those things at the bowling alley ..."

"Demons," he says for me.

Yeah, that's what I thought he'd say.

Wave upon wave of leaden perplexity swarm over me, teeming with concentrated defeat. A dense fog of uncertainty envelops my entire being, leaving me in a rattled and doubtful state. Staring into Sam's crystal blue eyes – *angel eyes* – and breathing in his concoction of heady lavender goodness, I realize that life as I knew it before has forever been changed, all thanks to an angel.

Sam's an angel.

Sam. Is. An angel.

"I'm trapped in a world I don't belong in," I mutter, staring up at the white popcorn ceiling. "A freaking nightmare."

Ignoring my comments, he asks, "Remember when I told you I've been by your side since the day you were born?"

"Vaguely," I honestly reply, keeping my focus upward.

"That's because I'm your Guardian, Clarity." My eyes lower and catch his as he adds, "I am part of the Heavenly Guard – and I'm your Guardian Angel."

"How is this possible?"

"With God all things are possible."

"But I don't believe – "

"Stop right there," he interjects sternly, standing to his feet, towering above me. "I don't ever want to hear those words out of your mouth again."

"But – "

He surprises me by pressing a finger gently against my lips, sending electric shocks through my body, touching every synapse that I own. My heart pounds ten miles a minute as I'm trapped in an angel's gaze. A real life angel!

Sam presses forward. "After seeing what you saw tonight, hearing and feeling everything around you, how can you continue to say God doesn't exist?" His finger slides from my lips and he steps back. "I've told you all I can at this present time. Besides, deep down you know the truth."

Unable to contain my distraught emotions any longer, I jump off the bed and get right in his face. "You haven't told me anything, and I know nothing!" My limbs shake uncontrollably as I continue. "I don't know why I have tattoos that are invisible to everyone else. I don't know why they burn like acid is being poured all over them. I don't know why they glow red, then green. I don't know why I saw what I did tonight, and felt what I felt tonight. I don't know why I can see angels and demons!" Out of breath, I push out, "And I have absolutely no clue why you stink of lavender!"

"Which you have smelled your whole life." A grin plays across his lips.

Considering his assertion, I nod. "Yeah."

Sam bites his lip, then declares, "I can tell you why your hands glow."

"Go on, I'm all ears." I gesture with my hands for him to proceed.

"At the bowling alley tonight, what color did they glow?"

"Red."

"And what did you see while they were glowing red?"

I shudder. "Monsters."

"Demons," he points out. "Anytime you are in the same vicinity as the enemy, your hands will glow red."

"Wow." Demons. Wow. "So red means demons, and green means...?"

"Angels." He breaks into a glorious smile. "When they glow green, it means you are in the presence of the Holy Ones, and in your case, a Guardian."

"You," I say.

"Absolutely."

Quickly, he walks over to my nightstand and starts rummaging in the junk.

"Hey, what are you doing?" I observe him with acute curiosity.

"Getting this." He turns around, holding something in his hand. When I see what it is my heart lurches to my throat

140

and my head fills full of air.

Sam's holding my mother's purple Holy Bible.

Visions of the past twist and turn in my memory. Mom's brown hair and laughing brown eyes, her beautiful smile. Her gentle touch.

"What are you doing with that?" My voice quivers with emotion.

He hands it to me. "I want you to open it up and read what's taped on the inside."

With trembling hands, I take my mother's bible, shocked that it's warm. I've never opened this book. Ever. Never wanted to. But with an angel staring me down, I feel a bit pressured into it, so...

Opening it, I find the little piece of paper taped to the inside and begin to read it.

Sam interrupts by saying, "Read it out loud."

I shoot him an evil eye, but do as I'm told. "For we are not fighting against flesh-and-blood enemies, but against evil rulers and authorities of the unseen world, against mighty powers in this dark world, and against evil spirits in the heavenly places ... Ephesians 6:12." My teeth brush over my bottom lip, while my brain combs over each word. Confusion starts enervating me. "What does this mean, and how does this affect me?" I wait for his response, but it never comes.

Glancing up I find that Sam is nowhere to be found. He's disappeared. *Again.*

"Really?" I call out loud. "You're going to leave me now, with no explanation or anything?"

Silence.

"Well." Tossing the bible on my bed, I place my hands on my hips and say, "The least you can do is help me clean up the spill downstairs. After all, you scared it out of my hands, so that makes it *your* fault."

Again, no response.

I sigh, admitting defeat. I'd have to clean up the spill. By *myself.*

Before I can open the door, I struggle to move the dresser out of the way. My adrenaline must have been supercharged when I'd put it there the first time, because it had only taken a couple of seconds to move the sucker. Now it was taking a full minute.

Plopping down the steps, I grab the broom and dust pan from the hall closet and start sweeping up the mess. Bending over to rake the broken glass into the dust pan, I eye the refrigerator and see there's a manilla envelope stuck to it with my name on it. Why hadn't I seen it before?

Oh yeah, probably because of the demons, and Sam...

Opening it and grazing the first couple of sentences, I quickly interpret what I'm reading. This is an acceptance letter – I'd been accepted into New York State!

For a moment I'm able to forget all of my troubles ... but only for a moment. I'd been dreaming of leaving this town for years, and now I have the chance to do so. Though now I'm not too sure that feat will be plausible.

Especially if Sam and demons trail after me.

# Chapter Twelve

# Clarity

*I'm lost.*

*Lost in a field of tall sunflowers, except they do not resemble your average sunflower. No, these have stalks twenty feet high and blooms as big as kiddie pools. They are colossal, and right now I'm lost in the bulk of them.*

*Lost in a forest of sunflowers. On steroids.*

*Lightning flashes and thunder rolls. The ground shakes beneath my feet. Peering up at the heavens, I see the sky is dark gray with seething, tumultuous clouds. A severe storm is brewing in a fleeting manner. Harsh winds toss the statuesque flowers back and forth, like ocean waves battling a fierce hurricane.*

*A chill cuts deep in my bones, the urgency to run shouting between my ears.*

*So I run ... and run ... and run some more. The wind disputes my steps, attempting to steal every ounce of energy that remains in my system. Deep huffs of breath elude my lips, and it feels like a drummer has invaded my heart, pounding away in demented, inconsistent thumps. Drips of sweat trickle down my face, stinging my eyes, but I push forward.*

*An opening appears in between the mammoth stalks. Yes, a way out!*

*The sizzle in my palms are near unbearable, but they are the least of my worries. I focus on the objective at hand — get to the clearing and out of this ridiculous maze!*

*The wind continues to howl. An invisible force of some kind is trying to tug me back into the sea of flowers. But I forge ahead, determined. With the last bit of energy I possess, I fly through the breech, landing hard on the ground.*

*Getting to my feet, I convey these new surroundings. I stare in amazed wonder.*

*I've landed in the middle of a circle, the immense flowers acting like a makeshift prison. The ground is charred to a crisp, barren of life. A sharp light burns my eyes, then fades, immediately catching my attention. A tall mirror slants beside me, and I flinch as my reflection comes in view.*

*For a tiny moment, I collect my mirror image. A white dress drapes my body, the hem reaching the ground and fluttering in the breeze. My hair flows down my back in beautiful brown curls, my dark eyes are glassy and confused.*

As I gaze into the out of place mirror, I start focusing on what's occurring behind me. The stalks are being violently tossed to and fro by the stark winds as dark clouds roll in insanely fast motions.

Something peculiar lurks in the forest of sunflowers, edging its way to the opening. My breath snares in my lungs as a deep frost singes my skin.

People.

People are making their way through the stalks, pushing through the large, foreign flowers. More people than I can count. Their bodies from head to toe are blacked out, as if shiny paint has devoured them, masking their true identities. Silhouettes of human-shaped bodies, nothing more.

The hostile winds quiet down as an acrid silence falls to the earth. Stillness settles over all existence, and the temperature drops. Circles of smoke form in the air as I breathe in and out. My heart beats frantically, trying to break free from my chest. Dread has its ugly grip clasped on every nerve in my body. The terror I feel is indescribable.

A bright light abruptly materializes and out of it steps Sam. He pulls me into his strong embrace, warming me instantly. But his arrival does nothing for my growing anxiety.

"Who are they, Sam?" I inquire in a small voice. He lowers his gaze. His eyes are the brightest I've ever seen.

"They know who you are, Clarity. They have found you." Anguish laces the edges of his voice.

"What am I? And who are they?"

Before he's able to respond, the ground shakes like an earthquake is busy ravaging the land. A cacophony of shrill voices, malicious and rich with fury, cry all around the circle, growling in anger.

"THIS ONE IS ALREADY TAKEN!"

"SHE'S OURS, ANGEL!"

"SHE BELONGS TO US!"

Cold fear swims in my blood, and I find my entire being thoroughly frozen. The cold is so rampant it pierces every cell my body holds. I'm forced to my knees by the incredibly potent frost. The heinous scene fades to black, though my ears still work.

Through all the torture and darkness, I hear Sam shout with authority, "She will never be yours – NEVER!"

I wake up to a girl screaming at the top of her lungs, only to realize that the girl is me. Like all the nightmares I've awakened from before, I find sheets soaked in a cold sweat – my sweat. The window is open, allowing the cool night air to sting my bare flesh.

Why is the window wide open?

Shuddering, teeth chattering, I quickly jump up and slam the window shut, pulling the curtains closed. The palms of my hands are the only warm points on my body.

Why me? Why am I being tortured?

The only answer I receive is silence.

\*\*\*

"Is Brenton meeting you after work?" inquires Janey. She's hastily wiping glass cleaner over the fingerprinted windows.

It's Saturday night at Baker's, and the two of us are diligently knocking out our closing duties. Casey left two hours earlier, feigning sickness. Mr. Baker had also left earlier in the evening, claiming he had a big date – we're pretty sure the both of them are fibbing.

With the boss out of the store, and no customers, we decided to finish up and close earlier than usual … maybe by only thirty minutes, but earlier, nonetheless.

Sweeping trash and dirt into the dustpan, I reply, "Nah, not tonight. He's working overtime at the garage."

Brenton is a very skilled mechanic and one day hopes to open his own garage. With news that I'd been accepted into New York State, I'd wondered how he'd like opening one up there. We still hadn't talked about it, though. I'm waiting for the perfect time to tell him I'd been accepted.

Thoughts of Sam enter my mind. Almost two weeks have passed since I've seen him, which has me confused. He said he's my Guardian Angel, yet he's nowhere to be found. As a Guardian, shouldn't he be, I don't know, *guarding* me?

"Bummer," Janey lightly laments, breaking me from my thoughts. She's on the tips of her toes, stretching to reach the highest part of the window. Her long blonde hair is pulled back into a messy ponytail, the tip of it resting in the middle of her back. I sigh, wishing that my hair was that pretty.

"No biggie," I remark, dumping junk in the trash can. "Besides, we don't have to spend every waking moment together like you and – "

I'm unable to finish the sentence. Janey catches me off guard when her face turns a sick green. She sprints over to the trash can I'm using and throws up. The taste of bile burns up my throat and spills onto my tongue. I've always had that problem. Whenever someone pukes in front of me, my body

150

reacts as if it wants to join them. I back away, covering my mouth and nose with my hand.

"Uh, you okay?" I ask, my voice muffled because of the hand glued to my mouth. Then I realize how dumb the question is. Of course she's not okay – she'd just blown chunks!

A few unpleasant dry heaves later, she straightens up and wipes her mouth with her sleeve.

"Oh, gross," she groans. "I think I'm sick or something."

Dropping my hand I dryly remark, "You think?"

"I've been feeling cruddy all week." She leans over, placing her hands on her knees and sucking in a couple of unsteady breaths.

"You probably have the flu that's going around," I opine, taking a mental note to wash the skin off my hands later.

Janey's eyes, darkened with circles and brimming with tears, deplorably gazes up at me. I can tell she's super sick. Her usual rosy complexion is tainted with grim pallidness.

"Probably," she replies a couple of eye blinks later.

Gently patting her back I say, "Go home. I can finish

up, there's not much left to do."

"No," she willfully declares, forcing herself to stand tall. "I don't want to leave you alone! Mr. B – oh crap!"

Again, she flings herself over the top of the garbage can and vomits, and again I cover my mouth and nostrils with my hand. When she's done, she slowly turns her head to the side, looking weak and pitiful.

"You're right, Clare. I think it's time for me to go home."

"Yeah, I know I'm right," I agree. "Go home. Now."

# Lukus

Standing atop the tallest building on Garlandton Square, the three of us keep watch on our target: Clarity Miller, teenage mortal and newly marked Seer.

"Is that her? Is it?" Markus bounces on the balls of his feet, panting like a dog … well, he *is* a dog.

A lone figure stumbles out of the door. From my vantage point I can tell it's not the Seer. This human has light hair, and is a bit shorter. Turning my head toward Stone, I watch as he sniffs the air, sucking in deep breaths. His black skin is tinged with an orange gleam, thanks to the large emergency light situated on top of the pebble-covered roof.

"Not her," informs Stone, grimacing. "But there is something wrong with this human, something not right."

The female mortal walks to a silver automobile, opens the door, then vomits on the ground.

"Eww, what is she *doing*?" Markus wonders, sounding appalled, and if it were possible, he appears to pale.

"Hush, hound," I snap, fighting the smile that's trying to penetrate my features. "The human is simply throwing up, which means it's sick. And besides, you've seen and smelled worse, my friend."

"Humans are disgusting beings," mutters Markus with a scrunched up face.

These hounds may be dense, but they are certainly entertaining.

"Right you are," I agree. "Humans are vile, destructive beings that carry many diseases and afflictions."

The sick blonde girl, who's stench is utterly atrocious, finally pulls out of the parking lot, disappearing down the empty street. Electricity surges around us, fueling us for what's coming next.

"Now what?" Stone asks, scratching at his bald head.

The hounds are still not used to their human skins, but after tonight the skins will not burden them anymore.

"Let's move," I promptly answer.

As a unit we jump off the five-story building, swiftly landing on our feet. The town square is devoid of any human life. Only one spark remains, and it's coming from the store on the outskirts of the square.

Looking to the skies I observe with delight the dark clouds rolling in, obscuring the moon and stars from view. They roll over and over each other in heartbreaking turmoil, which is exactly what I'm preparing to unleash.

Briskly walking toward the building known as Baker's Supermarket, anger flares in my veins when both Hellhounds throw arms across my chest, halting our steps altogether.

"Just what do you think – "

"Silence," hisses Markus, breaking off my words.

"And be still," warns Stone. "Very, *very* still."

It's at that point I watch as their eyes burn a bright red, with their noses lifted high. They're sniffing the air almost to the point of violence, combing through every floating particle that lingers in the atmosphere. Then, all at once, their reddened eyes look to me.

"The Guardian," they speak in unison, harboring identical frowns of pure revolt and terror. "He is near."

Taking in their hunched over, frightened postures, I start to laugh. Wonderment becomes deeply etched in their human skins, their expressions lost and forlorn.

"Why are you laughing?" Stone inquires thoughtfully.

"This is quite serious," counters Markus.

"I am laughing because..." I pause, quieting my cackles. "The angel can't touch us! And he definitely can't help her."

"What?" An incredulous look covers Markus's face.

"I am confused," Stone counters.

I roll my eyes. "You're always confused." Stone follows up with a frown. I continue, "No, the Seer is marked, but she isn't *saved*. She's been stating for years that God doesn't exist."

Again Stone says, "I'm still confused."

"Don't you get it, you weak-minded fool?" The hardness in my voice causes him to tremble. "She's still in the dark about who she is and what she can do. She's helpless and alone!"

Markus grins. "You mean – "

"The Light cannot interfere, the angel is defenseless!" I finish for him, deliciously beguiled. My eyes fall on Baker's

Supermarket, where Clarity Miller is located. With a snarl I say, "The Seer is *ours*."

# Chapter Thirteen

## Sam

I smell them before I see them. Demons. Three of them, making their way over to Clarity.

Standing on a hill that overlooks the weathered supermarket, I see shadows dancing through the town square at inhuman speeds. With my wings itching to be released, I'm ready to fight, but then a voice stops me. A familiar voice.

A voice of great authority.

"What do you think you're doing, Sam?"

Whirling around, I stare at the sudden newcomer. Standing at least six-foot five, he's wearing normal angel garb for earth – jeans and a t-shirt – though his long blonde hair is pulled back in a ponytail. Not the usual look for an Archangel.

"Gabriel? What are you doing here?"

"Stopping you," responds the messenger angel. With hands in the pockets of his jeans, he nonchalantly strolls to my side. "After all, you're about to make a grand mistake."

I stare at Gabriel with wonder. I've talked with him

157

before, even mentored under him, but I never thought the day would come when he stopped me from protecting my Charge.

"What are you talking about *mistake*? Clarity is my Charge and a newly marked Seer. Why do you not want me to interfere when angels of darkness are in such close vicinity to her?"

"The Lord sent me to stop you," he replies, his blue eyes shuffling from me to the supermarket below.

Perplexity slaps my angelic senses. "What?! Why?"

"Because," his eyes slip over and stay on me. "Clarity is a special Seer, one whose strength and power is more than this world has ever seen. Even the strongest of Seers cannot compete with what lies within her."

His response doesn't quell my distraught nerves. "You skirted around my inquiries, Gabriel. Why does The Almighty want Clarity to die by the hands of demons, especially if she's so powerful?"

Once again his gaze trails down to the supermarket. "She will not die tonight. You will be able to intervene. You just have to wait for the proper time."

"I can't believe The Father is allowing this," I remark helplessly, staring down at the building.

Gabriel's hand falls on my shoulder, sending over waves of comfort and peace. "Clarity will be tested multiple times in her life. Tonight will be a test that will show her exactly what lies in darkness, and what it feels like to be touched by the enemy." He pauses, so I focus my attention on him. His expression is indecipherable. "She's still unsure of herself, unsure of you, unsure that she's not going crazy. However, if she didn't believe before, she will have no other choice but to believe after tonight."

# Clarity

The night is cold, cooler than the norm for early November. A coat would be nice right about now, though that thought hadn't occurred to me when I left the house this morning. The scent of rain wavers on the breeze, and light sprinkles fall from the sky, tickling my cheekbones. My footsteps echo off the pavement as I make the way over to my car, which I'd parked in the very back of the lot.

Three of the six lampposts around Baker's are operationally, their dull orange glows barely lighting my footsteps across the empty parking lot. Clouds rumble from the heavens, alerting that a storm is fast approaching. It's depressingly gloomy without the radiant shine of the moon and the beautiful landscape of stars that usually paint the night sky.

The weather has been strange lately – one minute the sky is clear and devoid of clouds, though the next minute the clouds rumble in, with threatening lightning and rain. Crazy weather for November.

Halfway to my car, I halt my steps, noting a change in the atmosphere. The tiny hairs on my neck stand on end. Something is about to occur, something terrible and perilous. Don't know how or why I know this; I just know.

When I'd first stepped out of the store, the air had been chilly. But now it feels even colder, like I'm taking a stroll in Iceland. White cottony puffs of smoke pour from my mouth each time I exhale. The air has thickened tremendously as if a giant vacuum has attacked, sucking all the oxygen from the earth. It's becoming difficult to breath in and out, my lungs having to work overtime to battle the unusual thin air.

An eerie, creepy stillness has blanketed the region. No wind, no sprinkles, no nothing, except for the stinging coldness. Like someone hit the pause button to the planet, halting its continuous spin.

Yes, I'm freezing, though my palms are tingling with that foreign heat, which is starting to be a familiar feeling. A river of panic floods my veins when my hands begin to glow red.

Red. Red!

Red means I'm close to the enemy, and the enemies are demons!

Do I believe in demons? Or angels?

Do I believe that Sam is real?

What *do* I believe?

The three lampposts start to flicker on and off, snapping me out of my faraway reverie. I scan the lot, searching for anything out of the ordinary. A blinding flash of lightning causes me to blink.

What is up with the weather lately? I've never in my life seen so many storms this time of year.

The lampposts flicker a couple more times, then completely flit out. Total darkness swarms around me, my skin prickly with gooseflesh. My hands are the only source of light, but it's not a comfort. I'm cold, I'm scared, and the red glow radiating from my hands is telling me to get the heck out of there.

Spinning on my heels, I prepare to race to my car, but my feet become hitched. The hot blood flow within my arteries turn into a frozen lake of exhausted despair, and a bitter frost flies over my skin, glaciating deep in my bones. Leaning on the hood of my Honda are three guys – three mean-looking guys. From what I can tell, two are white and one is black. All dressed in black, and –

Wait. I've seen them before! One time after school, and once at the bowling alley. They had been with Nick. That night, right before my eyes, they'd vanished, taking Nick with them in a cloud of preternatural smoke.

My breath catches in my chest, while my heart speeds up, leaping to my throat. These guys aren't *guys* at all.

They are demons.

Come on, feet, move! Turn around and run to safety! Find Sam, call out to him, you idiot!

None of the above happens. Rather, I stand there unmoving, staring at three beings who don't belong in my reality.

When they peer at me with their shiny black eyes, I almost faint. Especially as a bolt of lightning creases the sky, illuminating the darkness and showing off razor sharp glints in their ebony eyes. A feeling of violation shivers down my back as they scowl with unblinking orbs. They appear insensate, harboring no feeling, no conscience, no emotion. What's weird is I know all of this just by taking in their solemn statures.

I don't know what to do, or what to say. When I open my mouth to talk, the one in the middle speaks, beating me to that unnerving punch.

"Good evening, Clarity," he greets with a tender yet malicious tone. "So nice to see you again." His hair matches his black eyes, which falls straight past his broad shoulders. When he takes a couple of steps forward, I notice how fluent and calculated his moves are. Like a predatory animal sneaking up on its prey.

The other two match his steps just as stealthily, though are careful not to pass him, which leads me to believe the one in the middle is in charge. Their eyes are black and dead … and terrifying.

A constricted grip of dread snakes through my disconcerted mind, but I force myself to squelch it. I may be alone, but I'm not going to let these … these *monsters* get the best of me.

Squaring my shoulders, lifting my chin, I inquire, "What do you want?"

The one in the middle narrows his eyes. "I believe the real question here is what can *you* do for us?" He gestures at me, grinning. The other two snicker, keeping their dead eyes trained on me.

A strained silence ensues. I take this time to soak in the appearances of the other two demons. The tall, skinny white one has a ridiculous looking blonde mohawk, perfect for a punk rocker in the eighties. He has a sleeve of tattoos on each arm. The other one is black-skinned and completely bald, more casual in his looks.

On the outside they seem human enough, except for their eyes. Those things throw out the human card immediately.

The head demon says, "My name is Lukus." He leans over and bows, almost gentlemanly. He's mocking me, I'm sure. Gesturing to the other two he orders, "Go ahead, boys. Introduce yourselves."

On cue, mohawk guy replies, "I'm Markus."

"Stone," says the black one.

Another round of silence hits, and I continue to stand a motionless pile of panicky nerves. I mean, what can I do? What can I say? Since I'd become burdened with glowing tattooed hands, I've been able to see angels and demons, and still have no answers as to why. Plus, I'd missed the class on *Demon Etiquette.* Apparently.

With my heart a frantic ball of meat in my chest, I ask, "What do you want from me?"

Moving inhumanly fast, before I can blink, Lukus is in front of me, right in my face. A heavy draft of raw sewage infiltrates the air, and I'm sickened to realize that it's coming out of Lukus's mouth. It's the most horrible, diabolical stench I've ever encountered. Then, in what looks like a dark, wispy smoke of movement, the other two move, trapping me in a tight, heinous circle.

Again, don't know what to do. Don't know what to say. I'm surrounded, with no place to go.

"We want what every angel of darkness craves," whispers Lukus, his features twisting into a venomous sneer. With his breath still bombing my face, he adds, "A Seer's soul."

Angel of darkness? Seer's soul? What is he *talking*

about?

To my shock, Lukus grabs hold of my arms, my breath instantly becoming snared within my lungs. His touch turns me into a human icicle – I can actually feel my heart turn to a hard ball of ice. The temperature of my body takes a downward plunge. My teeth chatter. My lips tremble. If this keeps up, it won't be long until I die of cryopathy.

The smell of death and decay thickly hang in the ice-cold air. Lukus tilts his head from side-to-side, studying me with acute curious fascination.

"You have no idea who you are." His words are more factual than a statement.

Markus snorts. "No clue, Lukus – no clue!"

"Can we take her now?" Stone growls, his tongue licking his lips.

My stomach contracts in horror as a feeble cry crawls out of my throat. The arctic air is so abrasive it has succeeded in stealing my breath, my lungs aching from the dense pressure. Voices echo in my ears, taunting me to no apparent end, their words forever being carved in my memory.

"Such a tasty soul!"

"Sweet little *Ra'ah*!"

"Let's take her, Lukus. Now. NOW!"

Lukus smirks, gleaming with satisfaction. "Boys, boys! Calm yourselves." Lifting his hand, he gently strokes my cheeks and adds, "Let's take our time with this *Chozeh.*"

*Ra'ah? Chozeh?* What's happening?!

"But there is no time!" whines Markus, his eyes wide.

"The angel is near," Stone declares. He takes in a deep breath, then lets it out. "Too near."

"S-Stop t-t-touching m-me," I stutter, with teeth clicking uncontrollably. His fingertips continue to graze my cheek, leaving a biting sting on my flesh.

"You are right, Markus," Lukus murmurs, then laughs. He takes his nose and roughly rubs it against my cheek, sniffing my skin. It's as if he's trying to breathe in my soul.

Numbness consumes my being, my legs failing me. Lukus lets me go, permitting me to fall to the pavement. I hug myself, wanting to escape – wanting to disappear somewhere within my mind. My car sits beyond them, waiting for me to get in and speed away. I'd been so close to getting home. So close.

Lightning continues to flash, the storm fast approaching. It's weird, a summer type of thunderstorm hitting in November. So, so weird.

For the first time in a while my palms are cold, icy, like they've turned into ice packs. Looking upward, I find that the demons have circled around me, like buzzards in flight searching for their next meal.

It appears that I'm next on the menu.

"Your angel has abandoned you." I whimper when Lukus bends down and licks my face, tasting my skin. He shudders, then whispers in my ear, "Yes, we are your enemies. Welcome to Hell." They start to chant in an unknown language, while I lay on the ground, frozen, completely open and unguarded.

I guess Lukus is right. Sam has abandoned me. All anyone has to do to realize I've been forsaken is to look at the position I'm in. Not for the faint of heart. And apparently not for me.

This is it.

I'm going to die.

By the hands of three demons.

# Chapter Fourteen

# Sam

"This is nuts!" A wail of agony evades my mouth. For at least the twentieth time, I try running down the hill, only to hit an invisible barrier that Gabriel set up to keep me from interfering the deadly confrontation. It's called a Heavenly Barricade, which blocks both angelic and demonic presences. And right now I'm wishing I had some supernatural dynamite to blow it up.

I pace back and forth, watching as Clarity is tormented by the demon Lukus and his Hellhounds. All I can do is watch. They've started chanting in Hell's language. I know what will happen if I don't stop it. Though she is marked, she is unsaved, and unsaved Seers go to Hell all the time.

Gabriel is leaned up against a pine tree, his eyes closed, as if meditating. His actions anger me. How can he stand there while one of God's children is being tortured by the enemy?

Finally, I can't hold in my choler any longer.

"Gabriel, I've got to get down there. Don't you get it?

They're *killing* her! Damning her soul for all eternity. This can't be what The Father wants!"

"Sam," Gabriel starts, but I continue my rant.

"If she is supposed to be a powerful foot soldier for The Light, then why let demons take her down? Why is this happening? It doesn't make any sense, no sense at all!" My pace quickens, my wings quivering under my skin, aching to be released.

"Sam," Gabriel tries again, but I'm on a roll.

"I'm her Guardian, and I'm unable to *guard* her. I've been watching over Clarity her entire life, not once leaving her side. I've done everything by the book! I haven't done anything to deserve a punishment this harrowing. I –"

"SAM!"

Gabriel's authoritative tone stops me in my tracks, both in my feet and mouth. His features are stern, his eyes blazing a luminous blue, his gaze intensely strict. But I'm undeterred in my thinking.

"What?" I spit out, lifting my chin with stubbornness. What do I have to lose by being insubordinate? Clarity is about to be taken away. A deep sadness pierces through me at such a thought, though when Gabriel responds, it dissolves immediately.

"The Father says you can intervene now."

Responsively, my wings spring from my back. I turn away from him, ready to battle and save my Charge's life. As I'm about to take flight, he calls out my name.

"Sam?" He walks up to my side, his eyes ablaze with Heaven's fire.

Giving him a sideways glimpse I inquire, "Yes?"

"Tell her everything she needs to know about being a Seer. But don't say anything about her parents."

"But she needs to – "

"Not yet – this is an order from The Throne." He points to the heavens, then adds, "Now, stop the enemy before they succeed in retrieving her unsaved soul."

Gabriel doesn't have to tell me twice.

# Clarity

A bright light suddenly illuminates the parking lot, the white glare so radiant that for a few seconds it changes night to day. The demons stop their incoherent blabbing, backing away and recoiling from the strong luminosity. They hiss and howl, clearly in pain, as if the light is burning their skin.

A hand touches my forehead, automatically warming my wintry bones. Relief overpowers the numbing fear, while the scent of lavender extinguishes the sewage smell.

My eyes flutter upward, my mouth agape.

Sam is kneeling beside me, and what I see causes my heart to skip a hundred beats. With amazement riding every nerve in my body, I'm left stunned, utterly hypnotized by what I'm seeing.

Wearing a white tee and jeans, he looks the same as he always does ... except for the wings. Just like the night at the bowling alley, he has white, fluffy wings jutting from his back, only this time I'm able to see them up close. They stretch out to outrageous lengths on each side of him. Transfixed on their beauty, I reach up and stroke a single feather. It's unreal how soft the feather is; amazingly unreal.

Sam's eyes are glowing an extra bright blue tonight, and those eyes are searching my own. Anxious concern flits across his flawless features, his expression chock-full of concern.

"Are you okay?" he wonders, his lavender-laced breath caressing my face. "Did they hurt you?"

I'm about to reply when an ugly, demented voice roars from a few feet away.

"You can't be here – that's not fair!" Lukus's tone is engorged with poison.

Sam ignores the interruption, his attention strictly on my well-being. "Clarity?"

"I-I'm fine." Something about being this close to him in his angel form has me captivated, making my words come out a babbled mess. I've always thought Sam was handsome, but seeing him like this, he's more than just resplendent.

Sam is powerful.

"Are you sure?" A look of worry cruises over his face, pulling his eyebrows together.

Blinking my eyes, still downloading his angelic beauty, I tell him, "You came for me."

"I never left you," he whispers.

"You're really an angel," I continue, still attempting to wrap my deluded mind around the in-my-face obvious.

He sighs. "I thought we discussed this already."

"Yeah, we did," I say. I shake my head, trying to clear the fog hovering over my brain. "Still, seeing your wings, up close ... wow, this is reality."

"Do you believe now?"

I nod, that disconnected feeling still in full swing. "Oh yeah."

Though I'd seen into this spiritual realm before, tonight cinches my belief in place. Angels are real – monsters are real. Though thinking like this is extremely unreal.

For some inexplicable reason I find myself stuck in the middle of a war that started way before I was created. The only question I have is this:

Why am I in the middle of this supernatural war?

"The *Ra'ah* is ours!" hollers Lukus. His effusion knocks me out of my cognitive state.

"They look human on the outside, but they're monsters underneath," I mumble, my terror amplifying.

A frown lines Sam's lips. "Yes. They wear disguises to blend in on the earth. Though in reality they are demons from the lowest regions of Hell."

I breathe out, not realizing I'd been holding air captive in my lungs. "Holy – "

"Clarity," he interjects. He hauls me swiftly to my feet, his tone full of urgency. "Listen to me. Get in your car and drive." Holding my face in his hands, he queries, "Are you hearing me?"

"Yeah, but Lukus and..." My gaze drifts over to my car. The demons aren't leaning on it, but standing a few feet in front of it.

"It's okay," he assures, maneuvering my head so my attention is focused on him. "They can't touch you. Not right now."

"But – "

"Clarity," he softly says, "whatever you do, don't look back." I want to protest, but he shakes his head. "You've got to trust me."

Cursorily, he gathers me up, enclosing my body within the safety of his wings. Two seconds later I'm behind the wheel of my car, the keys in the ignition and the seat belt clicked in place over my lap. My hair is a windblown mess and my head is stuffed with cotton wool.

What just happened? How in the world –

Dumbfounded, I gaze out the car window, eyeing Sam. He's facing the demons, his muscles rippling under his shirt as his shoulders roll. His wings extend to their maximum limit. I sit, observing, unblinking, completely dazed – then Sam's voice cuts into my crippled existence.

*Please, Clarity — drive and don't look back.*

A bright light starts emanating out of his body with so much force, the ground begins shaking. The pine-scented air freshener hanging from the rear-view mirror dances along with the otherworldly earthquake.

*Go, Clarity. NOW!*

That's the moment I wake up. The sharp insistence that tints his tone is like a shove to my back, a *get a move on* shove.

Twisting the key in the ignition, my Honda roars to life. I throw it in reverse, pedal to the ground, and hightail it out of there. Once in drive, I tear down the road, ready to get home. I'm nearly blinded by the cultivating light reflecting from the mirrors. Though my curiosity is growing exponentially, I don't look back.

I turn off the square and head for home, the engulfing darkness surrounding the car. Little dots dart across my line of vision because of how brilliant the light had been. Again, lightning rakes across the sky, coming with it hefty buckets of rain. The harsh drops pelt my windshield, blurring the road in front of me. With my wipers not up to par, I'm coerced to follow the speed limit.

"This isn't happening, this isn't happening, this isn't

happening..." I sound like a broken record the whole drive home.

The rain stops as soon as I pull up the driveway, parking in front of the house. The moon is bright, lighting my path. I quickly run up the path to the house, slipping on the wet steps and smashing my knees onto the drenched wood.

Biting back tears of muddled pain, I scramble to my feet and bring out my keys. I curse as I try to steady my hand, attempting to halt its excessive shaking long enough to slip the key in the lock. Eventually it meets its mark. I open the door, then slam it shut, throwing the deadbolt. Making my way through the house, I switch on every single light. Also, I go to each window, checking and double-checking that their latches are secure.

Once upstairs and locked inside my room, I fall into my closet, closing the door. I hunker down in the farthest corner when my hands run into my hidden bottle of vodka. Not thinking twice, I unscrew the lid and sling the bottle back, swallowing three huge gulps.

Closing my eyes, I decide to clear out my fuzzy, cobweb-filled mind. It doesn't work. My mind is set to overdrive mode, with no way of readjusting. Behind my eyelids, the demons and their tar-colored orbs are all I see. In my ears I hear their unrelenting voices of evil barking over and over again.

Lukus had called me a Seer. What is a Seer? Or a *Chozeh*? Or *Ra'ah*?

I need answers and answers fast. If not, off to the looney bin I go!

Popping my eyes wide, I stare out into the dark recesses of the cramped closet. Total unbalance tip the scales of my life over, sending bits and pieces of disarray to crash around me. Hoping to ease the momentum of my revolving thought train, I take another long pull from the bottle. The liquid burns my throat, but I don't care. Right now I just don't care.

Big fat tears spill over my eyelids, plunging down my cheeks. Screwed-up. That's how my life stands at the moment. A screwed-up pile of chaotic nonsense that continues to drag me further and further down insanity road.

Angels and demons, battling in the supermarket's parking lot – who would've thought that? And me, smack dab in the middle of it all.

Sam said that God had chosen me, but what am I

chosen for?

Suddenly, the door to my closest swings wide, and I scream as a hand grabs my arm.

# Chapter Fifteen

# Clarity

"Clarity!" Sam shouts, fastening his hands around my flailing arms. "Settle down, it's me!"

It takes a moment to discern that there's no danger. My eyes center on Sam, and like a hot spring, his celestial heat spills over me, warming all the way to my bones. I inspect him sluggishly, feeling arrant peace. His supernatural orbs are burning with broad interest.

"It's me," he whispers. His hand lifts to my face and palms my cheek, the touch so soft I almost can't feel it.

With my emotions flaring to the surface, I crash into him, locking my arms around his neck. His lavender aroma does little to halt my sonorous tears. They dampen his shirt, but he doesn't seem to mind. He rocks me back and forth, attempting to soothe my wrecked mind.

My Guardian, my *angel*.

Still captured in a tangled web of disbelief on the angel subject, still blindsided by the attack of demons – that's where

I am at this present second. A frantic ball of mess.

Sam lets me blubber a couple of quiet ticks, then declares, "You have much on your mind, and you believe now. You are ready to learn what gifts God has placed within you."

Tiresomely, *pitifully*, I gaze up at him and ask, "What am I? Am I human?"

The question amuses him, and as he laughs I become angered.

"Absolutely *nothing* about this is funny!" I snap. When he keeps up the laughter, I push him away and stand to my feet. In a huff, I walk across the room and stop in front of the window. Crossing my arms at my chest, I stare outside at the bleak darkness.

I can't believe the nerve of him, making light of all the trauma I'd just experienced! Angel or not, I don't deserve any of this. Not. One. Bit.

"I'm sorry," apologizes Sam as he walks up behind me. "Your question caught me off guard. But, yes, you are human, Clarity. One hundred percent human."

Somehow, with what went down, that statement is hard to consider.

I shake my head, rattling my brain. "No – that can't be true! What I'm seeing, what I'm feeling is nowhere near the norm for a human being."

"How do you think the first Seers felt?" he states. "Like Samuel, Gad, Nathan, and countless others. Do you think they felt normal? No, they didn't, because they knew that normal was to be part of the world, and the world was not meant for them. They knew they were above normalcy because they'd been called by God to accomplish mighty works for His kingdom. They knew that all of God's children were set apart from the traditions set in the world."

"Seer?" Languidly, I turn around, staring at him in a paralyzed stupor. "That word … that's what Lukus called me, but..." I swallow a bulky lump of angst lodged in my throat. "What is a Seer, Sam?"

His eyes glow slightly, with an intense look resting within them. "You may want to have a seat."

An uneasy vibe fills the room as a staring contest commences between Sam and me. He's waiting for me to make a move, to do as he says and take a seat, but I don't comply … not instantly, anyway.

With the intoxicating lavender saturating every inch of

my room with its relaxing chill, my limbs start to waver and go limp. Staggering, I take two steps and fall into my vanity's wrought iron chair. His scent circles around me with a calming sense of pure love.

"You and your lavender cologne," I drawl, adding, "That's part of you being an angel, correct?"

"A part of it, yes." He sits down on my bed and faces me, leaning his elbows on his knees. His blue eyes are aflame with fired-up serenity. "All angels have their own unique scents. Mine is and always has been lavender."

"Makes sense. I can't think of a time in my life when I didn't smell lavender."

"Now you know." He smiles. I watch as his lips fade into a straight line. "Now, are you ready to learn what it means to be a Seer?"

I nod my head, gesturing for him to move forward.

"Good." He reaches out to me. "Give me your hands."

A shiver flushes down my spine as I do what I'm told. He takes hold of my hands and flips them palms up so my marks are on display. A tranquil, serene expression shadows his features, and a soft smile touches his lips.

"These marks," he begins, lightly stroking my palms,

"are marks of the Seer. And I'm not talking about fortune telling or mediums – I'm talking true, biblical, God-chosen Seer.

"Biblical Seers can see into the spiritual realm. Not only can you see what's right in front of you, but you can also see what the majority of humans cannot. Both angelic and demonic beings are in attendance within the spiritual realm, and as your gift matures you'll be able to fight the forces of darkness alongside angels."

He pauses, his eyes raising to mine. "You, Clarity, are a Seer, a foot soldier for The Light, and tonight you got your first taste of darkness. Satan himself sent those demons to get rid of you, because he knows exactly what lives within you." His eyes narrow. "And he will not let up on the attacks. Not ever."

"They called me Seer," I tell him, my bottom lip quivering. "They also called me *Ra'ah* and *Chozeh*. What do those words mean?"

"Simple," he says. "Those are Hebrew words. *Ra'ah* basically means you're able to see, and *Chozeh* can be defined as an observer of visions."

"Visions?"

"Yes. A Seer's visions come mostly through dreams, but sometimes, when God permits, they happen when you're wide awake. As a Seer you may be able to see something that will happen in the future, or you will see it moments before it happens. Also, you'll be able to interpret dreams with help from the Holy Spirit."

Mystified I ask, "Interpret dreams? Holy Spirit?"

"Yes and yes," he confirms.

Amazement infuses my nerves as I try to keep an open mind. Just sixty some-odd days ago my life had presumably been normal, but now I find myself sitting in my bedroom having a stressful conversation with an angel.

My life is so far from normal it's pathetic.

In a few words, I'm totally floored and surprisingly speechless. Like a thunderbolt falling from the sky, his proclamation strikes every synapse my body holds, electrifying me from the top of my head to the tips of my toes.

*We want what every angel of darkness craves ... A Seer's soul.*

Lukus's voice echoes inside my head. The demons had called me a Seer. They'd known what I was before I did, but...

"How is this even possible?" I challenge Sam, unable to

digest the information he's feeding me. "Why me? I'm nothing special." My brows stitch together. "Out of the billions of people living on this planet, why me?"

"Because he chose you," he promptly responds, continuing to caress my Seer marks.

"But why *me*?" I press, still dissatisfied with his answer.

He sighs, eyeing my hands again. "God has a reason for everything. No human is a mistake, because the Creator doesn't make mistakes. In this case, you ask why because you feel too ordinary. Not at all special." His gaze travels back to me. "You are special in your own way. God places gifts and talents in every soul that walks the earth. One of yours just happens to be the gifts of a Seer, which allows you to see the world in a whole new light."

"In other words, I'm cursed," I remark bluntly, staring at him through teary eyes.

He frowns. "No, you are *blessed*."

A pounding attacks my head with a vengeance, my simple mind attempting to grasp all this inconceivable knowledge. It's as if he's taking a bundle of garbled mess and blending them together in a bowl of absolute disarray. Utterly and perfectly confusing.

How can he say I'm blessed when I feel like I'm living a nightmare?

"This isn't a nightmare, Clarity – this is reality." He gives my hands a gentle squeeze. "It's hard now, but one day you'll realize that your Seer gifts are a true blessing. A gift from God."

A shuffling noise sounds from on the roof, right next to my window. I almost cry out, but Sam quickly shushes me.

"It's okay," he assures. "It's only Brenton."

Studying him I wonder, "How do you know?"

"I hear his thoughts," he informs. "He's worried about you. He … cares for you." He drops my hands and stands to his feet. "I must go."

"Where will you be? What if I need you?" My words flow out in a rush. What if Lukus and his demons come back for me?

"Lukus and his hounds won't be coming back tonight," he tells me, hearing my thoughts.

"Hounds?" I query. "What do you mean by hounds?"

"The other two demons, Markus and Stone – they are Hellhounds. Big ugly wolf-like beast that track humans, angels, and even other demons. Lukus is their superior."

"Wow," I say, my voice trembling.

"You have nothing to worry about, Clarity." He smiles. "And besides … I am where you are."

And with that said, he disappears.

# Sam

Clarity glances around the room, her thoughts screaming disbelief.

*How can he leave at a time like this?*

*Why be my Guardian if he's just gonna up and leave?*

*Like most people in my life.*

"I'll never leave you," I say, though she can't hear me. I had to mask my presence with Brenton's arrival, which has me wondering – what is he doing here this late? His thoughts alone tell me he's been worried about her, but couldn't whatever it is wait until tomorrow?

Humans and their absurd, overbearing feelings – I'll never understand them.

Three knocks sound on the glass window, and Clarity promptly opens it.

"Brenton!" she exclaims, showing surprise. "What are

you doing here? It's a little late."

"I tried calling your cell, but you didn't pick up." He climbs in easily, the whole time looking a Clarity. "I was worried about you. Um, is A.C. home?"

"No, she's at work." Clarity smiles, though it's forced. "You don't have to worry, I'm fine, and..." Pulling her cell phone from her pocket, she examines it. "Yep, phone's dead. That's why I didn't pick up."

"Well ... okay, then." Brenton rakes a hand through his shaggy hair, continuing to stare at her with unblinking eyes. Hearing his thoughts, I feel of sense of agitation trying to ease its way inside my head.

*She is so beautiful.*

*I wish she would open up more.*

*I want to marry and spend every night with her.*

"So, what's on your mind?" she inquires, applying a kiss on his cheek. I want to shout when she takes his hand and leads him to her bed. When they sit down, he places a hand on her knee, giving it a squeeze. The Guardian in me wants to knock his hand away.

A teenage boy's mind can turn to putty when they're around a girl, and I've heard many fleshly thoughts come from Brenton...

"And from Clarity's mind too, Sam." I train my focus on Sarah, who has appeared outside on the roof, sitting next to the window. "She's not innocent in her way of thinking. Plus, nothing is going to happen tonight. He only came to check on her, and to ask her to the Thanksgiving dance that's in a couple of weeks."

I grimace. "Yes, they may be talking, but I know how their minds work. I also know how close they have come to succumbing to their fleshly desires."

"And I know for a fact that you have nothing to worry about." She sighs. "They're just *talking*, Sam. It's what humans do. Now come outside and take a seat. The sky is glorious tonight."

I don't want to, but I close my eyes, then open them. I'm now on the roof, out of the house – but I'm staying close to the window. Sarah is sitting down gazing at the stars, which are plentiful in the sky tonight. I rest next to her, eyeing the bright dots that blanket the universe.

Listening to Clarity and Brenton's conversation, I hear nonsensical, childish words pouring from their mouths. What they are talking about, like dances and such, are important to them. With all that's happened to Clarity the last couple of months I guess she deserves a little normalcy in her life, even if it's for a short time.

"Yes, it's important to them," points out Sarah, who has clearly been listening in on my thinking.

"There's too much danger in this town to let Clarity become unfocused," I readily say. "Lukus and those hounds of Hell are still around, though they are hiding, licking their wounds from earlier. They now know that Clarity is more informed on her supernatural gifts. They also know she's unsaved – I need more time to minister to her, to help her –"

"You can't hold her hand the whole time," Sarah scolds. "She's no longer ignorant to the unseen world, and you know as well as I do that with freewill she can decide if she wants to walk in light or remain in darkness."

I'm listening to Sarah, but also listening to the conversation going on in Clarity's bedroom.

"Will you stay until I'm asleep?" Clarity asks Brenton.

"Yeah, of course!" Brenton replies, clearly excited – too excited in my opinion.

"Great!" Clarity happily responds. "Just let me go to the bathroom and change out of my work clothes."

Ricking my head toward the window I say, "What is she thinking...?"

"Sam," warns Sarah, but it's too late. I'm already in the bedroom, ready to stop Clarity from making a stupid decision, like sleeping with Brenton.

Before I can show my presence, Sarah clamps a hand hard on my shoulder.

"No, Sam. You cannot intervene."

"I can't just let this happen!" I express. "I can't watch her destroy herself."

"And as I told you, nothing is going to happen." She drops her hand from my shoulder. "Brenton came over to see her, and to ask her to the dance, and that's it. Oh, and by the way, she said yes."

Swallowing down the concern wedged in my tonsils, I watch as Brenton's eyes roam over Clarity's room. He picks up a picture of the two of them at the beach – they were only four years old when it was taken. His fingers softly touch the frame, and a smile takes control of his lips.

"He does love her," I whisper.

"Yes he does," Sarah whispers back.

The door to Clarity's bathroom opens, and out she

steps, unaware that two angelic beings are in the room with them. She's wearing a t-shirt and sweatpants, her usual nighttime garb.

"Wow, you look beautiful," Brenton tells her, and he means it. His face flushes as he meanders closer to her, stopping just inches from her face.

She's blushing as well. "No, I'm not. I'm wearing ratty sweats and a stained t-shirt."

"Clare-Baby, you're beautiful because you … are you."

When he palms her face and pulls her closer, they begin to kiss. Again the urge to interrupt their moment barrels into every fiber my being holds. And again, Sarah places a hand on my shoulder.

"They can't do this," I grind out through clenched teeth. "They haven't taken vows, they're not married – "

"And you're the first angel with hearing problems." I cast her a sideways glance as she adds, "Look, the kiss is over. That's all it was, Sam. A kiss."

Looking back to my Charge, I see that she is already under her covers, resting on her side. Brenton lays behind her, snuggling against her, though he's above the blankets. That's when I ascertain that nothing is going to happen, but even still, I don't think the two of them should be alone.

Within minutes, Clarity is asleep, her breathing soft and balanced. I'm left all together stunned. After coming face-to-face with demons for the first time, and learning about her Seer heritage, her mind is at ease.

"She's at peace because Brenton is with her," Sarah apprises softly. "When she lost her parents, it created a fear within her, that lies and tells her that everybody she loves will one day leave her. Brenton has been by her side for as long as she can remember. He's a reliable, constant presence in her life – that is why she is at ease."

"You think I don't know this," I snip. "You think I don't know my own Charge?"

Sarah smiles daintily and replies, "Of course you know her. But I've noticed that when Brenton and Clarity are together, you become edgy and possessive – you can't be that way."

"So we're supposed to just stand around and allow them to sin?" I throw back.

"Sam, all we can do is watch out for them. In Brenton's case, all I can do is whisper encouragement in his ears. Clarity has an edge since she's a Seer – you can talk to her about what's right and what's wrong. After that, she will decide to either follow the rules or not. It's all about freewill."

"Trust me, I know about freewill," I mutter, my eyes on my sleeping Charge. "I've seen humans choose to live for Christ, and I've seen them choose not to, and that path leads to death."

"Letting your sinful nature control your mind leads to death, but allowing the Holy Spirit to guide your way leads to life and peace." Sarah quotes scripture, just as Brenton gets to his feet and pulls something from his pocket. We watch as he leaves a piece of paper on Clarity's nightstand, then places a gold chain on top.

"What's he up to?" I wonder, looking to Sarah.

She giggles, then says, "Leaving Clarity a present. See you around, Sam." She disappears, with Brenton climbing out of the window and onto the roof. He closes the window behind him as he goes.

Gazing down at what he's left, I smile. He's given Clarity a gold necklace with a sunflower pendant on it. Sunflowers are Clarity's favorite flower. I also smile at what's written on the note.

*I'm going to marry you one day.*

# Chapter Sixteen

# Clarity

Life has always been a game to me, one full of extreme happiness, devastating sorrow, and complete loss. I win some, I lose some, and at the end of the day I'm either impressed by my actions, or humiliated by what I've become.

Ever since I was twelve years old, my life has been a roller coaster ride, having the highest ups, the most twisted turns, and intense, stomach-dropping lows. Most people can analyze their lives as an enormous free fall, which contains a big climb of promise that ends with a great fall of failure.

My life has taken such a surreal turn, veering off the path of normality, imparting uncertainty as to where I belong.

Do I still fit in with my peers? Do I still fit in a world full of teenage drinking and parties? Can I even *attend* parties any more?

What about Brenton and our relationship? Can that still happen? He'd left me a note stating that he would marry me one day – can that happen now? Will any of my plans and dreams come to fruition?

Or...

Am I destined to live in the spirit realm, where angels and demons battle nonstop over unsaved souls? A dangerous, frightening world where demons lust over human souls, their only goal to kill, steal, and destroy.

Is that my future? A world unseen to everyone around but me; a world I still don't understand.

Do I belong in a Seer's world? More importantly, can I handle it?

I have a lot on my mind, a lot to ponder through, and a lot of decisions to make. Until I figure it out, I must act altogether ordinary. A perfect example of ordinary is spending a break at school with my boyfriend, enjoying an astoundingly mundane conversation – an ordinary, easy-going, *normal* conversation.

In the abandoned part of the school (which is condemned, but we sneak in anyway), Brenton and I sit gazing out the window of a small unused classroom. A turbulent storm is brewing in the outside world. Dark growling clouds cover the school as torrential rains transform

Garlandton into one massive puddle. Ferocious howls of wind and thunder rattle the windows of the ancient school, the storm hitting its peak with a vicious frenzy.

"I've never seen so many storms this time of year," Brenton murmurs beside me.

"Huh?" I'd heard him, but my brain is so majorly congested with this Seer business that it's hard to concentrate on anything else.

Three ticks of silence pass before he wonders, "What's up with you?"

Tearing my gaze away from the approaching storm, pursuing to sever all thought lines my brain has been trained on, I smile at him and reply, "Nothing's up. I've just been thinking about life and other … stuff."

"Like what?"

Lazily I shrug. "I don't know, just stuff."

"You know," he grins, nudging my shoulder with his, "the best thing you can do with stuff is share it with someone else, so share away!"

Considering the sincerity in his chocolate brown eyes, I realize how lucky I am to have him. More than anything I want to share what's on my mind. More than anything I want to tell him about the unseen world around us – angels, demons, Seers, and Sam – I want to tell him that I've been marked as a Seer; a *biblical* Seer.

However, telling him is not an option – not yet, anyway.

"Can I ask you a question?" I bite my lip, suddenly nervous.

He dips his head, takes my hand, and responds, "You can ask me anything."

I falter a couple of seconds before asking, "Do you believe in God?"

"Yes," he answers.

"In Heaven and Hell?"

"Absolutely."

"Angels and demons?"

"Why all the questions?" he wants to know, his eyebrows raised and his tone slightly inquisitive. "Why are you suddenly into God and all that religious stuff?"

Ignoring him I demand, "Yes or no?"

Giving in, he says, "Yeah, I guess I do. I mean, look around us – somehow the universe came into existence, and with all the bad in the world the devil has to be real. And angels have to be real, also, because demons were once angels, so I guess you can say I believe in God and everything else."

"Good," I exhale a breath, relief exploding in my bloodstream. Then, going a step further, I ask, "Will you start going to church with me?"

His eyes widen. "Whoa, slow down, now. Yes, I believe, but church – I'm not sure about all that."

"Why not?"

"Have you seen the kids that go to church?" he throws out, his head shaking in disgust. "They're the same kids who go to parties, drink, smoke pot, and hook-up with random people. Now I know I'm not perfect, but I'm no hypocrite, either."

"Understood," I say, squeezing his hand. "We'll take baby steps."

He grins, his dimples deep in his cheeks. "Yeah, I like that idea."

"I mean," I laugh, "look at Kora. She's as rough as rough can get, then she starts dating Kevin and now she's a different person. She took baby steps with Kevin, and now she goes every Sunday and Wednesday night. And the other day she was playing Christian music in her car – Christian metal, but Christian nonetheless."

"Can we talk about something else," Brenton proposes, eager to change the subject.

"Okay, what do you want to talk about?"

"Your necklace." He rubs the sunflower pendent between his fingers. "It looks marvelous around your delicate neck. Someone must really like you." I chuckle when he winks.

"Yes, it does look perfect around my neck, and as for that someone who likes me..." I return the wink. "I'm pretty sure I like him back."

Still fixated on the sunflower he inquires, "Did you read my note?"

My heart hikes upward, pounding in my throat. "Yes, I did."

"Well, what do you think?" His eyes travel back to mine, with an earnest gleam lounging in them.

"I think..." I pause, squelching down an annoying ball of angst. "I think I need to tell you something."

"Uh-oh, that doesn't sound good." Dropping the pendent, his smile disappears and he lets out a low whistle. Grabbing hold of my hand he queries, "What do you need to tell me?"

Not waiting any longer, I quickly respond, "I've been accepted into New York State."

A flash of surprise lands on his face.

"New York?" A vacant look glosses over his eyes as he fights to comprehend the news I delivered. Then, he lightens up and smiles. "You got into New York State. That's great news! When did you find out?"

"A few weeks ago," I say softly, almost a whisper.

With that answer, his gaze slides down to our entwined hands. "When did you plan on telling me?"

"Brenton." I take his face in my hands, coercing him to look at me. "I'm not going if you don't go with me."

"No, Clarity," he declares, his voice wet with sorrow. "You're going, with or without me. I'm not going to hold you back from your dreams."

"Brenton – "

"No!" Releasing my hand, he turns away and leans his head on the window, his eyes closed. "I love you so much, Clarity, but I will not be the one to ruin your future. So you're going."

Becoming agitated, I snap, "Well, I love *you* so much

that I will not go without you. I will *not* leave you behind."

He slips his head against the window, giving me an oblique glance. I think there's tears in his eyes as he says, "You're the best part of my life. Maybe I can go, but after a couple of years of saving and – "

"No, not good enough," I exasperatedly interject, hopping to my feet. "The only way I'll go is if you go with me, and that's that."

Crossing my arms at my chest, I defiantly glare at him. I know I sound immature and childish, but I don't care. A life without Brenton is not part of the plan. Never has been, never will be.

Matching my movements, he stands to his feet and faces me with a dumbstruck look etched in his features. "You are the most stubborn person I've ever known."

"Yes, I am." I'm quick to agree with this logic.

"Listen, it's not that I don't want to go, it's just..."

"Just what? Spit it out."

Sweeping a hand over his thick hair, he breathes out a sigh and replies, "I don't make enough money to support the two of us. When we live together, get married, whatever we end up doing, I want to be able to support you. I don't want us to end up like..." His sentence trails off as his eyes descend to the floor.

"Oh, Brenton," I whisper as a colossal dose of awareness pours over me. Wrapping my arms around him, we embrace, holding on to each other tightly.

I know who he doesn't want us to end up like, and that's his parents. His dad had been laid off months ago, while his mom earned minimum wage at a daycare center.

More than half of Brenton's paychecks go to fund his family's household. It's only the three of them, but it takes almost all he makes to keep them afloat. I want to slap myself for making him talk about his financial woes, but it's too late for that.

Luckily, I have some good news to share.

Leaning back so as to peer in his eyes, I carefully say, "Money isn't an issue. My parents left me well off."

Right away he backs up, gesturing with his hands. "No, that's not an option, not at all! I will not let you – "

"Shhh." I place a finger lightly on his lips, quieting him. "I get it when I turn eighteen, which is less than four months away. It's mine to do whatever I want with. And I'll do whatever it takes for us to be together. I promised myself I wouldn't use it until something important came along and I needed it."

"Clarity," he whispers, pulling my hand away from his mouth.

"This," I continue, touching my forehead to his, "is *majorly* important. There is no me without you, and this is a chance for the both of us to get out of this town. It's not about your parents, A.C., or anybody – just you and me." I recline back, staring at him, hard and serious. "Will you come with me to New York?"

My heart is a furious beast in my chest as I study his expression. I can almost hear the wheels turning over and over inside his brain, contemplating the whole scenario. Nervousness strikes my stomach as the wheels in my own head begin spinning out of control.

What if he says no?

"You'd do that for me?" he inquires, fixing a flyaway hair behind my ear.

I nod. "I'll do anything for us to be together."

With his eyes flicking to the ceiling, he sucks in a shaky breath, releasing it slowly. "I don't know..."

"Please," I implore, my arms a solid lock around his

waist.

Thunder rumbles outside, once again shaking the building. Sheets of rain hammer the roof so hard I'm afraid it will cave in. But what bothers me more is the troubled expression darkening Brenton's usual carefree face.

"Clarity, you deserve so much better than me."

"Don't you ever say that again! You are my everything, Brenton. My *everything*."

Kissing him firmly on the lips, we stay in that position until the bell rings. Our break is over, and now class awaits us.

Picking our book bags off the floor, I try assuring him, "It's going to work out. I know it will."

"I hope so," he says. Grabbing my hand, he leads us out of the old classroom and away from the abandoned hallway. My mind is in overdrive, the words he'd spoken reverberating in my head, bouncing off the walls of my skull.

*I hope so.*

Boy, I hope so, too.

# Lukus

The slap resounds all around the room, followed by a

soft whimper. Nick is giving the female human known as Daria her daily dose of punishment, embedding her in her place. The mouth on this one always gets her in trouble, sending Nick over the edge with acute fury.

"What did I do? What did I do?" she sobs. Her hair is tangled, and black streaks paint lines down her face, her make-up dripping from the wetness her eyes produce.

"What did you do? What did you do?!" In a fit of rage, he snatches her around the neck and bangs her head against the wall, choking her.

Lucky for Nick his mortal father is always away, leaving him in this stuffy mansion all by himself. If his father knew of the torture that occurred behind his bedroom door, I'm sure Nick would be seen as insane ... which he sort of is, thanks to his willingness to embrace darkness.

The walls are painted black and there's naked pictures of women hanging from the walls. A small table holds all sorts of bottles filled with amber liquids, and also a various amount of hallucinate drugs. Painted in red, a pentagram is showcased on the wall behind his bed, and a satanic bible sits on his nightstand. Nick has read it front and back.

Nick's heart is as black as mine – well, if I had a heart,

that is. And he's not hard to persuade in the ways of darkness. Easy target, that Nick Reece.

"It's not what you did," he growls, grinning maliciously. "It's what you're not *doing*."

Releasing her, he thrusts her against the wall and saunters away. Daria hits the floor hard, rubbing her neck and gasping for air. Nick unscrews the cap from one of the bottles and upends it, drawing long gulps into his mouth, letting the poison spread throughout his veins.

Smiling, I recline back on the opposite wall, enjoying the show. This disastrous couple has already taken Ecstasy, and they are acting out of their minds. They continue to ingest toxins into their bloodstreams, not knowing the damage they're doing. Not that I'm complaining. While they're slowly killing themselves, I have the satisfaction of watching them crash and burn.

Daria staggers over to Nick, hugging him from behind. He acts as if she's invisible. I almost want to call the hounds in so they can watch this hazardous yet amusing spectacle. But they're outside playing their parts, keeping their noses in the air, sniffing for any beings of The Guard.

"I'm sorry," Daria mumbles against his bare back,

laying light kisses on his skin. "What do you want me to do? Whatever it is, I'll do it."

Nick places the bottle on the table, staring ahead, his face reflecting off the mirror hanging on the wall. His eyes are dilated, almost black, his expression blank. A toxic grin slowly travels over his lips, so severe that it's hard for me to believe he's human.

"I'll tell you what you can do." Manually he unlocks her grip from around his waist, then turns to face her. "You can treat me like Kora used to."

A shrill, high-pitched cackle sounds from Daria. "Oh Nick, please! Look at me – I'm popular, a cheerleader, a Prom Queen, while Kora's just … just … skanky trailer trash!"

A mask of pure violence takes hold of Nick's features. In a swift movement, he seizes Daria by the hair, yanking her head back. The laughing stops and changes to screams as she pounds at his chest with balled-up fists.

"Yes," I say loudly, knowing he can hear my voice. "Make her fulfill all your darkest desires, Nick. Force her to satisfy your every need."

"Be more like Kora," Nick demands Daria. "Or it's over."

Defeated, she stops punching his chest, peering up at him with eyes full of tears.

"Why can't you love me for me?" she mewls pitifully. She cries out when he yanks her hair even harder.

"Oh, I love you, but you don't love me," he says gruffly, kissing her on the neck. "If you loved me, you'd do exactly as I tell you. You wouldn't argue or complain – you'd just be quiet and do it."

Whispering in his ear I tell him, "Force her to comply to your needs. You're her master and she is your slave. *Rule* her."

A gratified feeling scrambles over me as he pushes Daria to her knees. She gazes up at him through glazed, polluted eyes, a mixture of fear and doubt rolling off of her in stormy waves.

"O-Okay," she concedes, her spirit depleted. "I'll do whatever you want. I'll try to be more like Kora."

Nick simpers, knowing he's overcame the weak female. "Oh, you won't try to be Kora – you *will* be Kora. Now, be a good little girl and do what I say. I'll love you forever, and that's a promise."

They begin diving in to their sadistic, sinful desires, and I delight in their nasty display of affection. Humans and their flesh – gets the best of them almost every time!

Right in the middle of the wicked debacle, just as it's getting good, a thought hits me. Like I've grabbed hold of a live electrical wire, a knowledge like no other jolts through my corrupt being with a wild vengeance.

"I know," I state aloud, my smile so wide the human skin rips around my lips. "I know how to bring down the Seer."

Can't believe I didn't figure it out until now.

This will be too easy.

# Chapter Seventeen

# Clarity

"So I know I haven't ever cared about some stupid dance before, but now that Kevin and I are together I'm *so* ready for it!" Kora slams her locker shut and leans back on it, staring dreamily into empty air. "Kevin is just ... so sweet! I bet he's going to look so handsome in a suit."

Sighing, I close my locker and listen as Kora rambles on and on about Kevin's cuteness. It's Friday afternoon, just one week and one day away from the Thanksgiving dance, and Kora is beyond excited. Actually, I've never seen her this excited about anything.

"It's so romantic how he asked me," she murmurs, grinning from ear to ear. "He met me at the theater after work, like he usually does, but this time he brought a vase full of roses. No guy has given me flowers before."

"That's great, Kora," I tell her, though I want to scream *shut up, it's just a stupid adolescent dance*!

In the past when dances came around, Kora and I

213

would do something together, like hangout on my rooftop doing shots of tequila with music blasting from the radio. Not this year, though. This year we both have dates and we're both in love with outstanding guys who love us back.

Maybe I'd be more excited if the last couple of months hadn't happened, starting with the night Sam crash landed into my life. Oh, who am I trying to kid? I'm glad Sam appeared that night in the store. I love it when he's around. When he visits we spend time reading the bible. Most of the time is spent with him explaining the scriptures – the bible is so confusing!

Sam's also been explaining a little about my Seer qualities, leaving me intrigued almost every night. Like the white heavenly light that lives within him lives in me as well. Only mine is more potent, which surprises the heck out of me. He said that as my Seer gifts grow, I'll be able to send demons away by touching them with my palms.

"Hey, Clare, you there?"

Reality showers around me as I leap off my chugging thought train. Kora's voice has hacked through my thinking, instantly snatching my attention.

"I'm sorry," I contritely say. "I spaced out – what did

you say?"

"I was wondering if you'd thought about a dress, you know, since we're going dress shopping with Janey tomorrow." There's a twinkle in her green eyes.

"Dress shopping?" I scrunch my face in confusion. "Who said I was going dress shopping tomorrow?"

She gawks at me, her face flushing the same color as her hair.

"We – you, Janey and me – talked about this a month ago! Remember that one time during break?"

"Honestly, no, I don't remember." And that's the truth.

With the huge amount of changes exploding like dynamite in my life, I've been finding it hard to recollect the little things, like shopping and teenage stuff. It's as if I'm living a double life, and one is slowly taking charge over the other. I hate keeping this secret from my friends, but what choice do I have? How would that conversation go?

*Yes, nice weather we're having today. Oh, and did you know that I'm a Seer who sees angels and demons? Not only that, but my hands contain marks that you can't see and holds a celestial essence that destroys demonic beings. Cool, right? So, wanna hang?*

Yeah, I'm sure that would go over just swell.

"Well, we did talk about it," Kora continues crustily, her hand balanced on her narrow hip. "Janey said she fixed y'all's schedules and Mr. Baker agreed to work the register, plus Casey will be there."

"Mr. Baker agreed to work a register?" Wow, never thought I'd see the day where he worked outside his office.

"Yes," confirms Kora. "And we're going to the movies afterward, so no backing out – it's going to be a girls day and you're going to like it."

A girls day. Probably need one.

"I won't back out, pinky promise." I lift my pinky finger, looping it with hers.

"Sweet." Letting go of my pinky, she glances at her watch. "Whoa, dude! I've got to get to work!"

"You're working tonight?"

She sighs dramatically. "Yes, a night shift, the dreaded one night a month filled with cleaning the entire building from top to bottom. Luckily there's four others sentenced alongside me."

"Wait," I say, arching an eyebrow. "The theater is only cleaned like that once a month?"

"Yeah – I mean, we clean it nightly, just not to a great

extent."

"That's disgusting," I remark, blanching.

"Well, it is what it is." She pulls on her black hoodie and starts walking away. "See ya tomorrow."

"Kora!" I call after her.

"Yeah?" She stops in front of the exit door, glancing back.

I hesitate before saying, "Be careful out there – you never know who's watching you." An image of Nick flashes in my mind, while a cold shiver spreads goosebumps on my flesh.

"Don't worry, ma, I'll be careful." Laughing, she walks out the doors.

With Kora gone, I'm alone in the hallway. Everyone has headed home for the weekend, needing a break from the hell that is high school. I'm needing a break from teachers and tests, but now that I'm by my lonesome, thoughts begin driving in high gear.

Why had Nick cruised across my mind while I talked with Kora? Why had I felt a chill deep within my bones at the thought of him? Is it some kind of warning? Another Seer trait that I still haven't heard about?

Leaving school and driving to work, only one phrase repeats in my skull.

I'm one weird, messed-up individual.

\*\*\*

*I'm standing in the middle of a dark, wet alley. The orange glow from a nearby light casts eerie shadows on the brick walls that make up this dreary place. An unpleasant smell looms in the air, causing nausea to ram head on into my belly.*

*It's nighttime, and on eyeing my surroundings I see that the moon and stars are absent from the sky. Thick rain clouds have replaced them. A rumble in the distance threatens that a storm is in production.*

*On the ground trash is strewn in complete disarray, covering almost every inch of the pavement. The alley's one and only dumpster appears to be busting at its seams with garbage, which sheds light as to why it's so filthy.*

*Where in the world am I?*

*I'm cold, I'm scared, and most of all, baffled. Consciously I don't know how I've landed in the middle of this dark, repelling place. Being alone in a nasty alley full of garbage has never been on my list of sights to see.*

The wind blows, carrying with it a soft murmur. The sound of a girl crying bounces off the brick walls, flooding my eardrums. I take one step forward, then pause. Gooseflesh has risen up and down my bare arms, so I rub at them vigorously, hoping they can be subdued. I'm not too sure, but I believe the sobbing is coming from the back of the alley, in the darkest corner. Possibly on the other side of the dumpster.

"Hello!" I call out. "Is anyone there?"

The pitiful whimpering continues, and tears fill my eyes because of the sadness that's pouring out from the weeper. Against my better judgment, I begin walking forward, though my legs feel like they've turned to Jell-O. Trekking over piles of rotting food and trash, my eyes continue to tear up, but not from the crier. It's the horrible stench in the air that stings my eyes.

Rats crawl all over the place, some as big as small dogs. They squeak loudly as they scurry through the rank debris. My heart thuds in my ears, my mind screams at me to turn back. Instead of listening, I trudge ahead. I have to find out if the girl is okay, if she needs help.

"Where are you?" I call out again.

A weak voice answers, "Please … help me."

"I'm coming!" Adrenaline sloshes through my blood,

*pushing me to pick up the pace. When I get to the dumpster, I peer over its side ... and gasp.*

*Laying in a heap on the dirty ground is Daria Phipps. Her normally perfect blonde hair reminds me of a desert tangleweed. She gazes up at me, her wide eyes chock-full of terror, her mascara streaming down her tear-stained face. Red lipstick is smeared all over her mouth. The red mini-dress she wears is ripped on one side.*

*What horrifies me the most is all the cuts and bruises that color her bare flesh. She appears to have been beaten up, like one hellacious fight had taken place. There's not a single inch of her body that's not riddled with marks of brutality.*

*"Daria..." I try speaking as calm as possible. Bending to one knee I inquire, "Who did this to you?"*

*"He's coming," she announces with her swollen bottom lip quivering and eyes filled with magnetized fear. "He's going to kill me."*

*Taken back by her frightful admission, I ask, "Who, Daria? Who is going to kill you?"*

*Abruptly she sits up and seizes my shoulders, digging her long nails into my flesh. Her breaths are ragged, and her hands are ice cold. With our faces inches apart, our noses almost touching, I can see that her eyes are dilated; the whites of her eyes are close to* non-existent.

"You know who," she whispers, then, as if her life force has drained, she slumps to the ground unconscious.

Reaching for her wrist, I find her pulse – it's chillingly weak. Gently patting her face I push, "Daria, come on – wake up."

A cold wind suddenly blows in from behind, the ice picks of frost aimed straight at my heart. Someone is back there. I know this without looking. I can feel the eyes of evil drilling holes in the back of my head. My heart somersaults when a voice slices through the darkness like a knife.

"What are you doing, princess?"

Slowly, in no hurry, I lift to my feet. My legs shake uncontrollably. I spin around, deciding to face danger head on.

"Nick," I whisper.

Yes, the person in front of me is Nick. However he looks a bit on the strange side. He's dressed all in black, his skin is pale, and his eyes are the color of coal. When he smiles, it's malicious, a very hate-induced smile, and it's so obvious he's possessed. In his right hand he holds some sort of weapon. It's too dark to tell, thanks to the orange light flickering on and off.

"Answer my question, princess." His tone is dead and stoney.

*Rather than complying, I snap, "What are you doing here, Nick?"*

*The answer I receive comes in the form of barking cackles. I've never heard a laugh sound so malevolent. Not since meeting Lukus and his Hellhounds.*

*Like turning off a television, his laughter switches off. He sets his vacant gaze on me, tilting his head to the side.*

*"It's all part of his plan," he tells me, his voice detached from his body. Then, taking whatever he holds in his hand, he lifts it up and swings it directly at my head...*

Sitting straight up in bed, I awake from the head-spinning nightmare. My breathing comes in hefty pants, while my heart bounces around like a ball of loose meat in my chest, bruising my lungs. The palms of my hands are burning, while my pajamas are liberally doused with perspiration.

In a frenzied panic, my hands fly to my head to make sure it's still attached to my body. Realizing I still have a head, I chortle anxiously.

"Just another dream," I mumble, falling back onto my pillows.

Yes, a dream, but one that hits too close to home.

Sunlight bleeds through the curtains, immersing my

bedroom with its exquisite golden radiance. A beautiful start to a Saturday full of dress shopping, a cheesy movie, and stale popcorn. In one way I'm looking forward to spending the day with my friends, but then in another way I'm dreading it.

Truthfully I don't know how today will go, since these plans are so normal – *too* normal for a girl like me. Seriously, how can I concentrate on anything other than my hands burning like they've been sandwiched in between an ultra-heated flat iron?

"You have to warn Daria."

My bones attempt to dance out of my skin at the sudden sound of Sam's voice.

"Sam!" I exclaim, trying to calm the unnaturally fast beat of my heart. "You scared me! Sheesh, I about wet myself..."

"You've got to warn Daria Phipps." His expression lingers in serious mode.

"Why?" I question, appalled by what he's suggesting. "Daria hates me, and besides, it was only a dream."

"A Seer's dream can sometimes be a life or death situation for certain individuals. You must learn to take your dreams earnestly." His glowing blue orbs narrow. "Daria may

223

be in danger. She needs your help, whether she likes you or not."

Jutting my bottom lip out, I crisscross my arms and pout. So being a Seer means I have a duty to help all mankind, but Daria? Can she even be considered part of the human race? If she truly is human, where the heck did her conscience disappear to? Somewhere up her narrow behind?

"Fine," I concede in defeat. "I'll do it, though I'd rather stick hot pokers in my eyeballs than go to Daria's house and ... *talk*." I frown, shuddering. The thought of having a nonchalant talk with the school's biggest snob makes me sick with stabbing nausea.

"I know she's difficult – "

"That's a mega understatement," I interpose, throwing an eye roll his direction.

"But," he presses on, "as a Seer you must learn to work with all types of personalities, even with the mean-spirited ones."

I groan. "Daria's not just mean – she's atrocious." Also a slutty, hateful, controlling witch.

Sam's throat clears, and he shakes his head. A look of disapproval conceals his usual jovial features.

"What?"

"Your thoughts are unpleasant."

"Sorry, sorry," I say, mocking contriteness. "How about I call her an egotistical fudge-nut who reminds me of a female dog? Is that better?"

For the first time ever, Sam rolls his eyes. His eyes! It strikes me as comical since eye rolling is a human trait, not a celestial one. I mean, I *think* it's not a celestial mannerism.

When he vanishes, shock invades my system.

"Wait, Sam!" I shout, bounding out of bed. "I can't do this alone. How am I going to start the conversation, huh? *How?*"

Silence is my reply.

# Chapter Eighteen

## Sam

Clarity's radio is blasting vacuous music with empty lyrics as she drives down the road. It's hard to comprehend the words the singer is yelling. Horrible, meaningless noise, if you ask me. However, I know why she's listening to such a draining racket – she's trying not to think about her present situation.

Sitting in the passenger's seat, I observe as her thoughts go into a tailspin. She dreads facing Daria because she is such a detestable person. Her nerves are rattled because she doesn't know exactly how to go about the situation at hand. And she's confused because she doesn't understand why she's having to go through such torture.

That's partly my fault, I suppose. I've been focusing on teaching her the word of God, rather than getting her ready to approach humans who are in danger. Though before she can be a successful Seer, she must learn God's word. The problem is her soul is still hanging in the balance, sitting right in the middle. She's neither hot nor cold. She believes in God, but she is still unsaved.

True, she harbors the gifts of a Seer, but for her to reach her ultimate potential to be a mighty warrior for Christ, she has a decision to make.

Long ago, when she was a little girl, she'd asked Jesus into her heart. But her faith declined after her parents passed away. The light within her that once shined so bright slowly dimmed, until no light resided in her heart. A place that had burned so fervently in her soul had grown bitter and cold.

Clarity's light has been absent for years, and now as she heads to Daria's home, it's time for her to make things right. It's time to put just one of her many gifts to work.

It's time for her to burn as brightly as the sun.

# Clarity

Daria lives on the rich side of town, out of sight from the trailers and worn-down shacks that make up my side of town. Not that my house is a dump. It's just when you compare it to her mansion, my house can easily be described as old.

Princess Daria's house, I mean *castle*, was built ten years ago, when the elite members of Garlandton decided it was time to spruce up our quaint town. And that's how Garlandton Country Club was born.

The country club has all the accommodations rich folks could ask for – two swimming pools, golf course, state-of-the-art gymnasium with an indoor pool, hot tub, weight room, and sauna. Five tennis courts sit behind a five star restaurant that serves anything from hot dogs to lobsters.

Motoring through the open gates of the posh community, I spot Daria's red BMW parked in her driveway, with the three-story Phipps manor resting beyond. I park my rust-infested Honda at the end of the drive and survey the scenery. Nope, just as I thought. I'm the only one with a car produced in the early nineties.

An uneasy rock has settled in the pit of my stomach as I sit there pondering my next move. I can't start off the conversation by explaining the dream that starred her and Nick.

Sure, she'd believe every word, especially since we're so close.

*Not.*

Sucking in a breath, slowly releasing the air from my lungs, I open the car door and push myself up the steep driveway. With each step that pumps the asphalt, a queasy feeling grows in my belly. When I stand in front of the heavy mahogany door, I knock twice with a trembling hand.

My nerves are a bundle of jitters, and I'm tempted to leave when Daria opens the door.

Too late to wuss out.

"Oh, wow," she scoffs, leaning against the doorjamb. "What do you want, loser?"

Forcing down an explicit word, I greet her with a smile. "Hey, Daria. How are you doing today?"

I search her face for any signs of trauma, finding nothing but dark circles under her blue eyes. The fuzzy pink scarf she's wearing around her neck hits me as peculiar. The reason it's weird is because the weather outside is unusually warm, strange for November.

She smirks. "Either tell me what you want or go away. That piece of crap car doesn't belong in this neighborhood. People will talk."

Swallowing down yet again a nasty, vulgar word that's on the tip of my tongue, I answer, "I wanted to talk to you a minute. You know, a friendly conversation between two people which doesn't include being vile to each other."

"Friendly?" She chuckles, then quirks a sculpted eyebrow. "Are you serious?"

I comb my teeth over my bottom lip, really working on keeping my patience and anger under control. I declare, "It's important – may I please come in?"

A look of suspicion fogs her face as her eyes narrow. An eternity and a half passes before she responds.

"Oh, why not – come on in." She spins on her heels and walks away, leaving the door wide open. I step over the threshold, closing the door behind me.

Daria's house can be described in two words – massively *gaudy*.

When you first walk in you face a grand staircase, and your eyes see walls covered with classic paintings, most likely expensive originals. Hardwood floors and Persian rugs map out the entire house. Breakables are placed everywhere, from priceless Mint Eggs to five foot tall vases and statues.

Following her into a majestic dining room that leads to a huge gourmet kitchen, I wonder what her parents do for a living that allows them to live in such luxury. The floors in the kitchen are marble, the counter tops granite – it's intense and marvelous at the same time.

"Nice place," I say casually, trying to keep the mood light.

"What, this old shack?" She opens the refrigerator and retrieves two bottled waters. Throwing one my direction, I quickly grab it before it plummets to the floor.

"Thanks," I tell her, twisting off the top and taking a sip of the cool liquid.

"Whatever," she coolly replies, shrugging her shoulders. "Now, what did you want to talk about?"

I stare at her, unsure of how to start the conversation. When she opened the door and found me standing there, she apparently turned on her witch switch. Already, the urge to smack her across the face and rip her perfectly smooth blonde hair from the roots is hot in my blood.

Then an image of her from the dream traverses through my mind, all bloody and bruised...

Patience, Clarity. Perfect time to practice it.

"I wanted to ask..." I trail off when I eye dark bruises on her upper arms.

"Ask me what?" she snaps, seemingly agitated.

232

"What happened to your arms?" I bluntly inquire.

Patently surprised she replies, "Nothing. Go ahead, talk."

"Okay." Ripping my gaze from her arms, I peer directly in her eyes. "I was wondering how you and Nick are doing." I gauge her reaction with interest. It doesn't take long to receive a response.

"What?" she expresses, entirely puzzled. "You mean to tell me that you drove over here just to ask how me and my boyfriend are doing?"

Anxiously, I finger the cap of the water bottle, a sick feel nauseating me. "Well, yeah. I know this may sound weird – "

"Did Kora put you up to this?"

"What – no!" I'm appalled at what she's implying.

"Because if she did, you tell her to keep her slutty, little skanky hands off him because he's mine!"

"No, wait, you're not listening to me! This has nothing to do –"

"Then what are you doing here?" she interjects venomously, her hand playing with the scarf around her neck. "It's not like we're friends or anything."

I study her questionably.

"Why are you wearing that scarf?" I inquisitively ask, walking around the island and over to her. "It's not cold in here, and it's super warm outside."

Without another word, without thinking, I rapidly unravel the scarf from around her neck.

"What are you doing – no!"

However, it's too late. I have yanked the thick scarf from her neck. My hand rises to my mouth as a startled gasp peals from my lips. The scarf falls quietly to the floor, as soft as a whisper. Removing the cloth reveals what I've already feared. Bruises are all over her neck, the marks looking suspiciously like a pair of hands.

Silence occupies the space between us as the world goes still. A citrus smell arises in the air, like we've been transported to an orange grove. The temperature grows warmer, and my hands tingle with a familiar heat. Taking a peek, I'm not shocked that they're glowing green. Relief washes over me at the color.

An angel is in our presence.

With my gaze traveling to Daria, I'm unnerved that her angered expression still lingers on her face. She's unmoving and ... frozen? Is she *frozen*?

It's proving true. I wave a hand in her face, but her eyes don't blink. She doesn't flinch. That's strange, especially since I can move and she cannot.

The room is silent, except for the fast *thump thump* of my heart. The world is taking a time out. Everything in existence has paused but me. Daria, evidently, is stuck in intermission.

The citrus scent becomes stronger when a little girl appears by Daria's side. Maybe seven or eight, she wears a long white gown and has long blonde hair with bangs. Like Sam, she's simply resplendent with glowing blue eyes, though there's a bit of sadness in her gaze.

Yes, an angel – Daria's Guardian.

"Nick's been hurting her," the little angel says in a high-toned voice.

I look down at the small heavenly host. Her intense blue orbs stare back, her features soft and gentle.

"He tries to control her," continues the angel. "He attempts to change her into something she's not, and when she doesn't comply, he hurts her. Mentally and physically."

"But why?" I croak out, finding that the inside of my

mouth has suddenly gone dry. "Why is he doing this to her?"

The little angel's response isn't quite what I expect.

"Nick wants her to be like Kora."

My blood runs cold with apprehension, and my jaw drops at her admission.

"He *what*?" I'm having trouble grasping her statement.

"He takes out his anger on Daria because Kora rejects him," she clarifies, her forehead creasing as she frowns. "She is so weak, and if she doesn't get away from him she's going to die."

Speechless, with absolutely no words or thoughts, I watch as she vanishes before my eyes. The citrous fragrance melts away, and like someone flipping the breaker to the world, reality wakes back up. Daria wakes up as well, and I'm quick to see she's still in witch mode.

"What the heck is your problem?" she screams, her face three different shades of red.

Wow. She has no idea what occurred. She has no idea that time froze and her angel appeared.

This Seer stuff is proving to be one big headache.

Daria bends over and collects the scarf from the ground, frantically wrapping it back around her traumatized neck. Her eyes are filled with hate, shooting hard-edged daggers my direction.

Shaking my head, trying to dislodge the cobwebs from my distraught brain, I desperately work at controlling the spiraling-out-of-control situation.

"Nick did that – didn't he? Nick hurt you – "

"Shut-up!" she shouts, pushing me in the chest, but I'm undeterred.

"You need to break up with him. He doesn't care for you! If he did he wouldn't do … *that.*"

"I said shut-up!" Shoving past me, she stomps through the dining room, straight to the front door. Opening it and gesturing wildly with her hands, she orders, "Get out of my house!"

Any hope I'd had for helping her disintegrates into a fine dust. "I'm trying to help you," I tell her softly, making my way to the door.

She scowls, glaring at me with rage in her eyes. "Get. Out."

Slumping my shoulders in defeat, I throw her a sour look.

"Fine, I'll go. Just whatever you do, don't go down any

dark alleys with Nick."

Wonderment paints her face, but only for a couple of seconds. It fades into a menacing expression, her lips one big snarl.

"Get out and leave me alone." Forcing me roughly out, she slams the door in my face.

Well, so much for that.

Walking down the driveway to my car, a mixture of emotions cruise through my mind. Dejection, anger, perplexity, detachment – just to name a few.

Why me? Why did I have to subject myself to such horrendous agony? I've known Daria all of my life and I wasn't able to help her. She won't listen to me. She can't *stand* me!

If this is how the life of a Seer goes, then I'm not wanting it.

As soon as I sit in the driver's seat and shut the door, lavender instantly sates the air. Sam appears in the passenger seat, his expression brimming over with vexation. Usually his scent is a calming remedy for my agitated nerves, but today I'm too discombobulated to be comforted.

"What was the point of that?" I question angrily,

aiming an arrow of indignation his direction. "Why did you think I could help her? I told you, she can't stand me!"

"Clarity," he says, "not everyone will like you. Not everyone will want to be around you. But God has given you a special gift to serve others, and Daria, though she doesn't see it, is in distress." He pauses, his blues eyes blazing. "You have a good heart, and deep down you want to help others ... even Daria."

"Well, I did a horrible job at helping." I sigh, leaning my forehead on the steering wheel. "Daria has it in her mind that Kora sent me to spy."

"You helped her more than you know. You also met Mary Beth."

Lifting my head I glance at him. "Daria's angel, right? The one that smells like oranges."

"Yes."

"How do you know I helped?" I marvel.

"I know because at this very moment she's reevaluating her relationship with Nick. She's thinking back to all the hurtful things he's said and done, and she's boiling mad. She's on the phone right now canceling their date for tonight."

"Was it a date in an alley?"

"No ... at the movies."

Scrunching up my face in confusion I ask, "But why did I dream about her and him in an alley?"

"Because..." A shadow passes over his face. "She might have ended up there."

A shiver tears through my system as I digest his grave words. Maybe I *did* help Daria in a way, because if she'd gone on the date and made Nick angry, he might have killed her.

Another shudder rips through my body at the thought of Nick hurting Daria to the point of killing her. Did Nick have the nerve to take a life? Is he that cold of a human being?

"Yes," Sam answers, listening to my thoughts. "Like I told you the night we met – he's got demons all over him."

Wow. Those words make more sense than the night I'd first heard them.

"I don't think I can handle this, Sam," I confess wearily.

He assures me in a whisper, "I know you *can* handle this." He disappears, taking his lavender essence with him.

Turning the key in the ignition, the engine roaring to life, I mutter, "Yeah, thanks for the reassurance."

# Chapter Nineteen

# Clarity

"I am *not* sitting through some gushy love story," Kora blanches, sticking a finger in her mouth and making a gagging noise.

Janey, Kora and I have been standing outside the movie theater debating on what we should see. There's only three selections at the dinky Garlandton Theater: a sappy love story where I'm sure one of the lovers die, a gory horror flick with an ax-wielding fiend, and an animation film starring talking ladybugs.

Kora and Janey want blood and guts, while I opt for sappiness. With all the real horror occurring in my personal life, watching a killer stalk unsuspecting teens vacationing in a cabin doesn't fill my cup of tea.

Unfortunately I'm outnumbered, and to my distinct displeasure I'll be forced to watch ninety minutes of a bloody ax. To top it off, Kora wants to sit on the front row.

A day with the girls had been just what the doctor

ordered. We'd had a great time at Barb's Dress Boutique, each of us finding the perfect dress. During the trying-on process, I'd been shocked that I was actually having a good time. I was happy, despite the talk with Daria.

With Sam's reassurance that I had helped Daria, my spine had straightened back up, undoing the defeat that had stitched into my bones. Just knowing that she's rethinking being with Nick causes my ego to fluctuate, because I'd been the one to shed some light into the situation.

I almost feel proud. For the first time I think maybe, just *maybe*, I'll be able to handle this new world I've been called to.

For now, however, let the Hollywood fright begin!

The three of us take our seats right as the lights dim and the screen comes to life. There's only a handful of Garlandtonites in the theater, cueing me to believe that this movie is going to be a total bomb.

Digging into our dinners of greasy popcorn, candy and jumbo cokes, we watch as the beginning credits roll on the screen. Our crunching and slurping sounds throughout the theater, echoing off the concrete walls.

Fifteen minutes into the movie we realize what a

colossal mistake we've made – well, the mistake Kora and Janey made.

*"Wow,"* declares Kora abrasively. "This movie sucks so bad! And why are all the chicks wearing white t-shirts and no bras? They're in Colorado in the middle of the winter."

"Yeah, they should have called this film *Boob City Massacre,"* adds Janey as she sips her coke.

I laugh. "That's a good one, Janey."

"Thank you," Janey says. "Besides, the boobs in this movie are totally fake."

Kora raises an eyebrow.

"How do you know they're fake?" questions Kora.

"Look at them," proclaims Janey. She points a manicured fingernail at the screen. "Do real boobs float in hot tubs? I mean, geez! The jets aren't even on!"

Kora scoffs. "Oh, please! Just because boobs float in water doesn't mean they're fake."

"Real boobs don't float," insists Janey. "Those things are silicone or saline *blessed."* She shoves a mega-wad of popcorn into her mouth. I notice she's already eaten half of her large popcorn, but I choose not to point it out. I'm not doing too bad on my own tub of fatty popcorn.

Abruptly, Kora twists in her seat so as to look at me.

"Clarity," she says, "do your boobs float?"

"Why you asking me?" I inquire, taken back and appalled by her question.

She shoots me her biggest *duh* expression. "You know why." Her huge green eyes fall to my chest, then back up to my face.

"She's right, Clare," Janey barges in. "Your chest is as big as the hoochie mamas on the screen."

"Clarity's are actually bigger!" Kora giggles insanely.

"They are not," I tell them defensively, my face flushing hot.

"Oh, they *so* are!" alleges Janey, her mouth packed with candy.

"So, do they float or not?" Kora rudely asks, curiously awaiting my reply.

"Answer the question," pushes Janey.

"Yes or – "

"No!" I exclaim, maybe a bit too loud. So loud that someone in the back hollers for me to shut-up. I glance to the back of the theater, shooting an evil eye their direction, whoever they may be.

Turning back to my buds, I whisper, "No, they don't float."

With that argument settled, we switch our attentions back to the movie, which is extremely painful because it sucks so bad. However, after a few minutes, I'm amazed that the movie is grabbing my focus. Not the blood and gore, but the romance between the main characters. The ax-wielding maniac was busy chasing the guy, while the girl was trying to figure out how to save him.

I'm on the edge of my seat, inwardly rooting for the guy to survive so the couple can live happily ever after.

Being so involved with the movie, I almost don't notice the searing pain in the palms of my hands.

Almost.

# Lukus

"There they are, Nick," I whisper in his ear. "The girl that broke you and Daria up, and the one that rejected you."

"What are you going to do about it?" snickers Markus.

When Daria called and broke up with him, I'd been delighted when a violent rage overtook him. After his destructive fit, his wall was left with a hole the size of a basketball in it. It had been a fun show to watch, but what makes it even better is how the situation has shifted. With words of vile devastation being whispered in his ear, we'd successfully gotten his mind off of Daria. A plan has been set in motion, his focus now on the *Ra'ah* and her close friend.

Standing in the back of the movie theater, I observe the Seer with her friends. I know her warning signals are about to go off, and that's just fine.

The hounds and I are ready to battle and end this mission.

# Clarity

The glowing red in my palms catch me off guard. They're pulsating on and off, like a little kid playing with a light switch. I'm thunderstruck to see my personal alarms communicating that demonic beings are close, only because the last few hours had gone by completely normal. The intense burning takes my breath away – then changes become very apparent in the air.

All at once the temperature drops to freezing, my lungs

aching with every breath I suck in and release. Shivers assault my body inside and out, while my heart thumps like a cold rock in my chest. Shock swims through my veins, and dread digs its nasty claws into every inch of my flesh. And just like the night in Baker's parking lot, I have been morphed into a human icicle, except for my flaming hot hands.

A jumble of thoughts swirl within my head.

Why here? Why now? What do I do?

Then my thoughts travel to Sam. He's here, that I'm for sure of. Even if I can't see him, I know he's close. What I don't understand is why he doesn't intervene. I need help and he knows it.

Glancing over at Janey and Kora, I know they're not feeling what I'm feeling, or seeing what I'm seeing, which is crazy since the lights from my hands are bathing their faces with red. No, they're clueless, with their eyes glued to the screen. They both appear enthralled by the revolting movie.

Cautiously, I turn my head, taking a peek behind me. I can feel the demon's eyes drilling crevices in the back of my head. The brightness from the movie projection light plagues my vision. I squint my eyes, hoping to get a better look.

"Show yourselves," I mutter under my breath, careful

not to bring any attention to myself. I know someone, *something* is watching me.

It doesn't take long to find what I'm searching for.

In the back of the theater stands Nick, his gaze fixated in my general direction – and he's not alone. Three others surround him, blending with the darkness.

Lukus, Markus, and Stone.

A brief moment passes before Nick realizes I'm looking right at him. An expression of outrage distorts his features. Quickly he spins around and exits the theater. Lukus says something to the Hellhounds, gesturing with his hands. They obediently twist around and run after Nick, leaving Lukus behind.

I watch, unable to move, as Lukus traps my gaze within his. A hostile jeer forms on his pale face as his malicious voice speaks in my head. His lips never move, but that doesn't stop him from his taunting.

*Seeeer … come and get us.*

Still harboring a vicious jeer, he holds my gaze as he walks backwards out of the theater. Again, his voice rings between my ears.

*Come out and play, little Ra'ah.*

The temperature becomes normal when he disappears, though I'm still chilled to the bone. My hands are glowing a steady red, no longer blinking on and off. They want me to follow them, but at what cost? Deep down I know that it's a trap.

The sensible part of my brain is screaming for me to stay put, but the curious part is demanding that I run after them. I don't want to listen to the curious part, but it cannot be ignored.

Rising to my feet, I begin ascending the aisle, my focus totally set on finding Nick and the demons. Kora and Janey take notice of my sudden leaving, broadcasting confused expressions.

"Clare?" Kora calls out carefully. "Where you going?"

Without a glance back, I mumble, "I gotta check on something." That's when my limbs wake up, adrenaline taking control in a huge way. I start sprinting up the aisle, hearing Kora calling after me, but I don't look back. I'm sure they're thinking I've gone nuts, but I don't care. All I care about is catching up with the monsters.

So much for a normal, fun girl's day.

# Sam

Seated on the back row in the dark movie theater, I silently observe Clarity as she sprints up the aisle and out the doors. Lukus and his Hellhounds have baited her using their possessed pawn, Nick. At the moment they are setting a trap with her name on it.

Desperately I want to run after her, warn her, stop her from running headfirst into their diabolical hands. I want to appear directly in front of her and shout *No! Danger!*, but I cannot. Not with the messenger angel, Gabriel, lounging in the seat next to me.

"You know," he says, his glowing eyes staring at the screen, "I just don't get why humans enjoy watching such gory, brutal violence. Do they not realize all the real bloodshed that's happening in the world? All the unrelenting savagery that happens every second of every day? If they did, maybe they'd realize that watching people get chopped to bits and beaten to pulps is not entertainment."

"Gabriel." I glare at him. "Why are you keeping me from following Clarity? You know what the evil ones are planning."

"Yes, yes, I do." He nods his head. "The thing is, Sam, you've got a lot to learn about being a Seer's Guardian. You can't save her every single time the enemy chases her. She's got to learn to defend herself if she's ever going to help humanity."

"I *know* all this," I respond, becoming frustrated. "And I'm going to follow the rules, but – "

"Ah," Gabriel interjects. "You will follow the rules, but..." He laughs. "Saying *but* negates the former, my friend."

"She needs more guidance," I tell him. "Please, I've got to do my job. I've got to follow my Charge. And I will follow the rules. Please," I plead, "let me go after her."

He studies me a moment, then says, "You are right, Sam. Go after her."

"Thank you." I stand to my feet, but he halts my exit.

"Sam?"

"Yes?"

"Wait on The Father's word. Don't jump ahead of Him."

I nod. "Got it."

# Clarity

A cold breeze surrounds me as I bust through the exit doors of Garlandton Theater. For a Saturday night the town square is strangely quiet. *Too* quiet.

Along with the eerie silence, I'm stunned there's not one single soul walking around. Even Granny Mae's Creamery isn't busy, and with it being a teenage hotspot on the weekends it's a shock to see that the little ice cream parlor isn't packed.

Where is everybody? I mean, I feel like I've walked out of the theater and stepped into an isolated town, population Clarity Miller.

Though I know better than to think I'm all alone. I know everything around me isn't what it seems. What I'm experiencing is part of the supernatural world, full of angels, demons ... and really hot hands!

A familiar cry catches my attention. Listening, I follow it to the entrance of an alley. A heavy sense of déjà vu falls over me, so thick I think I'm about to faint. Taking in a breath, releasing it slowly, I'm able to squelch down the dizziness.

The orange glow of a light post, the unpleasant smell,

one overflowing dumpster, trash strewn on the ground – it's my dream all over again!

I guess Daria met with Nick anyway...

A rumble of thunder growls in the distance, alarming the town that another storm is headed our way. Nervousness gnaws ravenously at my stomach as a bitter taste splashes over my tongue. The sulfurous stench stings my eyes and throat. The déjà vu is growing stronger...

"Sam, what do I do?" I whisper. When I talk, little puffs of smoke float from my mouth.

"Help me..." a female voice weakly pleads. *Daria's* voice.

With those two words out in the open, adrenaline overtakes every synapse I possess, pumping through my veins and warming my blood. My feet wake up and start running, pushing me toward the lone dumpster. Rats scatter in all directions as I trek through the rubbish, but I pay them no mind. Since I'm being forced to relive my dream, I know exactly what to do.

Two things: Get Daria and *run!*

"Daria!" I breathlessly shout as I reach the side of the dumpster. "It's me, Clarity. Let's get out – "

Words become hitched in my throat, my eyes having trouble comprehending what they're seeing … or what they're *not* seeing.

Daria isn't here. The alley is empty.

Like an electric shock, puzzlement zings through my veins, leaving me dazed and muddled. I swing around, deciding Nick and the demons are gone, and … stop cold. Frozen in my tracks, my eyes finally catch hold of something, but it's not what I had in mind.

My heart goes into hysterics as I come to the realization that my worst nightmares have me cornered.

# Chapter Twenty

# Clarity

"Well, we meet once again, *Seer*." Lukus hisses through his teeth. A soft breeze pushes his black hair off his shoulder. Markus and Stone stand slightly behind him, with an orange glow reflecting out of their black orbs, thanks to the single light post.

A few heartbeats of silence tick by, allowing me time to calm the stampede galloping in my chest. It also gives me a chance to check out their appearances. When I'd first met them, their skin had been smooth and flawless. However now their skin is grayish, like flesh in the early stages of decomposition. Especially on Markus – strips of skin hang loosely on one side of his face.

"You tricked me," I accuse, glaring at them.

Lukus laughs, quickly closing the gap between us. A wave of sulfur and death rushes over me, my stomach lurching violently.

With his face inches from mine, Lukus growls,

"Anything goes in this war."

Before he can take hold of me, I shuffle back as far as I can go. Hitting the cold brick wall, the breath exiting my lungs, I actualize that there is no escape.

"You are right." Lukus smirks. "There is no escape, and your soul is still up for grabs."

"Tasty *Ra'ah*," sings Markus. A black tongue flicks out of his mouth, licking his cracked, dry lips.

"Are you ready to play, Seer?" asks Lukus.

Coldness has gripped my heart, while fear slashes furiously at my nerves. I try to rev-up my brain in a desperate attempt to stall them until a plan of escape appears. With three hungry-for-souls demons staring me down, I find it hard to concentrate on anything else but the danger at hand.

"Where's Nick?" I question, the whole time weighing my options.

"Nick?" Lukus tilts his head, then grins. "Oh yes, the human pawn." He pauses, his black orbs tapering to small slits. "He ran home crying like a baby, trying to figure out why his new girl broke up with him, and let me tell you, we had some big plans for Daria Phipps."

Stone barks out a laugh, sounding like the hound he

truly was under his black skin. "Yeah, that little wench was going to get what she deserved."

"But then a Seer came along and our plan went up in smoke." Lukus and his unblinking eyes blast me with coldness, his expression unreadable. A sizable chunk of trepidation forms in my throat, feeling like a boulder as I swallow it down.

"Lukus, what are we going to do with her?" questions Markus.

"What we've been sent to do." Lukus's eyes change from black to red, his voice becoming inhumanly deep. "Destroy her soul."

Panic strikes as his words sink in, the change in his eyes confirming the monster that hides underneath his human skins.

"Not this one."

Sam appears beside me, minus his wings. Leaning against the brick wall wearing his usual black t-shirt and jeans, he fixes his gaze on the angels of darkness.

Lukus is surprised to see Sam, his red eyes altering back to black.

"What makes you say that?" Lukus questions Sam. His

voice is not as deep as before.

"Because that's what my Father told me," replies Sam.

Lukus glances at Stone, at Markus, and then back to me. I cringe when they explode into evil cackles.

Snatching Sam's arm, I urgently cry, "We've got to get out of here!"

"Clarity," he speaks coolly, his sight thoroughly focused on Lukus and his hounds.

"Sam, *please*!" I plead caustically, "We've got to – "

"Touch his arm."

"What?!" I exclaim in total disbelief.

His shining eyes drift my direction. "Trust me. Touch his arm."

Shaking like a dried-out leaf, I do what he says – I don't want to, but I do it anyway. Reaching out, my hands burning like fireballs, I grab hold of Lukus's arm, a couple of inches above the wrist. I squeeze with all my might.

Lukus and his bitter laughter cuts off instantly. Stupor crawls across his pale gray face.

Then something new happens.

An electrified power deep within me begins to emerge. Every nerve in my body tingles to life as all my muscles tense with an unknown anticipation. I watch the demon's face as the power exits my body, through my hand, and enters his. The shocked expression on his face disintegrates into tortured pain.

What I'm feeling is hard to describe. It starts as a warm, heavy feeling, and as it's released, my body is so light I fear I may fly away like a wayward, helium-filled balloon. It's freeing and exhilarating, but the wail of agony spurting from the mouth of the demon I'm touching informs me he's feeling the exact opposite.

Lukus glances down at his arm, trying to wiggle it free from my grasp. His efforts are futile, for at the moment I'm stronger than he is.

Markus and Stone only watch, dazed and open-mouthed. The Hellhounds take a few slow steps back before disappearing into fast blurry blobs of gray.

I hold on to Lukus for about ten seconds, then let go because his howls of torment are near to bursting my eardrums. An angry mark surfaces on his arm. I gasp, shocked to see a Seer mark seared into his pale flesh.

The moment I free his arm is the moment he becomes quiet. The grungy alley is silent as he turns his attention to his newly scarred arm. Raising his black lifeless eyes, his face contorts into a mess of agony and hate. Growling sounds deep inside of him, his body trembling. Gradually the growls grow louder, even louder than his screams had been.

Strong winds come out of nowhere, swirling dirt and trash in the air. An unforeseen tornado has infiltrated the alley, Sam and I its targets. The howling wind is close to deafening, so I lift my hands to cover my ears.

Leaning into Sam, he wraps me in his arms, shielding my body with his. I pinch my eyes shut, waiting out the supernatural storm.

A few strained seconds pass, then all is quiet. The storm is gone, and so is Lukus. Stray pieces of trash dance in the air, eventually littering the ground. The stench of demons have left, though the dumpster scent still wavers, along with Sam's lavender essence.

With my heart a wild thud inside my body, I glare at Sam and ask, "What just happened? And please, don't skirt around the question. I want answers – real ones."

Sam squares his shoulders with mine. "You used your abilities against a demon."

"Is he *dead*?" I wonder.

"No," he readily replies, his eyes narrowed. "Just in a lot of pain. The dose of Heaven's Light you released was small, though as your powers grow, it will become stronger and more lethal."

Embarrassment floods my system. "They tricked me. Tricked me and used my dream against me. How did they know – "

Sam cuts off my words. "The enemy knows your every weakness, your every thought. I haven't told you this, but..." He pauses before he adds, "They've been messing with your dreams. The nightmares are because of them."

"But I thought my dreams came from God," I point out.

He nods his head and replies, "Yes, God sends you dreams and visions, though the enemy can sometimes twist what God sends you. When you're sleeping, you are vulnerable, at your weakest. That's why they go after humans when they sleep."

Gazing up at his angelic face with tears in my eyes I say, "What good am I if I can't tell which dreams are from God, and which ones … aren't?"

"The closer your walk with God, the easier to see through the enemies lies." He pauses, taking one of my hands in his. "Satan is the enemy, and he is the father of all lies. He fights dirty, efficiently, and aggressively. One day soon you will see clearly. Though you have to make a change – a *heart* change."

"What do you mean by that?" I inquire.

"You have to let Jesus into your heart again," he answers softly.

Staring at him, I think back to the day I had become saved, then to the day I'd been baptized. My parents had been so happy and proud of me. Thinking back I can almost feel the joy I'd experienced the day Jesus came into my heart.

Almost.

Like a dark cloud hovering above my head, my thoughts shift to the night my parents were taken away from me. Anger begins to boil in my blood. Why did God have to take them away? What was the point?

Shaking my head, I snatch my hand from his grip and back away.

"I don't want this," I confess, my tone emotionless.

"Clarity," he says.

"I don't want this life!" I exclaim. "Sam, I want to go back to the way it was before. Parties, drinking – don't you see? I want to go back to being clueless! I'm not cut out for this."

"You *are* cut out for this." He reaches for me, but I recoil from his touch.

"No, I'm *not*."

"Clarity – "

"Stay away from me," I snap. A sob builds in my chest. "I ... I don't want to see you again." Was I really saying this? Did I mean it?

Sam looks as if I've smacked him across the face. Dropping his hands to his sides, he closes his eyes, shakes his head, and disappears.

# Sam

Clarity is staring right at me, though she doesn't see me. She told me to stay away, but that's something I cannot do.

"I'm sorry Sam," she whispers. A tear slides down her cheek. I want to wipe it away, but fight the urge to do so.

Footsteps sound against the pavement and stop. Behind Clarity, at the mouth of the alley, stands Janey and Kora.

They're stunned, both wearing dumbfounded expressions.

"Clarity," Kora speaks, her tone cautious, "what are you doing?"

Clarity ricks around, shocked by their arrival. Her thoughts are screaming many different phrases in her brain.

*Oh, great, what do I say?*

*How does this look?*

*They must think I'm crazy.*

*How in the world can I explain this?*

"I, uh..." She stumbles over her words. "I needed some air. The horrible movie made me kind of sick."

Kora's eyes widen. "You needed air, so you ran out of the movies to hang out in a dark alley by yourself?"

"Which stinks, by the way," Janey quips, waving a hand under her nose.

Clarity doesn't know what to say. She only shrugs her shoulders and smiles.

"Okay, well," Kora sighs. "Come on, weirdo. Let's go to Granny Mae's and get a cone."

"Yes," Janey agrees, starting to walk away. "I'm freaking *starving!*"

Kora snorts. "What – are you serious? You must have a

tapeworm or something."

They walk away, chitter-chattering about how much food they can put away. Clarity follows after them. At the mouth of the alley, she halts her steps, giving a sideways glance my direction. A few seconds go by before she slumps her shoulders and walks away.

A sudden bolt of lightning hits, following up with a round of thunder. The heavens unleash hard, pounding rain onto the earth, but I don't feel it. Instead I feel a sadness penetrating Clarity's heart, which weighs me down in the process. She's confused and doesn't know what to think. She wants me in her life, but to have me in her life would mean the spiritual realm would always be there, giving her no choice but to fulfill her Seer heritage. And to get to that place, she'd have to do the one thing she swore she'd never do again...

Trust God.

As for me, I have to step back. I won't be able to reach out to her. All I can do is be by her side, but she won't sense me there. She won't even smell lavender. It will seem as if I obeyed her words by staying away.

"You are correct in your thinking, my friend."

"Am I, Gabriel?" My gaze slides to the messenger angel, who has appeared next to me.

"Yes," he iterates, the rain matting down his blonde hair. "Clarity has to learn that words have meaning, and that she must choose them wisely."

"But her soul – "

"Sam," he interjects, "she is not ignorant to the word of God. Freewill has come into play. She has a decision to make. Let's pray she makes the right one."

I'm irritated by what he's saying, only because every word is true. Spending the last couple of months with Clarity, I've been able to minister to her. She does know what salvation is, and she also knows what has to occur for it to be achieved.

As a Guardian I've done my job, and will continue to do it. The ball is in her court now. A decision will have to be made, one that could lead to life...

Or to death.

# Lukus

A bolt of lightning strikes a nearby tree. Thunder

shakes the ground. Rain falls from the sky, turning the stream I'm sitting by into a raging river.

I'm leaned back on a tree next to the brought-to-life river, still dazed by what happened between the Seer and me. What happened shouldn't have happened. It wasn't in the plan. The plan had been to trick the Seer by using the human pawn Nick, trap her in the alley, and destroy her.

It had all gone to plan, except for the last part – the *important* part.

The rain pours down onto my damaged arm, the Seer mark on my human skin taunting me, throbbing with acute pain. With my black claw, I slit open the skin and start peeling it off, my true self peeking through. I bellow, the pain near unbearable. Never in my existence have I suffered such agony – no pain in Hell touches what I'm feeling.

My screaming has disturbed a flock of crows. They scatter among the treetops above the forest, my wails sending them into flight.

"Lukus," Markus says. "Is it … is..."

The Hellhounds hover above me, with fear rushing in their blood. Their eyes are wide, wondering the same thing I was...

Did the Seer mark taint my true skin?

Using one swift movement, I rip the rest of the human flesh, exposing my red skin below my elbows to the tips of my fingers. The freshly peeled skin hangs loosely from my claws – I don't shake them off. I center my focus on my arm.

"NO!" I cry out, not wanting to believe what's embedded in my arm, possibly permanent.

A set of wings, a cross, and a crown. Outlined in black on my red skin.

"The *Ra'ah* has … *marked* you!" exclaims Stone.

"A demon marked by one of God's foot soldiers is a disgrace to lord Satan," Markus whispers, shuffling back a couple of feet.

Red. All I see is red. Flying from my seated position, with my talons growing from my natural hand, I slash at the tree. Immediately it falls to the ground.

Breathing hard, I look to the Hellhounds, awaiting their response. They stay silent, their eyes unblinking, their bodies trembling. They're smart for keeping their mouths shut, because the rage I'm feeling is like nothing I've ever felt before. Rain falls onto my shoulders, with steam rising from my body.

Able to stanch my anger, I set my sight on the town and growl, "The *Ra'ah* must pay. If it's the last thing I do, I'll make sure she dies."

# Chapter Twenty-One

# Clarity

Excited voices sound throughout the halls of Garlandton High the whole week before the Thanksgiving dance, and frankly I'm sick of hearing about it. Girls are obsessing over hair appointments and manicures, while guys are swapping secrets on how to impress their dates. Posters adorn the walls, announcing the date and time of the dance.

*A Night to Remember* – such a generic theme.

Discussions on where to have an after party is the topic of the hour on this rainy Friday. Wherever it will commence, alcohol and pot would be the prime party favors, along with some grudge band from a couple of counties over.

Yes, a magical, booze-filled evening where every teen's dream will hopefully come true. All I want is a normal night with my friends, which shouldn't be too hard to accomplish. It has been a week since I've seen a demon – or an angel.

Sam.

"Don't think about him," I grumble to myself, slamming my locker shut.

He's gone. Sam is gone. I'm getting exactly what I want, but...

I'm not happy.

Six days pass with no sign that a supernatural world exists, and no nightmares plague my sleep. My life has shifted back to the way it was before I met Sam, back to a time when I was a clueless, carefree teenager who knew nothing about the invisible world. Problem is...

I'm not clueless.

The truth is I am not ignorant to the invisible world around me. The truth is I know there are hideous demons lurking in the darkness, waiting to devour the souls of the lost. I know about the glorious angels that watch over mankind who battle the forces of evil nonstop.

Truth is, I know too much. I will never free my mind of images from the supernatural, or flush the knowledge of spiritual warfare from my brain. I've seen it firsthand. There's no going back – the marks on the palms of my hands are proof that my life will never be the same.

Walking to my car, I feel more weighed down than

ever. The hole in my heart aches with a loneliness so profound that only a celestial being can cure.

\*\*\*

Stocking shelves on a Friday evening, all by my lonesome – yep, that's how this chick rolls.

The dull music that Mr. Baker uses to torture his customers and employees has shut down for the night. Only the sounds of the freezers switching on, the florescent lights humming, and cans hitting the metal shelving echo through the empty store. Usually I can't stand stocking shelves, but tonight I embrace it. This type of manual labor helps to keep my mind off things. It's a job where I don't have to talk, and I don't have to think.

For the first time ever I'm happy that Casey called in sick, and that Janey wasn't answering her phone calls. I'm glad there are no customers to annoy me. I'm glad that Mr. Baker is unsociable and locked behind the closed door of his office.

"Hey, princess."

Unloading a startled gasp, I drop a can of green beans. Turning around, a large ball of anxiety rolls down into my belly. Nick stands at the end of the aisle with his hands in his pockets. He peers at me with dark, vacant eyes.

I am shocked to see him, mostly because he hadn't been to school the entire week. The last time I'd seen him was at the movie theater. Thinking on that certain night causes shivers to flow down my spine, though I readily squash down those disquieting emotions.

"Nick, where did you come from?" I hadn't heard him come in, which surprises me. Another thing that has me surprised is my hands – they're not tingling with the usual brazen hotness that comes with iniquity being in my presence.

I guess that means there's no demons close by.

"So, the Thanksgiving dance is tomorrow night. I guess that means Kora will be Kevin's date."

"Well, yes," I nod my head slowly. "They've been a couple for awhile now. You know that."

"Yeah, I know." His tone is flat and soft. He's wearing all black, which strikes me as odd. Most all of his outfits were made by popular designers. Tonight he's wearing something that looks like it came from the local Goodwill.

"I'm really busy, Nick," I say, my eyes raking over Mr. Baker's closed door. "What do you want?"

Something about the way he's glaring causes my heart

to thump madly in my chest, riling up a fear from deep inside my being. His face is the palest I've ever seen, and his eyes are almost black, with dark bags circling under them.

When he doesn't answer, I ask, "Nick, have you been drinking?"

He grins. "Nah, princess. I'm feeling just fine."

"Okay, then what do you want?" I fight to control the waver in my voice.

"I wanted to tell you something." The strange smile is still present on his face.

"What?" I wonder, becoming frustrated.

When he answers, his smile melts into a frown. "Tomorrow night … is going to be a night to remember."

"Yes, Nick," I scoff, quirking an eyebrow. "That's the theme of the dance – A night to remember. Thanks for the reminder." Why is he quoting a stupid dance slogan?

A muscle twitches in his jaw before he announces, "See ya later, Clarity." Spinning on his heels, he shuffles out of the store.

I stare after him, not understanding the reason behind his visiting me at the store. Obviously he's lost his ever-loving mind.

Getting on my hands and knees, I retrieve the can I'd dropped. It had rolled underneath a shelf when I'd released it. I sigh, shrugging my shoulders, and pick up the pace, not thinking another second about Nick or anything else.

Thinking is overrated, anyway.

# Sam

Clarity goes about her business, nonchalantly humming a tune. She's not giving Nick a second thought, which has me on edge. It's like she's forgotten what a threat he is, that Nick Reece isn't constantly surrounded by demons. It's as if she's forgotten all she's seen and heard, like she doesn't see the signs so prominent in the palms of her hands that mark her as different. It's like...

It's like she's forgotten about me.

"Suck it up, Sam," Gabriel orders. "The human mind is a fickle beast."

I sigh, shooting the messenger a sideways glance. Gabriel has been hanging around, making sure that I fulfill my promise of stepping away from my Charge. Though I have the utmost respect for him, I can't stop the annoyance attempting

276

to creep into my system.

"Why can't I know?" I ask him, clenching my teeth.

"Know what?" he shoots back.

I start pacing the aisle, passing by Clarity – she has no idea I'm there.

"Something is about to happen, I can feel it." I halt my keyed-up steps. "There's a reason Nick came into the store tonight, talking about the dance. What's the reason?"

Gabriel's expression changes from relaxed to grievous. "You know I can't say." He walks over, stopping next to Clarity, studying her closely. "I can tell you that your Charge will be one of the most powerful Seers in the world. If, and only if, her heart changes."

Clenching my fists at my sides, I close my eyes and ask, "Is there anything I can do for Clarity? Is there any way I can talk to her?"

Gabriel glances my way and tells me gravely, "You can't show yourself now – she's got a decision to make. Her and her alone."

"Then what can I do?"

"The only thing you can do – what you've been doing since the day she was born." Pausing, his blue eyes starting to glow, he adds, "Pray."

# Clarity

*Rain hits my face as I run through the woods. Pumping my legs as hard as they'll go, I dodge tree limb after tree limb, my heart close to exploding because of its fast beat. The ground is mushy under my bare feet as the sky continues to unleash heavy amounts of water onto the earth.*

*Trepidation scores through my veins, while a deep sadness begins devouring my soul. Tears dribble down my face, and I release a desperate cry that echoes throughout the dense forest.*

*Someone is chasing me, and whoever it is has done something terrible. Don't know how I know – I just do. There's a wrongness in the air that's undeniable.*

*Pain.*

*Sadness.*

*Confusion.*

*Guilt.*

*Whoever is after me has caused inexorable destruction, extreme misery and chaos, that my life, and the lives of others, has become completely unraveled. Can these lives be fixed? Or will they* be broken forever?

Suddenly a clearing appears in front of me, halting my steps immediately. A drop-off about thirty feet down greets me. The river below is flowing fiercely, all thanks to the storm succeeding in deepening its depths.

Like a punch in the gut, I realize something...

There's no escape.

Sensing someone behind me, I slowly turn around, ready to face the one pursuing me. I can't see who it is, for the darkness has them completely swallowed. The figure is male, but that's all I can tell, since shadows conceal his facial exhibits.

When I notice something shiny in his hand, a heavy dose of déjà vu blankets around my body. That's the moment my palms catch on fire, so intense I bite my bottom lip to keep from screaming out from the unwarranted hurt.

Lightning strikes a nearby tree, and the force is so great the ground shakes. The rain pours even harder now, stinging my eyes. I can barely see in front of me.

"What have you done?!" I yell.

The shiny object he holds trembles in his hand. Something horrible has happened, like someone's life force has been dimmed forever – I can feel the soul leaving the earth.

*The man runs at me, and then I'm falling off the ledge, diving headfirst to the rocky creek below...*

I wake up from the nightmare, hollering at the top of my lungs. The window is wide open, allowing the rainwater from the raging storm outside to soak the walls and hardwood floor. My ears pop like I'm driving around a mountain, my equilibrium off and unbalanced. Sweat has my pajamas glued to my skin. A burn emanates from my hands. I don't bother looking at them – I already know they're glowing.

"Clarity, what's wrong?!" A.C. suddenly busts into the room. She's wearing flannel pajamas, the countenance on her face that of shock and concern.

Flipping on the light switch, she rushes over and embraces my shivering body. Rocking me back and forth like I'm a terrified child, she tries consoling me, assuring me that everything is okay. Unable to contain my emotions, I cry, hugging her tightly with all my might.

A few minutes pass before I get myself under control. Lying back on my fluffy pillows, I stare at the ceiling while A.C. pushes wet strands of hair off my face. She grabs my blankets from the floor and covers me, then swiftly walks over to the window and closes it. I still don't know how it became opened.

A.C. stands in front of the window, with one hand resting on her hip. Her body trembles as she quietly stares out at the stormy weather. Lightning flashes, the thunder that follows causing the house to shake.

"A.C.?"

She flinches, my voice apparently interrupting her deep thoughts. Walking over to the bed, she sits on its edge. Worry flickers in her hazel eyes as she runs a hand through her disheveled brown hair.

"Clarity, is … everything alright?" she questions. Her eyes are bloodshot from working too much and lack of sleep.

I nod. "Yeah, I just had a bad dream. That's all."

She opens her mouth as if to say something, but quickly shuts it. Leaning over, she kisses my forehead and smiles.

"You know I love you, and you can talk to me about anything."

"I know," I grin, adding, "I love you, too."

Searching my face she inquires, "Is there something I should know?"

I shrug my shoulders. "It was just a dream, A.C. – no biggie." Closing my eyes, I roll over to my side, hoping she takes the hint that I'm done talking.

She sighs and stands up. "Well, I'll be in my room if you need me," she says reassuringly. Turning off the light, she leaves, closing the door behind her.

Curling up into a fetal position, I bury my face in my pillow, attempting to block out the world. It's kind of hard to do, thanks to the booming storm. My hands slowly stop their incessant burning, giving way to relief. A few moments tip-toe by when I feel a presence in the room, and smell a familiar perfume in the air.

Lavender.

*Sam.*

"I know you're here," I whisper against my pillow, not bothering to lift my head.

Expecting to hear his voice, I instead receive a long silence. In a subtle way he's telling me that my wishes are being honored – the wish for him to leave me alone.

Rolling onto my back, I once again stare up at the white popcorn ceiling. Hot tears sting my eyes as a sob threatens to explode from my throat.

"I know you're here," I repeat, swallowing down the sob, "and I know you're my Guardian, but ... I'll never live up to what He wants me to become. I don't want to be a Seer – I want to be normal. You might as well give up on me."

When Sam speaks, his words slice deep inside my heart.

"I love you too much to give up. The Father does, too."

Tears cascade down my cheeks as I pinch my eyes shut.

Doesn't Sam get it? Doesn't God get it? Do they not understand that I want to be left alone to live my life – my own *ordinary* life?

Did I ask to be different? Absolutely *not*. And since I have freewill, I have a say on whether or not I want to follow that path.

"I don't want that life," I say, my jaw ticking. "I just … don't."

Pulling the blankets over my head, I try hiding from reality; I try hiding from everything. The storm eventually stills, and the familiar presence disappears along with it. The usually calming lavender is the last to go, fading slowly from the air until it's completely gone.

I am alone.

# Chapter Twenty-Two

# Lukus

Nick paces back and forth in his room, drunk on alcohol and fevered rage. This whole week the hounds and I have been busy planting seeds of destruction into his tortured existence, poisoning his thought process. He thinks his thoughts are his own, but he is sorely misguided.

"Tonight's the night, Nick," I strongly declare. Those words halt his excessive pacing. He turns his gaze my direction, as if he can see me.

"I don't know if..." His words trail off as he starts pacing again. He pulls at his hair, clearly frustrated.

I laugh, loving this display of rabid chaos. He feels he's losing it, becoming completely unhinged – that he has nothing to live for.

We've got him exactly where we want him.

Getting right in his ear, I ask, "Don't you want the ones who rejected you to pay? Don't you want revenge and power?

You can't let them get away with it, Nick. You are better than them. They need to know where they stand – they need to be put in their places. Only you have the power to put them where they belong..." I pause, then whisper, "In the ground."

Once again he stops pacing. He stares at the pentagram crudely painted on his wall, saying nothing. His thoughts swirl around like a tornado in his head, his brain downloading my crucial, extremely detrimental words.

"Yes, that's where they belong," he says, his eyes still studying the pentagram. Leaning over, he opens his desk drawer and pulls out one of his most prized possessions – a pistol.

"Yes!" I shout with exhilarating emotion. "You know what you must do."

"Yes, I do," he replies, robotic in his tone.

It won't be long now. The town of Garlandton will never be the same after this night.

The Seer will fall.

# Clarity

"A.C., hurry up!" I shriek as I catch sight of my digital

clock. At any moment Brenton will be walking through the door to escort me to the dance. However A.C. is still putting the "final touches" on my hair.

"Take a pill, Clare!" she bristles back. "Patience is a virtue – you should practice it."

"Whatever." I roll my eyes, tapping my high-heeled foot impatiently on the floor. A.C. has been working on my hair for an hour, and I'm anxious to see what she's come up with. The suspense is killing me, especially since she has my chair turned away from the mirror.

"Can I at least see what I look like before Brenton gets here?" I'm becoming more and more antsy with each second that passes.

A few seconds later, A.C. steps back and announces, "Done!"

I retort with, "Finally!"

Twisting around in the chair, a full minute of silence goes by before I realize the person in the mirror is me. There's only one word to describe how I feel, and that word is *astonished*.

Usually my brown hair is a wavy mess, but tonight it's half-up/half-down with loose curls flowing down my back.

Whatever eye shadow A.C. used is smoky in shade, my eyes sparkling with life. A glossy pink covers my lips, causing them to appear shiny and plump.

All the work she's done on my hair and face compliments the dark green color of my floor-length gown. She's transformed me into an entirely different person.

"Is it too much?" A.C. wonders, her teeth scraping over her bottom lip.

"No, I love it." I smile, continuing to soak in my appearance.

She smiles back, then suddenly exclaims, "Oh! One more thing." Picking up the sunflower necklace she adds, "*This* is the final touch."

Clasping the dainty gold chain around my neck, she studies me with a bit of rarity.

"What is it?" I inquire.

"Nothing," she replies. "It's just that you look a lot like your Mama."

I grin. "What about Daddy?"

She scrunches her face. "Not much in looks, but more in the attitude department."

I laugh, though it sounds sad. "I miss them."

She sighs. "Me too, hon."

Taking a deep breath, shaking off the depression trying to sneak in, I say, "Thank you, A.C., for fixing my hair, make-up – thanks for everything."

"My pleasure, kiddo." Leaning over, she gives me a hug.

The doorbell rings, breaking us apart.

"He's here!" I squeal, immediately hating that I sound like a boy-crazed freak.

"Relax," A.C. soothes. "I'll answer the door and send him up." Throwing a wink my direction, she scoots out of the room and closes the door.

While A.C. bounces down the stairs, I again catch sight of myself in the mirror. Emotions dance and swirl around me, the mixture causing a dizzying affect. I feel anxious, excitement, happiness and dread, all at the same time.

Is Brenton feeling the same way? What will he think of my girly transformation? Glancing down at my palms, I allow my thoughts to drift from Brenton to Sam.

Is Sam here right now, experiencing my emotions? I can't help thinking about what he would think or say if he was here with me.

Then my thoughts take a surprisingly wide turn: What would Mama and Daddy think? Would they be proud of me? Or disappointed?

A light knock jolts me from my thoughts. Standing up, careful not to step on the hem of my dress, I swing the door open. Brenton and his dimpled grin greets me.

"Wow," he whistles, "you look absolutely – *wow!*"

An involuntary giggle pushes from my lips. "And you look as charming as ever."

He really looks handsome, wearing black dress pants, a black button-up shirt, and dark green silk tie, the exact color of my dress. He holds a clear plastic box in his hand. A wrist corsage rests inside, adorned with a mixture of wild flowers with three small sunflowers.

"My mom made this," he announces, retrieving it from the box. Taking my left hand, he slides the homemade corsage on my wrist. "Is this, um, *right?*"

"No clue." I shrug my shoulders. "I love it, though."

A blush slowly crawls across his face, his dimples deepening in his cheeks.

We walk down the staircase together. Being chivalrous, he holds my elbow so I won't slip – these high-heels are pretty, but horrible to walk in. A.C. is waiting at the bottom of the stairs, ready for work wearing her hospital scrubs. A satisfied grin is plastered on her face.

"Y'all look great!" she gushes. Pulling out a digital camera, she exclaims, "Picture time!"

A few minutes of picture taking goes by before we're finally able to walk out the door. His truck is parked in the driveway, ready to take us to our first dance. Expecting Brenton to open the passenger side door, he instead turns around to face me. He leans back on the truck and crosses his arms at his chest, grinning broadly. Surprisal takes over as he begins to take his tie off.

"What are you doing?" I ask skeptically, studying the tie in his hand.

"I'm going to blindfold you."

"Um, *why*?"

Smirking he replies, "It's a surprise."

I respond with, "Surprises can be overrated."

"You'll love this surprise," he assures as he covers my eyes with the tie.

Since I can't see, he helps me into his truck and secures the seat belt around my waist. On the way to … wherever we're going, he holds my hand, squeezing it gently. Soft music plays on the radio, though I can hardly hear the music thanks to my heart beating in my ears.

I hate not being able to know where we're going, and really, I have no idea what he has planned, but what am I to do? Brenton is being a hopeless romantic, and I'm not going to complain about it. Most girls would kill to be in my position, to have a guy plan a romantic surprise on a special night.

Every synapse in my body is electrified with nervous anticipation and crazed excitement. My heart falls to my stomach as the truck comes to a halt.

"We're here," Brenton says.

"Great, now I can take off this thing..." I reach up to untie the blindfold, but he grabs my hand.

"No, not yet," he says mysteriously.

I sigh, listening as he gets out of the truck and slams the door. A couple of seconds later the passenger side door opens. Unlatching the seat belt, I gasp in surprise when he lifts me into his arms.

Holding onto him I query, "What are you up to?"

"Almost there," he whispers. His footsteps make crunching sounds, as if he's walking on dead leaves. A gust of wind hits us, causing a tremble to encompass my body. A black stole is wrapped around my shoulders, but it's extremely thin. It doesn't do much to keep the cold fall air from reaching my skin.

All of a sudden he halts his steps. Gently, he places my feet on the ground, keeping a hand on the small of my back to balance me. As the tie falls from my face, my hand raises to my mouth to cover a shocked gasp.

We're standing in front of a small shack, only it's more than that – it's our old hideout from when we were kids, located way behind his house. Though there's been some modifications done to the wooden retreat since the last time I'd seen it.

A few heartbeats later Brenton asks, "What do you think?"

"It's our ... our old hideout." I gaze up at him in complete amazement. "I'm simply speechless."

"Come on," he smiles, taking my hand, leading me up the steps to the wooden door. He opens it, gently nudging me over the threshold.

What I see next has me entirely floored.

Candles are placed everywhere, burning bright and

smelling sweet. A small round table with two chairs sit in the middle of the room, with a covered silver platter placed on top. A couch sits in a corner next to the only window in the hideout.

The hideout is nothing more than a little shack, but if there was plumbing and electricity, it could pass for a small apartment.

"Why did you do all this?" I wonder, soaking in every little detail. "We haven't been here in years."

He stands behind me and wraps his arms around my waist, resting his chin on my shoulder. "Just thought we could use it as a hideout again. Like, whenever we want to be alone, or escape from the world." He turns me around in his arms, my dress swishing around my ankles.

He continues, "I thought this would be the perfect place to tell you that I've decided to go to New York with you."

I lean back to study his face, my breath hitching a bit at this awesome news. "Really? That's great!"

"Yes, it is," he agrees, grinning. "Told my folks last night."

"What did they say?"

"They're all for it."

Taking his face in my hands, I inform, "Brenton, you just made me the happiest girl in the world."

Pressing my lips to his, I push all negative thoughts out of my mind. For a few brief moments I'm able to forget all my troubles, forgetting all about nightmares, angels, and demons. I lose myself in the kiss, and we stay lip-locked for a long while.

For dinner we indulge in pizza and drink coke out of red plastic cups. Yeah, not the most romantic dinner, but to us it's simply perfect.

On the way to the dance, I can't stop smiling. Brenton has certainly impressed me, his actions verifying how important I am to him. He loves me, I love him, and nothing will ever come between us.

Nothing will wreck or destroy this night.

Nothing.

# Sam

Noise comes from the large gymnasium, which is holding the Thanksgiving Dance. Humans are decked out in their finest, laughing and joking amongst themselves.

Though I'm not here to monitor the dress code of young humans. Rather I'm studying the skies, watching out for the enemy. Lightning strikes above. I know that whatever Lukus and his hounds have planned, it will be happening soon.

Looking to Gabriel I ask, "What is their plan of attack?"

"You will see shortly," is his vague reply.

A horn blast sounds from above and a bright light appears, lasting for a few seconds. As the light dissipated, I'm shocked by what I see. I have no words to speak. I am ... *enamored.*

"You see, Sam," Gabriel laughs. "You are not alone."

I nod, feeling a smile creep across my face. "Talk about reassurance."

Immediately I drop to my knees and give praise to the Lord.

Even angels receive answered prayers.

# Chapter Twenty-Three

# Clarity

Opening the doors of the gym, a blast of cool air welcomes Brenton and I, along with the scent of lemony floor wax mixed with sweat-soaked socks. The school has dug deep into their stingy pockets and hired a surprisingly good DJ to work the dance. The wood floor beneath our feet vibrates from the club-like music blaring from multiple speakers.

The decorations are made up of tacky streamers, paper-mache turkeys and pilgrims. Leaves of every shade have been tossed all over the gym floor, giving the dance an earthy Fall feel. A refreshment table overflowing with junk food and two punch bowls are placed in front of the stage area. Six smaller round tables dressed with black tablecloths reside in one corner of the gym, every seat taken. Each table holds a lit candle and (something I actually like) a vase full of real sunflowers. I take a mental note to swipe one of those after the dance.

A group of girls, obviously dateless, are out on the dance floor dancing *extremely* badly. Some students point and snicker at them, but they don't notice.

Just minutes after arriving, Kora runs up to us, with Kevin trailing behind.

"Omigosh, Clare, you look *amazing*!" she raves, pulling me into a hug. She looks pretty amazing herself, wearing a long, fitted black dress. A slit slides up on one side, stopping midway up her thigh.

Hugging her back I say, "So do you, but what up with the heels?" I gesture at her four-inch heels. Mine are pretty high, but I'd break my neck if I tried dancing in them!

"Oh, please!" Playfully, she slaps my arm. "I'm still a lot shorter than you."

Brenton and Kevin greet each other with their dude-like salutations. Kevin looks dashing in his suit, and actually has his hair styled, parted to the side. Usually his hair is plastered against his head due to his excessive hat wearing.

After mingling with friends, drinking some stale punch (nobody has spiked it yet), and getting our pictures taken by the photographer, Brenton and I make it to the dance floor. The music is fast and I soon find out how hard it is to dance in high heels.

Brenton notices my awkwardness in the heels, so he wraps his arms around my waist and lifts me off the ground. I feel like a nerd as he tries to keep dancing, all the while keeping my feet from touching the floor. Instead of being embarrassed, I start laughing uncontrollably. Really, I am surprised to be having a good time.

To my relief, a slow song comes on. On cue, he places my feet to the ground, keeping his arms around my waist. On the other side of the gym I spot Kevin and Kora. They sway back and forth to the music, gazing sweetly at each other. Janey, wearing a short, silver dress, is standing next to the refreshment table with Casey. They seem to be engaged in deep conversation, both gesturing animatedly at one another.

Briefly I wonder what Casey and Janey are discussing, but Brenton erases that thought when he asks, "Having a good time?"

"It's okay," I answer, shrugging my shoulder. Then I break into a huge smile.

"Come on," he says, grinning his dimpled grin. "It's got to be better than okay."

I roll my eyes. "Fine, fine. I'm having a *spectacular* time.

There. I said it. Are you happy now?"

"Quite," he answers aristocratically. Pulling me close to him, I lean my head against his chest, catching a whiff of his cologne. I love the smell of him, almost as much as lavender...

No. No. *No.* I'm not going there.

No angels. No demons. No more supernatural mumbo-jumbo.

No, tonight is about fun and friends. Plus I'd received the best news in my young life. Everything at the moment is perfect; all the pieces are falling into place. I'm happy and, most importantly, I feel *normal.*

So since I'm feeling normal, I bury my head in his chest and close my eyes, relishing the closeness of our bodies. The slow music is hypnotic, almost sounding like it's coming from a tunnel. Sweat trickles down my back, a cold shiver sending goosebumps up and down my body. A sharp pain –

Whoa, what's happening?

Slumping over in pain, I clutch my stomach as a rush of nausea hits me like a wave in a hurricane-riddled ocean. The jab feels like someone kicking me in the gut, over and over again. My mind blanks for a moment, causing a disoriented sensation to rust my brain. My energy level dramatically drops, and then a familiarity, one I wasn't expecting for tonight, fogs my senses.

No. No. *Please* no!

This is not good. Not at all.

A deep chill has frozen all the way through to my bones. My lungs ache and feel heavy. My hands...

I gasp in a muted shock as I catch sight of my burning palms. They're different than before, not glowing red, not glowing green. No, this time they're black. Black as the night sky, black like I'd stuck my hands in a bucket of black paint.

As black as demon eyes.

*Death.*

That one certain word reverberates in my mind, pounding against my skull. Panic surges through my veins, freezing my blood on contact. I scan the crowd of clueless, dancing teens. They're oblivious to what's happening – or what's about to happen.

I know exactly what to look for: three black-dressed freaks with pale faces, black eyes, and wickedness sketched on their features.

"Clarity, what's wrong?"

I hear Brenton, though he sounds like he's inside a

bubble ... or maybe it's *me* inside the bubble. Instead of answering, I continue to search the crowd. My eyes pause in Kevin and Kora's direction, the couple still enjoying a couple's embrace. But they're not what I'm focused on.

Rather I'm concentrating all my attention on Nick, who appears deathly pale and dressed all in black. With an expression of anger and fierce determination, he makes his way over to Kora and Kevin, though I can tell his eyes are solely on Kevin. Frost blankets my skin when I catch sight of the gun in his right hand.

I try to scream; I try to run. I want to warn them of the impending danger stalking toward them, but to my dismay I find my legs have turned into cooked noodles, while my mouth feels full of thick cotton.

The pain in my gut doubles, my eyes blur with tears, and the biting burn in my palms intensify – they're still the color of black ink.

Helpless, I watch a true horror movie unfold in slow motion. Nick walks up to the dancing couple, an argument ensues, and Kevin gets in between Kora and Nick. With words being thrown in all directions, Kevin pushes Nick away from them, unaware that Nick possesses a gun.

A look of acute rage blisters Nick's face, then quickly twists into an evil sneer as he lifts the gun, pointing it at Kevin's chest.

Like the slow motion button on a DVD player has been pressed, the terrifying scene unwraps into a chaotic mess. When I find my voice, I begin screaming, just as Nick pulls the trigger. The blast echoes off the gym's walls, and from where I stand I can see the smoke pouring from the end of the gun. The music turns off immediately, followed by frantic screams of confused and scared teens.

With my body finally coming back to life, Brenton and I start pushing through the crowd, both of us desperately trying to reach our friends. We press forward, but it seems like we're walking in quick sand. No matter how hard we push, it feels like we will never get to them.

The scene can be measured into one single word:

Pandemonium.

People are attempting to exit the gym at the same time, shoving each other forcefully, not caring who they're hurting. Boys and girls alike are falling to the ground, some being trampled upon. Brenton and I are being tossed in all directions, but we stand our ground, almost reaching our friends.

Kora is having words with Nick, tears causing her black mascara to run and paint ribbons down her cheeks. I cry out as Nick takes the gun and strikes her against the head. Instantly she falls to the ground.

"No!" Brenton yells. He pushes me back, getting in front of me as we navigate through the thick of panicked teenagers.

Where are the teachers and parents chaperoning the dance? Are they already outside of the gym? Were they the first ones out?

Nick holds the gun to Kora's head, but before he can pull the trigger, Brenton tackles him around the waist. The gun goes off, luckily nowhere near Kora or anyone else. Brenton and Nick are a tangle of legs, rolling on the ground with fists flying in the air.

When I reach Kevin and Kora, I drop to my knees, resting in between them. Kora, who is unconscious, has blood on the side of her head and face. Checking her pulse I blow a sigh of relief. She has a pulse, though it's extremely weak.

My attention switches to Kevin. His eyes are wide with fear, and his chest is a massive swell of blood. He looks up at me, with blood dripping from his mouth. Blood is pooling all around him – my knees are warm with it.

Not good. Not good at all.

"C-Clarity," he manages to speak. A coughing spasm hits him, sending out a heavy amount of thick blood.

"Kevin!" I sob, placing a hand on his cheek.

Suddenly he grabs my arm and says, "Tell Kora I-I love her, and to not..." Another round of coughing attacks him, sending blood all over himself and my dress.

"Take it easy," I soothe, knowing full well what the outcome will be. Tears spill down my cheeks as I look down at the good-natured, caring Kevin Davis. The first guy Kora has ever truly loved.

Again he says, "Tell K-Kora not to be upset. Tell her … God will take care of her."

"Kevin, hang on," I whisper sadly. "Help's on the way."

He drops my arm and stares straight up at the ceiling. A smile caresses his lips.

"They're already here," he whispers, sighing. Then, closing his eyes, he takes his last breath. The world seems to vanish around us.

"Kevin?" I breathe out, shaking his shoulders. But I know he's gone; he's no longer feeling pain. He's no longer here.

"No!" I shout out. Trembles take my body captive, and once again I'm ice-cold.

This isn't happening. This *can't* be happening!

This is all a dream. Yeah, one of my nightmares that feels like it will never end. I'll be waking up any minute now, tucked safely in my bed.

As another gunshot explodes, I realize that none of this is a dream. On shaky legs, I stand to my feet, my gaze traveling to the corner of the gym where Nick and Brenton are standing. My stomach drops to the floor as Brenton crumples to the ground.

Nick won the fight.

"NO!" I cry, my hands pulling at my hair.

Please, not Brenton. *Please!*

Nick turns to me with a maniacal grin on his face. From what I can tell, his eyes are black, with a shiny gleam coating them. When he begins strolling towards me, taking long strides, he lifts the gun and points it at me. Fear has its ugly claws clutched around me, so tight I –

I can't move.

Just as I think my life is about to end, Nick freezes mid-stride. Teenagers trying to exit the gym are also frozen, standing like well-dressed mannequins from a high-end department store. All is quiet, the only sound my heavy breathing and hard-beating heart throwing itself against my chest. Everyone is immobile, with me being the exception.

A flash of light fills the gym, so bright I shield my eyes. An overwhelming perfume smell bombs the air. I feel like my nose has been shoved into a potpourri dish.

When the light dims after two seconds, I'm amazed to see around fifty or sixty angels hovering in the air, their glorious wings jutting from their backs. Some descend and stand next to frozen teens, most likely their Charges.

Sam appears right in front of me, reaching out and touching my shoulder. A warm calmness touches every nerve I have, and his lavender scent tickles my nose. The sight of him, and the other magnificent angels, has taken my breath away. I've never seen so many angelic beings in one place. It's simply mind-boggling!

They're here to make everything right, to save us from this hellish nightmare!

"Sam!" I exclaim, throwing my arms around him. Leaning back to look in his pale face I plead, "You've got to help them! Help Brenton. Help Kora. Help Ke – "

I stop myself before saying Kevin's name. The angels can't help him now – he's already gone.

Sam takes my hand, his blue eyes showing signs of sorrow.

"Clarity," he says, his voice calm and collect, "listen to me. You – "

"No, you listen!" I scream, punching at his chest. "You've got to help them – "

Before I know what's happening, Sam wraps me in his wings. With my feet no longer on the ground, a rush of wind overtakes us. When he unwraps his wings, lowering me to the ground, I'm shocked to see we're now outside. Rain pours buckets from the sky – when had it started raining?

"What are we doing out here?" I glare at Sam, with anger rising within me. "We've got to help them."

"Their angels are with them," he informs softly, his eyes glowing. "Right now you must get out of here."

Confused, I stare at him and say, "No – NO! I can't just leave them."

"You've got to run, Clarity."

"No."

"You don't have much time."

I'm about to offer a rebuttal, though when I hear Nick's voice coming from the gym, I shut my mouth.

"Princess! Where are you?"

With rain drenching the both of us, I gaze up at Sam, reading the desperation in his eyes. It's not over. The horror, the pain, the … reality is not over.

"I am where you are." He touches his forehead to mine, but the moment doesn't last long.

A gunshot explodes in the air, hitting a nearby tree. Nick stands just outside the gym, looking to his left, then to his right. His darkened eyes find me.

"There you are, princess," he spits out nastily, quickly walking toward me.

"Run," Sam tells me, then disappears. Then his speaks in my head, *You are not alone.*

Without looking at Nick, without a second thought, I spin around and start running into the woods behind the school gym.

Running directly into yet another nightmare.

# Sam

Harsh laughter sounds behind me, my celestial alarms going off, prickling my skin. Turning around, I come face-to-face with Lukus, Nick's main tormentor and the one sent to destroy Clarity.

"Well, little angel," Lukus smirks, "how do you like the makeover we're giving this town?"

"Not impressed, demon," I respond. "But I guess it's to be expected from one of Hell's underlings."

The grin erases from his face as he retorts, "I'm not an underling. If I were an underling, why would lord Satan send me on this mission?"

"None of that matters, especially when that mark on your arm is seen by every demon in Hell." A sword of light appears in my hand. He hisses, observing the sword with acute hatred. He knows that with one touch from Heaven's Light, he'd be sent on a one-way trip back home.

"The Seer will fall," Lukus tells me with finality. "She will die a horrible, painful death. And you will lose your Charge. Wonder what your Father will say to that?"

I shake my head. "She will not die tonight – the Lord

has many plans for her." I pause, then add, "It's sad, really. You can't see it, but your mission has already failed. It failed before you set foot on earth. You and your hounds have lost."

"Oh yeah?" he scoffs. "And how has our mission failed, little Guardian?"

Narrowing my eyes I answer, "Because you're going back to Hell in a couple of seconds."

Or so I thought.

Before I can attack, the ground shakes beneath my feet. I stare down at the muddy ground, disbelieving what I'm seeing.

Tall beasts around nine-feet tall ascend from the ground, closing me in a tight circle. They wear armor over their bodies, looking like hairy ogres. Carrying a multitude of weapons, I can tell the favorite among the demon warriors are large battle axes.

I'm not afraid. Not at all. Lukus's disappearance is what has me on edge. But for now I'm trapped. Trapped in a circle of Hell's most devious beasts, and before I can run after Clarity and make sure she's safe...

I must fight.

# Chapter Twenty-Four

# Clarity

One thought is driving my body forward – I have to disappear, and disappear fast. I dart into the woods, maneuvering through various tree limbs and overgrown vegetation. Sharp thick briars pull and rip my dress, feeling like tiny hands snatching at the fabric, attempting to slow me down.

At one point my left shoe becomes lost, stuck in the mud, causing me to run lopsided. The wrist corsage that Brenton's mom made gets mauled off my wrist by razor-like briars, the fabric holding it all together becoming detached. A sob of desperation bellows out of me as I trip over a dead oak, falling face first into the swampy earth.

Momentarily dazed, I roll onto my back and gaze up at the falling rain. My heart is functioning at triple time, my body one big tremble as I lay motionless on the drenched ground. I flinch as lightning flashes and thunder booms.

313

Kevin is dead ... dead! Kora, Brenton, and many others might be, too. Lives are being torn apart, including mine. Why is this happening? Why –

The dream. The dream from the night before. I'm living it. We *all* are.

I should have seen this coming. Seers can receive messages from God through their dreams, though it's hard for me to decipher if they are from God, or from the other guy.

Even though I don't want this extraordinary life, it wants me. Again the overwhelming feeling to go blind, to be uneducated in the spiritual realm weighs down on top of me like a concrete slab. Then I instantly know...

I can never go back.

Guilty emotions produce more tears as I lay here in the mud. I just want to give up. It is my fault, after all. Yeah, sure, I'm not the one who pulled the trigger, but ... I shouldn't have ignored my calling. I had let my selfishness bring everyone down, and now I find myself sinking in the mud, descending lower and lower into the ground.

"Princess! Where are you?"

Nick's singsong voice forces my adrenaline to start pumping again. I crawl behind a huge oak tree, being as quiet as possible. Taking deep breaths and letting them out, I struggle to slow down the rapid beat of my heart. Glancing down, I notice I've lost the other shoe. Probably stuck in the dead tree I'd tripped over.

Barefoot and soaked to the bone, I strain my ears and listen for Nick. All I hear is the heavy drum of my heart and the relentless thunderstorm. Closing my eyes, I tell myself that everything is going to be okay, that Nick will not be able to find me in these dense woods.

"There you are, princess."

I'm wrong. Dead wrong. I realize this as Nick whispers in my ear, his hot breath hitting the side of my face.

Not turning around, I once again find myself running, unable to see two feet in front of me. A gunshot blast bounces around in my eardrums, the noise so loud I'm afraid they will burst. The bullet ricochets off a tree next to my head, splintering wood that hits my face, neck, and arm. I don't stop to think how close that had been. With my adrenaline still fueled-up, I ignore the stitch in my side and the throb in my ankle – pretty sure I'd sprained it.

"You can run, you can hide, but I'm still gonna get ya!" Nick's taunting recites in the air, making it sound like he's right beside me. And maybe he is. I can't tell, thanks to the imbruing rainfall.

Continuing on, I hike my dress up to keep from falling again. It's shredded and stained, totally ruined. The silly part of my brain laughs, saying there's no way this dress will be wearable again. The sensible part of my brain is wishing the silly part would be quiet and concentrate more on staying alive. As for me, I wish they'd both shut-up.

As the two parts of my brain have a back and forth with each other, I almost don't see the clearing leading out of the woods. A clearing that leads to a ledge with at least a thirty-foot drop.

I slide to a halt before plummeting over the rocky crag, the mud so deep it buries my feet. A river is located at the bottom, the raging water deeper from all the rain that's been attacking the town.

Looking to the left and then to the right, feelings of dread, fear, and panic stream hot in my veins. This debilitating feeling creeps from the top of my wet head to the tips of my grimy wet toes. Lightning ignites the sky, the rain pouring harder and harder. Thunder rumbles, shaking the ground. Rain, trees, and an overflowing river. That's all there is.

"Found you."

If I wasn't already frozen, hearing Nick whisper those two words would have done the job.

I don't know what to do. My head is full of wool and my legs feel like they're made of jelly. There's no place to go, no way to escape. I have to face the cold hard fact...

I'm trapped.

My eyes gaze down at the river. I don't know how deep it is, but I contemplate jumping, falling head first into the water. If I'm going to die anyway, I may as well get it over with. To me that would be a better death than to die at the hands of some deranged teenager.

**STAND FIRM.**

Completely and utterly taken back by this new voice in my head, I find myself whispering, "I'm too scared ... what do I do?"

The voice, strong and majestic, answers, "**BE STILL. TRUST IN ME.**"

All at once my body tingles with electricity, my hands burning and glowing, but not the usual green or red, or most recently, black. Instead a white light radiates from my palms, reminding me of the celestial essence Sam possesses inside of him. A mystification takes hold of my being, and an extreme rush of power surges through my body. Almost like the sensation I'd experienced the night I'd touched Lukus, only multiplied by a million.

Feeling an eruption of bravery (I have no idea where it's coming from), I turn around to face the gun-toting Nick. A huge weight of déjà vu slaps my face as I realize that this is exactly like the dream.

I guess if I live through this night I'll be taking my dreams more seriously.

Sam had told me that Satan and his evil angels recruit humans to do their dirty work, and being so close to Nick I figure that he's been their most recent yard dog.

Black clothes, pale face, holding a gun, and yes, black eyes. Completely black. Nick's newest look.

Lightning flashes, following with a violent clap of thunder while Nick and I wordlessly stare each other down. The rain has flattened his blonde hair to his head. Tiny beads of water drip from the ends. His lips, which are blood red against his pale skin, curl up into a sneer. That one move transforms his face into a picture of pure malice.

"Honestly," he says, his tone dark, "why run? You'd never get away."

Anger boils in my blood. I glare daggers at him, balling up my fists. My hands are the hottest they've ever been, most likely from the new bright celestial essence flowing from them. If I live through this horror, I'm going to interrogate Sam thoroughly about, well ... *everything*.

"Why, Nick?" I yell. "Why did you kill Kevin? Nobody deserves to die that way! Nobody!"

He laughs an evil bark of laughter – I'll never be able to forget that laugh. "That Davis guy deserves what he got for taking Kora away from me. If I can't have her, no one can."

"So why hurt Kora? Why shoot Brenton? What did Brenton ever do to you?"

"Sparks wasn't supposed to get shot. He just got in the way." He narrows his newly blackened orbs. "I was going to kill Kora, then myself, so that we could be together in the afterlife, but," he wags his finger at me, "*you* interfered."

"Me?" I react in confusion. "What did I – "

He briskly interrupts, "You and your goody two-shoes boyfriend decided to play heroes, which didn't pan out too well, did it?" He pauses, his lips drawing into a thin line.

"After I shot your beloved, all I could think about was putting a bullet through your pretty little skull, and with all that said..." He points the gun at me. "It's time for you to get what you deserve."

"You ... you *planned* this," I stutter in terrifying amazement, recalling his words from the night before.

*Tomorrow night is going to be a night to remember.*

"Nick, this isn't you," I say cautiously, my eyes on the gun. "So Kora rejected you, but killing is not the answer. Can't you see that? Stop listening to the voices in your head, Nick. They're using you. They are evil! You've got to fight them! Don't let them win."

He shakes his head. "It's too late, Clarity. There's no going back." He cocks the gun. "I ... I have to finish the job."

I stare at the gun in disbelief.

So this is it. This is how my life ends. Who would have guessed it?

Taking a deep breath, I decide to make one last attempt to change his mind. While doing this, I busy my brain into formulating some kind of escape route.

"Fine," I huffily say, clenching my teeth and narrowing my eyes. "Listen to them – listen to their squeaky evil voices.

Let them control you. Be their puppet. I don't know what they've told you or what they're saying now, but I guarantee you they are feeding you a bunch of lies." I shake my head and smirk. "They don't care about you. All they care about is bagging human souls to keep their master happy, and you know how they get their jobs done? By using small pathetic losers like you, who choose not to think for themselves."

He ricks his head to the side. "What are you talking about, princess?"

"What I'm talking about," I answer swiftly, "is that all you are to them is a little pawn in their game. They sought you out because you're weak." I pause, shooting him an angry sneer. "You're nothing but a sucker, Nick. Plain and simple. Oh, and the little plan you had about spending an afterlife with Kora by killing her and yourself? Not gonna happen."

He lowers the gun.

"I will spend an eternity with her," he adamantly speaks, his eyes wide. "That's part of the deal. They said if I did everything they told me to do, then every wish I had would come true. And they wouldn't lie."

Despite the imminent danger I'm drowning in, I let out a harsh cackle.

"Oh, please! Lying is what they do best! How stupid are you?" Crossing my arms in front of me I add, "Like I said – they go after the weakest, meanest, and apparently, the *dumbest.*"

As I'm speaking, I take small sidesteps to my right, preparing to sprint into the woods. It's the only chance I have ... either the woods, or take a swim.

"You better watch your mouth," he expresses, his shoulders hunched, his body trembling.

Again, I chortle, knowing the sound will crawl underneath his skin. "You know what's going to happen, Nick? Even if you kill me, Brenton, Kora – whoever they want you to kill, they're not going to give you what you want."

"Shut your mouth," he warns, his pale face turning crimson.

I press on. "Even if you kill yourself, you're not going to get what they promised because they are deceitful little smelly fiends."

A shudder tears through me, not from the rain, but from the sinister growls sating the air. If Nick is possessed, then most likely I'm rattling the demons inside of him. Plus, Lukus is probably still angry that I'd scorched his arm with my Seer mark, adding more fuel to their bitter animosity.

Still, I keep up the banter. "I mean, come on, Nick! Really? Who gets everything they want? It's the stupidest thing I've ever heard, thinking you can kill someone and spend an eternity with them – especially with someone who can't stand you, nonetheless. Anyone with half a brain could figure that for deceit!" The growls grow louder, but I'm undeterred. "And where do you think you're going to spend eternity, Nick? Huh? On a tropical island, living in complete paradise? No, I think not. I'm sure where you're going is hot, but it won't be pleasant."

I can see that my words are generating angry spores within his brain. His face has turned blood red, and his expression is so furious it looks like at any minute smoke will pour from his ears.

"Let me tell you what I think," I continue, smiling sarcastically and taking a couple more steps to the right.

"Shut-up!" he screams. I'm not sure if he's speaking to me or the demons that possess him. He's pacing back and forth, clutching his head in his hands as he slings obscenities out of his mouth.

Wow. Guess I got the demons all riled up.

Good.

Edging closer and closer to the woods I softly say, "I think I know what your paradise is called, Nick."

Stopping his obsessive pacing, he steers the gun my direction, figuring out what I'm up to. "Shut-up! Don't move!"

"It's called Hell!" I shout.

At that moment, I spring forward, escaping into the woods. Only I don't get far – Nick tackles me around the waist. I lose my balance.

Before I know what's happening, Nick and I both fall over the ledge, descending toward the icy waters below. On the way down the side of my head connects with a rock that juts out from the ridge's wall. A pain explodes in my head, and as I hit the water my body stiffens, then becomes limp.

# Sam

The demons of Hell keep coming. When I slash one down, two more arise from the ground in its place. I know this is a ploy from the enemy, to keep me sidetracked and busy, but they don't know the devotion I have for God and my Charge.

They are strong, but I am stronger. They are determined, but I have all of Heaven on my side. They will not win.

Clarity. I've got to get to her side, and fast. Knowing she's in the woods, alone with Nick and his gun – that thought keeps running through my mind, round and round like a car on the racetrack. Also knowing that Lukus and the Hellhounds are after her as well...

I've got to get to her side.

She's not dead, of that I am sure. I still feel her soul, the bright light The Father placed within her when he knit her together inside her mother's womb. However, that can change in a split second.

"Father!" I cry to the heavens, taking out five demons at one time with my sword of Heaven's Light. "Please help!"

The angels in the gym are having their own battles, so I have no other choice but to call out to God. Thankfully, an answer arrives promptly.

An abrupt light morphs night into day, destroying all demons that have me circled. It also takes out the ones waiting to rise from the ground. Relief surges through my being. Glancing down I discover where the light is coming from.

As the light fades, receding back into the messenger angel, Gabriel lifts from his crouch. A look of fierce tenaciousness has spread across his face, his eyebrows sewn together.

"Go to your Charge. She needs you." With his gaze set on the gymnasium, he begins trotting toward the building's door.

"What about you?" I call out.

Halting his steps, giving me a sideways glance, he responds, "I am done playing this game with the enemy. Every demonic being in this gym and in close proximity to this town will be sent back to Hell tonight."

Nodding I say, "Bye, Gabriel, and thank you."

"It's what I do." Swords of light appear in both of his hands. I watch as he focuses his attention on the gym and releases a battle cry. Then, crossing the gym's threshold, he jumps right into the never-ending war between good and evil.

As for myself...

Clarity needs me.

# Chapter Twenty-Five

# Clarity

The water is dark and murky, devouring my body completely. My dress soaks up the dirty river water, pulling me lower into its cold depths. The gown rapidly absorbs the water, and eventually I reach the bottom of the river. When I gaze up I can see lightning flash, the storm still busy attacking the earth.

Attempting to move my arms and legs, I find that my limbs don't want to work. The hit I'd taken to the head has left my body depleted, with absolutely no energy.

I can't see. Can't breathe. Can't move.

I am dying.

Sam is nowhere in sight.

Who will save me?

God.

Please help me.

Closing my eyes, I wait for death. What's the use? If I

struggle, it will be for nothing. The bang to my head has sucked out my vitality. My will to live has abandoned me. With my lungs aching and burning, my head pounding, I give up. I'm done.

Finished.

Suddenly a light emerges, along with a face, one I haven't seen in five years.

"M-Mama?" I whisper, sounding far, far away.

Mama looks the same as she always did, only a bit younger. Her smile is vivid, her brown eyes twinkle. Her brown hair sways around her shoulders, with curls flowing down her back. I try to reach out to her, but again my arms don't lift. It's like I don't have a body anymore. Maybe...

Maybe I'm dead.

"Open your eyes, Clarity," she gently murmurs.

"My eyes are open," I protest, not understanding her soft request.

"No, no they are not." Lifting her hand, she touches my forehead. She smiles. "There ... now they're open."

A radiant light sears my vision, and I'm saddened to find out that I'm back in the river. A deplorable feeling ensnares me. This isn't fair. Mama was just here, and I talked to her. Why am I still here?

Looking up, I observe a light slowly radiating on the surface of the choppy water. As it breaks through the water's barrier, the light transforms into the shape of a hand. A hand of pure light.

Heaven's Light.

Entranced by this otherworldly spectacle, I'm surprised that I feel absolutely no fear. Rather I'm fascinated by this awesome sight. My heartbeat quickens as the hand of light descends closer and closer, and just when I think it's going to crush me, it turns to the side, moving behind me.

A warmth like no other floods my spirit, and I am astounded to be able to breathe again while still underwater. Water is all around me, yet I'm breathing in air instead of water. It's insane, totally irrational.

The biggest wonderment of all happens when the hand palms my body and lifts me upward. I'm rising higher and higher, and before I know it I break the surface of the river. Rain batters my face, but I'm too transfixed on what's happening.

The hand of light takes me to the water's edge, gently placing me on the muddy bank. I fall to my knees when it disappears from sight. My energy is still depleted, my head is pounding, and my mind is unable to comprehend the miracle that took place.

"The Hand of God."

Lifting my gaze, I find Sam standing a few feet away. The rain has his clothes soaked, the material clinging to his skin. A flash of lightning strikes, illuminating his pale face, which is flooded with concern.

"What?" I wonder.

He replies, "For I hold you by your right hand – I, the Lord your God. And I say to you, don't be afraid. I am here to help you."

I recognize this particular scripture from the bible. One of many that Sam has recited to me over the past month.

"You mean what just happened..." My words falter, my reasonable thought train plunging off the track.

"Yes," is Sam's response.

I stare down at the mud I'm sitting in, my emotions spinning out of control.

Moments ago I'd fallen off a rocky ledge and nearly drowned. I'd been ready to give up, to let death consume me. But God had other plans ... *obviously.*

From what I'm gathering, with what I saw and the information Sam had just fed me, it came to this: God reached into the water and pulled me from the deep depths of the river. He placed me in the palm of his hand, placed air in my lungs underwater, and...

Saved me.

Tears fill my eyes as images of the night's events swim through my mind. My hair, which had been perfectly styled two hours ago, is hanging in my face, dirty and tangled. I gaze up at Sam, barely able to see him thanks to the storm.

"Sam," I whisper, my body trembling and my lips quivering, "why did He save me? I'm not – *worthy*."

"Clarity, you – "

Suddenly a gray blur attacks Sam, and he goes flying back in the air. They crash somewhere deep in the woods. I don't have time to scream – I don't have the energy to. When something growls a few feet away, my blood turns glacial. Funny, I didn't think it were possible to be any colder.

Cautiously, I glance up – and scream.

This nightmare is never going to end.

# Sam

The blow from the Hellhound has sent me deep in the woods. We crash through trees and land in a small clearing full of thick vegetation. Quickly I rise to my feet, my focus directed on the demon a few feet away. The huge, repelling beast gets on all fours, stumbling as if dazed. It shakes its head, rainwater flying off its black fur. Then it turns its glowing red eyes at me and growls, baring long, sharp teeth. It's trying to intimidate me, but that's not going to happen.

We have a stare down, good against evil, neither one of us making a move. Harsh winds batter the treetops above, the storm becoming stronger with each passing second. I clench my fist, anticipating its next move. Instead it speaks.

"The end is upon the *Ra'ah*," it snarls, twisting its black lips into a wolfish grin. "The plan has come to fruition – you lose."

"No," I shake my head, my sword appearing in my hand, blazing in all it's heavenly glory. "It is *you* that will lose."

Seemingly it doesn't agree. Crouching low, it then pounces, taking flight with mouth wide open and claws outstretched. When it's almost on me, I step to the side. The hound rams headfirst into an oak tree. Laying on its side, its red eyes glow brighter and it howls, releasing its fury into the wind. Standing up, it paces back and forth, its gaze never leaving me.

"Your demise will be long and painful!" the hound bellows, adding, "And the Seer's death will be even more grotesque."

Again, I shake my head. Slowly I unfurl my wings and reply, "Don't think so."

And again, the hound doesn't like my response. It squats down on its hind legs, then leaps in the air, charging full force. I, in turn, spring to the air, with my sword pointed at the beast.

The fight continues.

# Lukus

"You seem a little broken, Seer," I smirk. "A little beaten-up and ... *defeated*."

She doesn't respond. Rather she continues to stare at me in horror, which is pleasing. Stone stands on all fours, growling at the dispirited *Ra'ah*. She's realizing that the inevitable cannot be stopped. That after tonight she will be dead.

"The angel almost got away with you," I point out, making a *tsk tsk* noise. "Though the key word here is *almost*."

"That's right," echoes Nick, who is limping over, favoring his left side. The fall had broken his foot, but since he's hopped-up on drugs, he's feeling no pain. Stopping next to me, he points the gun at the Seer and says, "And now it's time to die, princess."

She pinches her eyes closed and bites her lip, making no attempt to fight. Tilting my head I study her a moment. Do I want Nick to have the pleasure of taking her life? Would he really appreciate it as much as I would?

"No, Nick," I snarl. "You will not be the one to kill her."

Confused, he shoots me a perplexed expression. "But..."

"No," I interject. Lifting my chin, I square my shoulders with his, though I tower over him. "Now is the time for you to leave this earth. Remember what we talked about?"

"Yes," he answers, his eyes glazing over.

"Do you want to spend eternity with your beloved Kora?"

"Yes," he adamantly replies.

"So you are ready for paradise?"

"Absolutely."

Grinning sadistically I ask, "Are you ready to pull the trigger?"

"Yes." His tone is empty and robotic – he's totally under my control.

"Good," I say. "Go ahead, Nick. Pull the trigger so you can receive your prize. Pull it, and you'll wake up in paradise."

"No, Nick, don't!" shouts the Seer. She flinches back when Stone lurches at her, barking and growling.

With malevolent delight, I watch as Nick lifts the gun, presses it to his temple, and pulls the trigger. The Seer is screaming in the background, but I'm laughing as the human pawn I'd used for months does himself in, dead before he hits the ground. In a few moments he'll be meeting his Creator. He's going to be real surprised when he's sentenced to an eternity in Hell.

A howl of death sounds through the woods. My

features twist into a scowl. Anger rises in my throat because I know what that sound means. Markus has been overcome by the angel.

"Stone, attack the angel," I order gruffly. "Keep him occupied for a few minutes."

Stone nods his head, then takes off after the angel. He knows that Markus has been defeated, and that the angel has sent the hound back to Hell. This fuels the Hellhound tremendously, and I know Stone will give all he's got. Most likely Stone will fall, but it will not be an easy battle for the Guardian.

The rain continues to pour, the lightning continues to flash, and darkness is still in control. The night was far from over.

Glancing down at the Seer I mischievously say, "Now it's our turn to play. Just you and me."

# Chapter Twenty-Six

# Clarity

Shock has overridden my existence. A knot has twisted around my stomach, like a snake squeezing the life out of its meal. I'm afraid that at any moment I will throw-up, the doleful events of this night taking its toll.

Nick is laying face first in the mud, dead. Someone I've known my entire life just killed himself. A bullet rests in his brain, ending his young life.

And the night isn't over.

"Look at me," Lukus orders. When I don't comply, he shouts, "LOOK AT ME!"

The demon's earsplitting command forces my attention his direction. The rain buffeting the earth has plastered his black hair to his face. Orbs the color of coal glare with scourging menace, his lips twisted into a deep glower. A slight gasp spills from my lips when I lay eyes on the arm I'd grabbed in the alley. The human flesh has been ripped away,

337

replaced with bright red skin. The hand of that arm holds long black talons.

I catch sight of the Seer mark – it looks as if it's been seared into his flesh. Only on his skin, the mark is outlined in black.

"Your a-arm," I stutter, "it's..."

"What about my arm?" he snarls, lifting it up as if to investigate it. Dropping it back to his side he says, "Yeah, about that – that wasn't very nice. After I defeat you and go back home, I'll be the laughing stock of Hell."

"S-Serves you r-right," I stammer, my teeth chattering. With the rain freezing my entire body, and the acute pain in my head, I can hardly see straight. The world is all topsy-turvy, keeping me dazed, while sharp fear stabs into my heart. Over. And over. Again.

My statement angers Lukus. "You will pay. Your death will be slow and unmerciful, but first ... let me show you the *real* me."

Shaking my head, I open my mouth to protest, but nothing comes out. I don't want to see the beast that resides underneath the skin. The last couple of months I'd witnessed too many disturbing things. I want this nightmare to end –

this is all too much for me to handle.

Though the next few seconds that follow inform me that what I want and what I get are two *extremely* different things.

Lukus lifts his hand to his head, his eyes glued to mine. I watch in utter revulsion as he takes a talon and slides it down the middle of his face. Then, taking both hands, he begins peeling the fake skin off his head.

The first thing I notice are the red horns protruding from his forehead. The second thing is the black, cracked lips. The third – bright red eyes. The rest comes out in a blur of strict disbelief.

Like unzipping and stepping out of a costume, Lukus shifts from his disguise. He grows to at least ten feet tall, his whole body bright red and muscular. Black leathery wings emerge from his back, so long that the tips of them hover just a couple inches off the ground. Casting the skin to the side, he leers.

Being down wind from Lukus, I gag when the scent of death and decomposition sates the air. The odor burns up my nose, and I know at any minute my dinner from earlier would be making an appearance.

"Stand to your feet," he tells me, his tone deathly grave.

On unsteady legs, I force myself up. Though I'm scared to death, frozen solid from the inside out, and convulsing with shivers, I lift my chin in defiance. It's all a show, really. I'm weak, I'm tired, I'm weary. I have no fight left in me.

Accepting my fate I spit, "Go ahead, demon. Do your worst."

In response, he kicks me in the stomach. I fly through the air and connect with a nearby tree. The pain radiates throughout my nerves as I land, rolling over onto my side. Along with the aching throb in my head, my ribs now twinge excessively. Pretty sure a couple of them are broken after that attack, the hurt keeping rhythm with my heart.

Wheezing, finding it hard to breath, I fling onto my back, attempting to stanch the sting my body is suffering. Lukus doesn't allow any time to go by before he seizes me around the throat, shoving me up against the tree. Bark bites into my bare flesh, bringing forth an agonizing cry from my lips.

Releasing his hold around my neck, he takes a step back and stares with unblinking eyes. "You know, I'm ready to go home. I'm done with you." Slinging his arms out, stretching his sharp, knife-like talons, he clamors, "Goodbye, Seer."

As his arm rears back, preparing to attack, I close my eyes and await impact. However I immediately open them when the faint scent of lavender permeates the air. A bright light singes the atmosphere, and relief shoots through my system as Sam appears in between Lukus and I, with his white fluffy wings unfurled. The sword of light Sam holds is sticking in the demon's stomach.

Lukus's expression is that of saddened shock, his red eyes wide and bulging.

"No, this can't be..." The demon's face screams defeat, his gaze strictly on Sam.

"Don't worry," Sam whispers. "It's almost over."

Sam drives the sword deeper, and the demon discharges a gargled moan, then explodes into a fine, silvery dust. The rain quickly washes Lukus's ashes away; he's on his way to Hell this very second.

Turning around, Sam gently takes hold of my arm, inspecting me. His sword occupies his other hand. "Are you alright? Are you hurt?"

I open my mouth to answer, but a terrified scream

comes out instead. Flying up behind him is one of the Hellhounds. In one quick movement, Sam twists around and cuts the demon in half, its dusty remains falling on the both of us. Thankfully the rain washes the remnants off our skin.

Pivoting back around, the sword disappearing, Sam insures, "That was the last one. It's over."

I shake my head. "No ... it will never be over."

"Clarity." Frowning, he lifts me into his arms. "Everything will be okay."

"Sam," I say, suddenly becoming fatigued, "I'm so sorry..."

"Shh," he consoles. "Relax. Close your eyes."

"But..."

"I will take care of you." He takes to the skies and adds softly, "I am where you are. Always."

I try to fight the drowsiness edging its way into my system, but in the end I lose that battle. Granting his calming lavender substance access to my body, I quietly immerse myself into a deep unawareness.

No dreams allowed.

# Sam

Landing next to the edge of the woods, I stand still, watching the scene at hand. People are everywhere – police officers, EMT workers, firefighters – assisting the traumatized teens. I can read their thoughts, and they're all thinking the same thing.

How can we help these kids make sense of what's happened, when we don't understand ourselves?

The lightning has stopped, though the rain continues. Gazing at the sky it's as if the heavens are pouring down God's healing rain, and that's what this town will need – a heavenly healing.

Angels are scattered amongst the crowd, some guarding over their Charges, while others aim to soothe frantic teenagers. There's an immense amount of sorrow oozing down the brick walls of the gym, soaking into the ground and poisoning everything it touches. If this town ever wants to overcome this catastrophe, it has a choice to make...

Sink into a damaging depression, or call out to God.

I train my eyes on the crowd, searching for an earthly helper in the sea of chaos that's raging outside the gymnasium. Zeroing in on a man rummaging through medical supplies in the back of an ambulance, I sprint over, cradling Clarity tight to my chest.

"Hey, you!" I call out to the man. "This young woman needs assistance!"

The paramedic swings around, his eyes catching sight of the precious commodity in my arms.

"Here, lay her on this stretcher." He points to a flat gurney.

I place her gently down, and say, "There's a young man next to the river in the woods."

"Does he need a stretcher, or can he walk on his own?" When I don't respond, he lifts his gaze. Confusion racks his brain because I've disappeared from sight. He quickly forgets about me when a voice rings in the air.

"Let me by – I'm her aunt!"

Clarity's aunt Caroline has arrived on the scene, and her attention is focused on my Charge stretched out on the gurney. There's a frenzied glow in her eyes as she grazes past two policemen who try holding her back. As she rushes over to Clarity's side, she notices the EMT working on her.

"Omigosh, Doug!" she cries, falling to her knees next to

her niece. "How is she?"

"She's pretty banged up," he admits. "But I think she'll be okay. We need to get her to the hospital."

"How did she get here?" Caroline wonders. Retrieving a towel from the ambulance, she wipes the rainwater from Clarity's face, even though the rain proceeds at a steady pace.

Backing away, I let the pair work on Clarity. She's in good hands with them. She'll be safe. She'll be okay.

Allowing my wings to unfold, I take to the skies.

Lukus and the hounds are gone, but darkness still resides.

# Clarity

A clean antiseptic smell assaults my nose. Opening my eyes, I take a gander around the room, quickly coming to the realization that I'm laid up in a hospital bed. An IV is stuck in my arm, dripping fluids into my veins. My right ankle is wrapped in an adhesive wrap, along with my midsection. The bandage around my stomach is so tight it's hard to take a deep breath. Touching my head I learn it's bandaged, as well.

I try to sit up, but stop moving immediately when an

agonizing pain surges from the top of my head, down my spine, and into my toes. Sighing, I once again glance around the overly sterile room. Garlandton has the saddest, most depressing hospital in the entire world. It's just like the rest of the town – old, outdated, and decrepit. What makes the room a little less dismal is the vase of sunflowers placed on a table next to the window. Sunlight splashes its red orange glow on the gray walls. I'm so glad the rain has moved on, and I hope it stays away for a long while.

As I attempt to sit up a second time, the pain is so intense that I fall back against the flat pillows. My body is one big throb of hurt, the pain pulsating with my heart.

"Ow!"

"Don't move!" A.C. severely exclaims, running into the room. She must have been right outside the door.

"A.C., I – "

"Shh," she hushes, pulling the blanket up to my chin. "Don't push yourself. You've got a couple of broken ribs, a sprained ankle, and a slight concussion." She gently sits on the edge of the bed, careful not to jostle me. Though she smiles, there's a sadness penciled into her features. "You were beaten up pretty badly."

I close my eyes. "Sounds like." I feel her hand as she brushes a strand of hair from my forehead.

"It's going to take awhile for everyone to get back to normal," A.C. says softly.

My eyes pop open. "Where's Kora and Brenton?" I question in a rush, the memory of the night before flashing through my brain.

"They're fine," she speedily informs, using her calm nurses voice. "Kora suffered a head concussion and was released from the hospital this morning. Brenton will be released here in a little while. They were able to get the bullet out of his shoulder and fix him up. Luckily the bullet didn't hit anything major."

I blow a sigh of relief. "Oh, thank God! So, Kora only had to spend a few hours in this horrible place and soon Brenton will be able to escape." I grin, trying to lighten the mood. "When do I get out, Nurse Caroline?"

Concern suddenly fills her brown eyes.

"Clarity, what's the last thing you remember?" she inquires cautiously.

"Um ... I don't remember."

Oh, I remember. I remember every single detail.

However, with the lethargy attacking my body at the moment, I'm wary about speaking on the subject.

She pushes on. "Okay, I was afraid you may not remember. Let me start off with this – you've been here three days, unconscious. The IV in you arm has been supplying you with fluids so you wouldn't become dehydrated, along with painkillers."

My heart rate speeds up tremendously and I feel on the verge of a panic attack. As she spoke every ounce of my blood froze up in my veins. Taking a few deep breaths, I'm able to settle my heart, keeping the attack at bay. Still, that knocked down, floored sensation keeps a firm grip on my mind.

Clearing my throat I whisper, "I've been in here three days?"

She nods. "Yep, and there's more."

I listen as she tells about Kevin being shot by Nick, and about how the paramedics found Nick's body deep in the woods. Of course I already know all this. I'd had a front row seat to the deadly drama, watching the whole scene with my very own eyes. But I can't let her know this. Too many questions would roll if I told her the whole truth.

"This is all so weird and tragic," I express when she's

finished talking.

"It gets weirder." She leans in and narrows her eyes. "And it revolves around you."

"Me?"

"Where did you go after the shooting occurred?"

Flustered, I react with, "What do you mean – I already told you I don't remember!"

She takes my hand and pleads, "Clare, please! I can't figure this out by myself. When I arrived on the scene you were unresponsive, soaked to the bone, your dress torn up – a complete mess."

Pulling my hand from hers, I reach up and touch my neck.

"Where's the necklace Brenton gave me?"

A.C. frowns. "You must have lost it, hon."

"Oh." I cluck my tongue. "I really liked that necklace."

"Do you remember anything about the guy who found you?"

My heart leaps to my throat, but I don't skip a beat. "No. Like I said – I don't remember."

"Well, shoot," she says in a huff. "Doug, the paramedic who helped you, said he ran over carrying you in his arms. He also knew where they could find Nick's body."

A few quiet moments tick by in silence. I can't say anything about Sam, or Lukus, or any of it. I have to play dumb, which isn't that hard thanks to the bump on my head.

"You want a drink of water?" she asks, breaking the quiet in the room.

I force a smile. "Thanks, that would be great."

She smiles back, then gets to her feet and walks to the door. Abruptly she stops and looks at me. "Oh, I almost forgot – you know your friend Janey?"

"Yeah." Dread pours into my stomach. I don't want to hear any more bad news.

"Janey was pushed down during the chaos and stomped on." She pauses, her gaze drifting to the floor. "She ... she lost the baby." With that spoken, she walks out the door, closing it behind her.

I stare at the space where A.C. stood just a second ago, my mouth hanging wide open. Janey had been pregnant, and I hadn't known. How could I have *not* known? How could I have missed the signs? And why hadn't she told anybody?

One of my close friends had been pregnant, and lost the baby by being trampled on at a school dance. Another tragedy added to the long list of disasters this town has experienced.

As I sit in this hospital room, all my mind can ponder on is this:

Is it over?

Or has it just begun?

# Chapter Twenty-Seven

# Clarity

Kevin's funeral was held on a Thursday. A sunny, beautiful day with no storm clouds in sight. The whole town had come to pay their respects for a young man cut down in the prime of his high school life. A young man who had devoted his life to Christ. A great athlete, a sincere friend, and a good son.

During it all I watched a mother and father mourn their only child. A mother and father that had worked hard to give their son a Christian upbringing. They would now have to live the rest of their lives knowing that when they wake up every morning they will find an empty bedroom at the end of the hall. The only thing that will keep them moving forward is the knowledge that their son is in Heaven, and they will see him again.

I witnessed Brenton fall to pieces at the sight of his friend's casket being lowered underground. I held my best friend as she grieved over the first guy that truly loved her for who she was, not for who she wasn't. Losing Kevin will most definitely push her over the edge, but I will be there to help her through it. Just like I'll be there for Janey, who also lost someone in the midst of turmoil.

Nick's family took his body to their hometown of Atlanta. The Garlandton Press had questioned Mr. Reece about the incident, and just like the lawyer he was he replied, "No comment".

Through it all I saw a town in shock. Who would have thought a murder/suicide could occur in our quaint little town? What could fuel a young person to be so heartless and violent?

Questions fly from one direction to the other, but I know answers will be hard to come by. When the enemy is involved, we as humans have the freewill to choose which path to tread.

Some of us decide to take the easier path, allowing evil to enter our lives and control our thoughts. That path is full of darkness and shadows, only leading to an imminent death.

Some of us take the narrow path full of hope and light, where each step we take is closely watched by the enemy in hopes that we fall flat on our faces. Though along the way we have celestial beings protecting us every step of the way. The path lit with joy and peace leads to eternal life, where no sadness or pain exist.

As for the town of Garlandton, a healing will need to take place, one that no mortal man can accomplish. Only God has the power to mend a broken city.

\*\*\*

When the sun rises in the east, a new day is born, leaving yesterday in the dust. A time for change, a time for new beginnings, a time to move forward and to not look back. Maybe for me a chance for my life to get back to normal.

Wait a minute … did I say normal?

HA!

What in the world am I thinking? No chance for normality in this life, especially since I've decided to take my being a Seer more seriously. I mean, really, *normal*? I'm so far from normal as any human could possibly be.

Being able to see into the spiritual realm, fight demons alongside angels, have visions and dreams sent from God

Himself – I'd have to be crazy to think I'm anywhere near the norm, but you know what?

I'm cool with it.

Okay, I'll admit that I have a lot to learn, but I'm not worried. What helps me to see a brighter future ahead is knowing that I'm not alone in this new chapter of my life.

We are *never* alone.

When we fall on our faces and feel we can't go on, we need not worry. There is always someone there to help us up. The only problem is most of us don't think about the spiritual realm. Most of the time we are too caught up in our mundane priorities to think about the heavenly angels by our sides, watching after us as we go through our daily routines. In reality, many people don't believe there's a Heaven or Hell, God or Satan.

Well, I'm here to tell you this – I'm a believer.

I've seen what comes from Heaven, and I've seen what crawls up from Hell. I've gazed into the beautiful eyes of an angel; I've stared into the malicious eyes of demons.

I've witnessed what Hell is capable of – anyone who watches the news can figure that one out.

I don't know why God has chosen this path for me, and

I have no clue of what lies ahead, but there is one thing I am absolutely certain of...

Next time I'll be ready.

# Note from the author....

Hello readers! I wanted to give a huge THANK YOU for purchasing Seer Society, Book One: Clarity. I hope you enjoyed a story that is so dear to my heart.

This book was recently titled "Clarity", then later "Mark of the Seer". Many people have wondered why I've taken the story and rewritten it. Well, it's simple, really. The way it was written before only gave the reader one side of the story. Adding different POVs gives more insight to what's happening, letting the reader see all sides of the story. Clarity (the Seer), Sam (the Guardian), and Lukus (the demon), and their thoughts and feelings can be read throughout the whole book. The story changed a bit, though spiritual warfare is the common focus.

Book Two will be coming Summer 2014, recently titled "Broken". It's being rewritten as we speak, shedding light on two other characters (Kora, Livian, and, naturally, Clarity and Sam). And like Book One, the story has changed a little.

Book Three will be coming 2015, titled "Masquerader".

Again, thank you for reading the Seer Society. Be on the lookout for future works. You can keep up with me on

Facebook, Goodreads, Twitter, and LinkedIn.

God Bless each and every one of you!

Jenna Kay Pridgen

# Thank You!

First and foremost, I want to thank God for blessing me with the stories I write. You are the reason I breathe. You are the Way, the Truth, and the Life. Thank you for blessing my socks off.

To Rocky, thank you for supporting me when others would not. Thank you for encouraging me to continue and keep moving forward. Couldn't do it without you. I love you.

Ryder, Wyatt, and Sarah Kay – you are perfect examples of God's blessings. You three keep me determined and focused. Whatever you guys do in life, keep God at the center and you'll accomplish whatever you set your minds to. Love y'all lots!

Kay, my precious Mama, I love you so much. Thank you for believing in me and supporting me these past few years. I can always count on you, no matter what. I thank God for you every single day. Best mom ever!!

Danny and Brenda, thank you for being there when we've needed you. Hope you know we'll always be there for you, as well. Love you both.

To my LifeLine family, I love you all! God is good, and

I'm looking forward to see how God works in each and every one of us.

Thank you to my family and friends for all the support and encouraging words.

And to my fans – the pen keeps moving for you all!

www.ingramcontent.com/pod-product-compliance
Lightning Source LLC
Chambersburg PA
CBHW070733180626
46818CB00007B/2823